Paulo, Karen.
America's long distance challenge : the complete guide to the sport of endurance and competitive riding / Karen Paulo. -- 1st ed. -- North Pomfret, Vt. : Trafalgar Square Pub. ; New York : E.P. Dutton, c1990.
vi, 166 p. : ill. ; 25 cm.

Includes index.
ISBN 0-525-24845-5 : $19.95

(Cont'd on next card)

AMERICA'S LONG DISTANCE CHALLENGE

1. Rider Rod Berry cantering past some dramatic rock formations on the Ken Caryle 50-mile ride, Colorado.

AMERICA'S LONG DISTANCE CHALLENGE

The Complete Guide to the Sport of Endurance and Competitive Riding

KAREN PAULO

Trafalgar Square Publishing
NORTH POMFRET, VERMONT

DUTTON NEW YORK

DUTTON
Published by the Penguin Group
Penguin Books USA Inc.,
375 Hudson Street, New York, New York, U.S.A. 10014
Penguin Books Ltd,
27 Wrights Lane, London W8 5TZ, England
Penguin Books Australia Ltd,
Ringwood, Victoria, Australia
Penguin Books Canada,
2801 John Street, Markham, Ontario, Canada L3R 1B4
Penguin Books (N.Z.) Ltd.,
182–190 Wairau Road, Auckland 10, New Zealand

Penguin Books Ltd, Registered Offices:
Harmondsworth, Middlesex, England

First published by Dutton,
an imprint of Penguin Books USA Inc.,
and by Trafalgar Square Publishing,
David & Charles Inc.,
North Pomfret, Vermont 05053.
Published simultaneously in Canada
by Fitzhenry & Whiteside Limited.

First printing, April 1990.

1 3 5 7 9 10 8 6 4 2

Library of Congress Cataloging-in-Publication Data

Paulo, Karen.
America's long distance challenge : the complete guide to the
sport of endurance and competitive riding / Karen Paulo.—1st ed.
p. cm
Includes index.
ISBN 0-525-24845-5
1. Endurance riding (Horsemanship) 2. Trail riding—Competitions.
3. Endurance riding (Horsemanship)—United States. 4. Trail riding—
United States—Competitions. I. Title.
SF296.E5P38 1990
798.2′4—dc20 89-34993
CIP

Printed in the United States of America

Designed by Mark Gabor

We have made every effort to obtain permission for all photographs used in this book. In some cases, however, the photographers were not known and therefore are not identified. Should any names become available, the photographers will be credited in future editions, assuming permission is granted.

Photo number 3 facing page 1 by Jimmy Butler

Contents

Acknowledgments

I have many people to thank for the development of this book, which in itself is a dream fulfilled.

To my family, husband, Al, and daughter, Andrea, who tolerated my sometimes poor disposition as I wrote the manuscript. They seldom complained about my lack of time for them and often helped out whenever it was possible.

To the many veterinarians whom I've quoted in this book, for allowing me to bend their ears at endurance rides and AERC conventions. Their help is most appreciated, not just by me but by the many horses who will benefit from their shared knowledge.

To all of my best riding buddies who encouraged me years ago to begin writing magazine articles, then to tackle the task of this book.

To my parents, because it was their life-style with the thoroughbreds at the racetrack that enabled me, as I was growing up, always to be learning from many of the best trainers in the industry.

To my own endurance horses, because they have been my companions and my teachers through 13,000 miles of endurance rides.

To the many people who so generously furnished the photographs that allowed this book to come to life. I'd like to give special thanks to AERC's Hall of Fame winner Charles Barieau, who supplied many beautiful photos that are an integral part of the history of endurance riding. The people at Phelan's in Sausalito, California, especially Patty Phelan, also deserve special thanks for their crisp shots of tack and riding apparel.

This book's existence is due to the efforts of Caroline Robbins, who saw to every minute detail that goes into the publishing process. She spent countless hours and late nights working on the text, organizing photos, and bringing the project to fruition. She also had some truly wonderful people working with her, and to them I am also grateful. To Robin Culver, who spent a great deal of her time working with Caroline and also for supplying so many fine photos. To Mike Noble, who took the time to travel and capture some perfect shots necessary for the book. To the artist, Carol Wood, who did a superb job on the detailed drawings. And to Mark Gabor for the many hours required in the editing of text and captions—and for designing the book itself.

When I first began this project, I had no idea of the immense amount of work entailed, nor did I have an inkling of how many people it would take to do all these special tasks. Thank you, everyone, for all your efforts—for turning a rough diamond into a jewel of a finished product.

Karen Paulo

This book is dedicated to the horses that died at the hands of uneducated riders on June 13, 1987, at the Catoosa "Suicide" Races in Oklahoma. May no other horses ever have to suffer as they did.

HONORING THE ENDURANCE HORSE

—A poem by Ed Johnson, 1965

Through the early morning twilight
Along the dusty trail
A phantom horse and rider
Determined not to fail

A stallion's scream of challenge
For all the world to tell
A soft clatter of hoofbeats
And the call of Bezatal

A fleeting glimpse of shadows
Gliding through the trees
A phantom horse and rider
Moving like the breeze

To the snowcapped mountain peaks
Where the wary eagles dwell
A world above the silver clouds
There goes Bezatal

A pause to quench a mounting thirst
Where icy waters flow
The beauty of the sunrise
Upon the frozen snow

Hear the echo of the hoofbeats
Of this faithful steed
And the murmur of his nicker
That all is well indeed

They traveled onward through the day
Towards the setting sun
The phantom horse and rider
The ride this day was won

Preface

This book describes and illustrates the many facets of the sport of distance riding—preparation, technique, equipment, training, and competition. You'll experience the joy of completing a challenging course, the exhilaration of cantering through the wilderness, and the thrill of being a winner. Together, you and your horse will become an inseparable and unbeatable team, conquering your adversary—the trail. You'll learn the discipline needed to pace your horse through the demanding miles. With this book—and a little bit of luck—you may never experience the heartache of having to pull your horse from a competition just a few miles from the finish line.

Distance riding is addictive. After only a couple of rides, you are hooked. Once the ride is over, you'll be thinking about the things you should have done differently—as you steer your truck and trailer home, sore muscles and all. But once you unload your cargo and take a deep breath of relief, you'll find yourself—yes, it's true!—looking forward to the next ride. Your new riding friends have now become your favorite people, offering help and advice whenever you need it.

Some of your old riding friends—not yet into distance riding—may not understand what inspires you to go on these rides in all kinds of weather over wild and wicked terrain. They may even stop riding with you the way they used to, complaining that you ride too far, too fast. You and your horse will inevitably spend many lonely miles together, conditioning and strengthening yourselves as a team, a unit.

Once prepared, you and your truest friend—your horse—can ride as far and fast as your bodies and spirits will allow. If you enjoy the commitment, dedication, and perseverance that go into this sport, you'll find the greatest satisfaction and success on the distance trail.

This book focuses on the sport of distance riding. But it's very clear that most of the concepts and techniques apply equally well to all other equestrian sports. Conditioning is, inevitably, the key to success in any athletic endeavor.

2. Ed Johnson on Bezatal, the winning team at the 1965 Tevis Cup ride. Bezatal went on to become an AERC Hall of Famer. Photo: Charles Barieau

Part One

Starting Out

1 *The Sport of Distance Riding*

Distance riding has become one of the fastest-growing equine activities in the world today, and thousands of people are realizing the rich possibilities and rewards that the sport holds for them.

Almost everyone answers the distance challenge for different reasons. Some do it because horses are their business and they want to prove the soundness and sturdiness of the horses in their breeding program. Some simply love to ride, enjoying their horse in the beauty of the countryside and looking to meet other people who share the same satisfaction. Some have become bored with the show ring, or with formal equine activities, and want to do something new and exciting. Some do it because they enjoy the very process of getting themselves and their horses really fit—and this is the ultimate test of fitness! And of course there is always the hotdogger who feels that his horse is faster and stronger than anyone else's. This is the chance to prove it.

No matter what the motives are for trying this sport initially, there are many other reasons for staying with it. Distance riding offers recreation and relaxation separate and distinct from the real world, the drudge of the day-to-day routine. While there are some people who find their escape route through television, a paperback, or a bottle of booze, horsemen prefer to gain their freedom with a horse!

Distance riding offers families a special and unusual sport that they can all compete in and enjoy together—whatever their ages. One mother said to me, "Where else can my teenage son and I spend six hours talking and joking together?" Long distance riding appeals to riders age eight to eighty. The horse becomes the equalizer—enabling a child to compete with grown-ups and providing an elderly rider with a new source of strength and speed.

You need a great deal of time, experience, and money these days to succeed in most other equine sports, so often dominated by professional horsemen. But in distance riding, the horse's owner is usually his rider, trainer, groom, and friend. In this competition, riders have an equal chance so long as they discipline themselves, condition their horses, and prepare well for the ride. It is simply one horse and rider *pitted against the trail*, testing and combining their talents to emerge as a winning team. There are seldom money purses—only trophies, T-shirts, and nominal prizes. Official winning aside, however, there is a *lot* of satisfaction to be gained in just completing a ride. "To Complete Is to Win" is the first motto of this sport.

4. A most happy Mae Schlegal, 75-year-old retired X-ray technician, riding 20-year-old Khala Suraka as they complete the 1985 Race of Champions. Photo: Purina

Comparison of the Two Sports

The American Endurance Ride Conference (AERC) defines *Endurance* riding as "An athletic event with the same horse and rider covering a measured course within a specified maximum time." An Endurance ride is a race normally 50 to 100 miles long per day, in which all horses are under strict veterinary control. The first horse to finish in "acceptable condition" is the winner. In addition, out of the top finishers, one horse—not necessarily the first horse over the finish line—is judged to be in Best Condition. This is based on vet score, weight carried, and riding time. All horses that finish in acceptable condition are given Completion awards. Many riders participate solely to complete the distance within the prescribed time—not to win.

A *Competitive* ride is different from an Endurance ride in that it is not a race. It is judged *totally* on the horse's condition at the finish as compared to his condition before the ride began. There is a minimum and maximum time in which to complete the ride; horses arriving at the finish

5. Multichampion Endurance rider Lew Hollander together with his son Lewis Hollander III. Photo: Karen Paulo

Distance riding has grown immensely in the last 20 years. Before that time it was not generally accepted as a bona fide sport. Over the years it has gained respectability owing to several important factors: uniform rules were established; strict vetting procedures were adopted and enforced; and a number of national and regional organizations were formed to sponsor scores of rides annually. As a direct result of all this structuring, many more riders participate with each passing year. They are no longer regarded as oddities by the rest of the horse world, but rather as respected athletes.

There are two kinds of distance riding: *Endurance* and *Competitive*. Although they have different goals, they are similar in many respects.

too soon or too late are penalized. These rides range from 25 to 40 miles per day, and 100 miles are ridden over three days. The horses are judged and scored by veterinarians and other experienced trail riders. The highest-scoring horses in different weight divisions are the winners (see p. 14).

History of Distance Riding

Distance riding has been around for years and was once a way of life. American pioneers traveled thousands of miles to reach the West, enduring hardships that are difficult to imagine; settlers depended on the pony express riders to bring their mail; Indians bred horses for strength and stamina because their very existence depended upon the horse for hunting and tribal warfare.

Organized Endurance rides were held in the United States as early as the mid-1800s, though not always with care or concern for safety. Trotting races of 30 to 40 miles, with huge money purses of up to $4,000, often resulted in dead horses—all in the name of "sport." Humane societies were formed to discourage the "hard drivers" and these events in general. For instance, the Massachusetts SPCA was started in 1869 as a direct result of the death of two horses during a 40-mile, $1,000 trotting match. At the turn of the century certain European military horse trials, whose purpose was to determine the best breeds, body types, and age range for top performance, also resulted in high death rates. The worst was the Berlin-to-Vienna Ride in 1892, which was a competition between Prussian and Austro-Hungarian soldiers. Over a distance of 350 miles, the winner rode a Hungarian mare in the time of 72 hours at an average speed of 5 miles per hour. However, out of 199 entries, 26 horses died, the winner included.

Meantime, in the United States during the 1880s, frontiersman "Buffalo Bill" Cody and others held fast to the theory that by regulating riders and imposing controls, good horsemanship would have to be practiced and damage to horses could be

7. Winner of the 1984 Oregon 75, Maggie Price of Pennsylvania rides her purebred Arab mare Ramegwa Kaffara. Photo: Terry Halladey

6. Junior rider Heather Kinney and her Appaloosa mare Nifty Image. In 1987 they were first in the Junior Division at the Oregon 100 ride. Photo: Terry Halladey

prevented. In 1886, Frank Hopkins—a military dispatch rider and a man who in his time won over 400 long distance races on horses that finished in good condition—rode a seven-year-old, 800-pound stallion named Joe to win a 1,799-mile ride from Galveston, Texas, to Rutland, Vermont. Hopkins weighed 152 pounds and his saddle 34. All horses were monitored along the route; those who could not continue without injury were eliminated. The rules allowed one horse per rider; no horse could be ridden more than ten hours a day; and judges along the route saw to it that no short-cuts were taken. It took Hopkins and Joe 31 days to collect their $3,000 purse. They averaged 58 miles a day—and the horse actually *gained* eight pounds over his starting weight, suffering no ill effects whatsoever from the race. Seven years later, in 1893, Hopkins and Joe raced 1,100 miles and won $1,000. From Kansas City to Chicago, the route wound through obscure wilderness in an

9. Junior rider Bruce Moore on 20-year-old Tonkawaikah in the Oregon 100 ride. At right is his sponsor, Al Paulo. Photo: Terry Halladey

8. Septuagenarian Web Coleman on Arabel and friend Judy Voll on Wild Acres Popcorn during the 1987 January Thaw ride in South Woodstock, Vermont.

effort to avoid a number of towns having over-zealous humane societies.

Perhaps the first modern, organized Competitive ride held in the United States was sponsored by the Morgan Horse Club of Vermont in 1913. Strict rules were enforced for the entire ride to reassure anyone who was concerned about the horses' welfare. No horse was allowed to exceed an average of 6 miles per hour over the 154-mile course. All horses had to carry a minimum of 160 pounds. The winner was an Arabian whose time was 30 hours 42 minutes. He was awarded a silver trophy and $100 for his efforts.

In the 1920s the U.S. Army Cavalry introduced the United States Mounted Service Cup competition. These were races of approximately 300 miles, with a daily average of 60 miles over five consecutive days. Each horse carried 200 to 245 pounds (rider plus gear), an average of 23.6 percent of its own body weight. Again, strict regulations were employed. In one race, for example, controls were so tight that one Arabian stallion, El Sabok, was disqualified after winning because of a lump on his back caused by the saddle.

What is significant about the Mounted Service Cup competition is that among the finishers there was often a separate prize given to the rider who took the best care of his horse and used the best judgment in riding the course. This is historically the first time riders were rewarded in a race not for coming in first, but for coming in *best.*

11. At the 1987 Green Mt. Horse Assn. 100-mile ride, Betty Welles leads on Hawk's Nest Capri, followed by Jane Graffam-Maine (center) on Nabarra, who went on to win this ride.

In 1972 there were 696 known Endurance riders and 24 rides. In 1987 the AERC sanctioned 646 rides, which included 539 rides of 50 to 150 miles in length, plus 107 limited-distance rides (25 to 35 miles long). More than 2,300 AERC-registered riders participated, for a combined total of nearly 700,000 miles. Another organization that sanctions Endurance rides, UMECRA (Upper Midwest Endurance and Competitive Riding Association) had over 50 rides on its 1988 schedule.

Competitive rides have enjoyed comparable growth. In the early 1970s the main Competitive riding organizations—UMECRA, NATRC (North American Trail Ride Conference), and ECTRA (Eastern Competitive Trail Ride Association)—sanctioned just 30 rides altogether. By the late 1980s, approximately 250 Competitive rides were being held annually with combined membership of nearly 4,000 people.

Distance riding affords a special opportunity for virtually anyone on horseback. It does require that the horse-and-rider team possess the qualities of strength, perseverance, and dedication—because the time and effort involved in this sport are immense. But then, so are the personal rewards.

10. Trot, Trot, Trot—This is where the endurance horse lives! *Shown here is the author (right) with Terry Crawford.* Photo: Terry Halladey

12. Nina Warren and Amir after winning the 1983 Scutchalo Hills ride in Michigan. It was a long day with high winds, severe thunderstorms, and pelting rains. Photo: Nina Warren

2 *The Endurance Challenge*
A Race Between the Fittest

The famed Tevis Cup (officially known as the Western States Trail Ride), first run in 1955, and the Old Dominion 100, which started in 1974, are both billed as the toughest 100 miles you'll ever experience on horseback. The Tevis Cup is held in California, and the Old Dominion in Virginia. The two rides have attracted competitors from all over the United States and inspired the development of many new Endurance competitions.

Origin and Purpose of the AERC

These new competitions led to the formation of the American Endurance Ride Conference in 1971. Its main purpose was to establish a set of standardized rules that would create a common format for riders across the country—riders who might never actually compete against each other on the same trail. Thanks to the efforts of the AERC founders Phil Gardner, Charles Barieau, Marian Robie Arnold, and cofounders Kathie Perry, Todd Nelson DVM, Hal Hall, and Julie Suhr, Endurance riding has come into its own as a bona fide sport. Any person interested in trail riding may join the AERC, and certainly all riders who intend to compete in Endurance rides should join. The AERC provides you with copies of rules for riders, lists of ride managers and experienced ride veterinarians, as well as dates and information on sanctioned rides. It also keeps a permanent record of the mileage and points accumulated by all members and their horses.

13. A misty morning during the Sun River 100, September 1977. Left, Nancy Springer on Rakar and, right, the author on Sunny Spots R—following their first vet check.
Photo: The Photographer

14. Winners Jan Worthington and Mary Koefod toasting each other after the 1985 Race of Champions (ROC) in Sedalia, Colorado. *Photo: Darrell Doddo,* Appaloosa Journal

Endurance riding has been called a "renegade" sport. This is no doubt due to its spotty history and the fact that many competitors are rebels or dropouts from other equine sports. Endurance riders tend to be an outspoken group, fighting for the principles they believe in—one of which is to maintain the sport's simplicity and not allow it to become bogged down with excessive official regulations. The AERC rules are very basic, leaving ample room for the ride managers and veterinarians of AERC-sanctioned competitions to adapt them to different terrains and climates. There are also about a half dozen regional groups that sanction rides: nearly all of them recognize the AERC rules, adding a few regulations of their own.

Length and Time of Endurance Rides

The most common Endurance rides are 50 miles long, with a maximum completion time of 12 hours; 100 miles within 24 hours; and 150 miles within 36 hours. Most rides are held over one day, but occasionally a 100-mile or 150-mile ride is broken up into 50-mile segments per day. The multiday rides described in chapter 25 cover 200 to 300 miles.

Controls and Conditions

At all AERC-sanctioned competitions, the ride veterinarian sets maximum pulse and respiration limits, known as parameters, eliminating any horse that may be in danger if allowed to continue. The AERC requires that all horses must be at least 60 months of age, calculated from their actual date of birth, in order to compete in rides of 50 miles or longer. This age limitation is set because horses seldom reach physical maturity before they are five years old; in fact, some breeds take as long as seven or eight years to mature. Horses of 48 months are allowed in rides of 25 to 35 miles, but the AERC will sanction these rides—called limited-distance rides—only on the basis of completing the distance; speed is not measured or recorded. This policy was established to protect the novice horse from injury and allow the rider to gain experience. The ride management will also reward the horses that have the highest vet scores at the end.

Scoring and Awards

The AERC maintains a record of all bonus points and mileage points earned by members and their horses. Points are issued to all members riding in sanctioned rides (excluding limited-distance rides) at the rate of one point per mile, plus bonus points for winning or for a Top 10 placing. At the end of each year, the horse-and-rider teams with the highest points are honored at the AERC's annual banquet. Before 1988, awards were based on an overall national "Top 25 Senior" standing, but now they are based on weight-division classifications—Lightweight, Middleweight, and Heavyweight. (Junior riders compete in their own division.) These classifications are determined by the weight of the rider plus his tack. Any regional groups that sanction rides give similar awards.

Points also determine other AERC honors, such as regional awards, family awards, husband-and-wife championships, and 1,000-mile standings.

15. The silver buckle awarded to every rider who completes the Tevis Cup. Photo: Charles Barieau

16. The amazing team of Cortez "Smokey" Killen and Bandit represent what the sport is all about. Killen is the leading high-mileage AERC rider with 21,500 miles, and his horse has gone 15,700 miles. Both horse and rider are now in the AERC Hall of Fame. Photo: Charles Barieau

Total mileage is tallied for a special annual championship, and Best Condition points are scored for yet another important prize.

Mileage awards are given by the AERC at 1,000-mile increments to individual horses and riders. There are many 1,000-plus horses, but only a handful have ever reached more than 7,000 miles. One outstanding grade gelding, Bandit, has managed to reach a phenomenal 15,700 miles—and his owner, Cortez "Smokey" Killen, has amassed over 21,500 miles! This team has set a standard for Endurance riders everywhere, and both horse and rider have been inducted into the AERC Hall of Fame.

Pit Crew

Most Endurance competitions permit riders to have a pit crew help them throughout the day (see ch. 20). There are, however, special awards at some of the prestigious 100-milers for riders who complete the distance without assistance.

17. Kathy Ray and Easter Charm, winners of Best Condition at the 1987 ROC, overall winners and Best Condition at the 1989 ROC, and overall winners of the 1986 ROC and the 1987 Tevis Cup.
Photo: Kathy Ray

Importance of the AERC

The AERC has developed an acceptable and sensible standard for all Endurance rides. I would discourage any person from entering a ride that fails to provide proper veterinary control, allows horses to be drugged, or doesn't generally follow the AERC rules and guidelines. Such rides do exist—so be very careful about what competitions you enter, since you don't want to put your horse or yourself at any unnecessary risk.

It is not difficult for rides to receive AERC sanctioning. Application must be made to the AERC at least 120 days prior to the ride date and the ride management must agree to follow all AERC rules and regulations. After the ride is over, the management must submit the results to the AERC. The information is recorded and saved on a computer. An AERC sanction gives a ride credibility, which in turn attracts more riders who are keen on competing for official points and riding under well-controlled conditions.

Rise of International Competition

In past years, a number of American distance riders have visited their European and Australian counterparts, borrowed their horses, and ridden in foreign Endurance rides. Reciprocally, their friends have come to the United States and also competed on borrowed horses. This cultural interchange led a few dedicated people, in the early 1980s, to develop a plan for international competition. In 1985 several American riders went to France as a team, borrowed horses, and rode in the first European Championship. In 1986, Americans *and* their horses flew to Rome and earned a silver medal in the Federation Equestrian International (FEI) 100-mile World Cup Ride. In 1986, the first FEI-sanctioned 100-mile ride in the United States—the North American Championship—was held in California. Its success paved the way for more North American Championships to be held on a biennial basis.

Endurance riding has come a long way—from a handful of unnoticed, scattered rides in the late sixties to the international competition widely practiced and recognized today. The sport offers limited-distance rides for beginners, 50- to 100-milers for the more experienced riders, and multiday rides for the teams that are truly fit and superbly conditioned.

3 *Competitive Riding*
A Test of the Best Conditioned

As mentioned earlier, the sport of Competitive riding differs from Endurance riding in that the latter is essentially a race where *time* is the major factor, and condition is judged mainly on the basis of the horse's ability to continue on. In Competitive riding, by contrast, the horse is judged primarily on his condition, with consideration sometimes given to manners and way of going. Speed is not a major factor. Time is relevant only in that the horse-and-rider team must complete the ride within preset minimum and maximum limits. Failing to do that, they receive penalty points.

Competitive trail rides cover from 25 to 40 miles per day at a pace of 5 to 7 miles per hour. These rides may be one day only. But some run up to three days, covering 100 miles—which is considered the ultimate competitive challenge.

The speed differential is the distinguishing factor between the two distance sports—and the reason why some prefer one discipline over the other. Competitive riding also affords the opportunity for green, or young, horses to participate, and a chance for less experienced riders to learn the thrill of distance rides. Of course, it is possible to compete in both sports with the same horse.

Scoring

At Competitive rides, each horse starts with a score potential of 100 points. The preride inspection establishes the horse's starting condition. As his condition changes during the ride, points are deducted. These scorings are particularly important in the final inspection at the end of the day's ride. The most important factors under consideration are: *pulse and respiration* (P&R); *mucous membranes* and/or *capillary refill time* (CRT); *dehydration; soundness; muscle fatigue* and any related changes in the horse's way of going; *bodily damage* or *inflammation* in tack areas and legs caused by the tack itself or by the horse hitting one leg against another (interference or overreach); *injuries* caused by objects along the trail; NATRC (see page 15) also scores *manners*; good manners are extremely important, since they affect the safety of those involved with the horse, as well as the horse's ability to do his job.

18. Robin Culver on Rosebud's Tango and Steve Rojek on Perkion. Rojek is a well-known competitor from the Northeast. Photo: Warren E. Patriguin

Judges

Competitive rides are usually judged by a veterinarian (preferably a distance rider himself) and a second person, usually referred to as a "lay judge," who is a horseperson knowledgeable in the sport of trail riding. All horses in the ride are under the jurisdiction of both judges—from the preride check through the final inspection. Apart from evaluating and selecting those horses who have performed best throughout the ride, the judges are responsible for the safety and well-being of all animals, monitoring them at every checkpoint along the trail. Judges have the final word on which horses may safely continue and which will be withdrawn, depending on their general condition.

Rules and Procedures

At Competitive rides, the horse-and-rider team starts out individually at 30-second or 1-minute intervals, usually at a trot. They proceed along the marked course at their best working pace—the idea being to use up the horse as little as possible, yet reach the finish within the minimum/maximum time limits. On a typical 40-mile ride, for instance, the preset limits would be 6½ to 7 hours, leaving a half-hour leeway. In this way, all the horses are subjected to pretty much the same stresses of speed and trail conditions.

The judges may stop and check a given horse at any time along the trail. And there is usually a mandatory midpoint rest stop of ten minutes or more, at which P&R recoveries are taken and soundness is checked.

While groundwork (where the rider dismounts and walks or runs with his horse) is allowed in Endurance rides, Competitive riders must always be mounted when any forward progress is being made. However, riders may dismount at any time and for any reason, provided they don't proceed down the trail. Doing so would result in disqualification unless the rider returns to the point of error before riding on.

19. Group of riders wending their way along a dirt road in the lovely countryside on the annual Vermont 100-mile ride. Photo: Mike Noble

20. Lucille Kenyon (#33), veteran of over 100 100-mile rides, during a Competitive ride in Ocala, Florida.

21. Jessica Smith, junior rider from New York, well equipped for a day on the trail.
Photo: Mike Noble

Equipment

Generally speaking, similar equipment is used for Competitive and Endurance riding. The main exception is that protective hoof and leg boots, or wraps, are not allowed in Competitive rides. Certain Competitive rides ban pads under the horse's shoes. And Easyboots may be used only to get the horse to a blacksmith if a shoe is lost.

Pit Crew

Most Competitive rides do not permit pit crews for the riders. But considering the relatively easier pace of this sport, a crew is hardly necessary.

Sanctioning Organizations

While all Endurance rides in the United States are governed by the AERC, Competitive trail riding is not centrally organized and has a number of different sanctioning bodies around the country. The North American Trail Ride Conference (NATRC) covers rides in most regions of the United States. The Eastern Competitive Trail Ride Association (ECTRA) covers the East Coast and reaches west to parts of Ohio. The Upper Midwest Endurance and Competitive Riders Association (UMECRA) sanctions rides in that region of the country. (The addresses of these organizations are in appendix I.)

All these groups have generally similar philosophies and rules, but there are enough differences in the specifics to warrant the attention of any prospective rider. It's important that you know as much as possible about the group that sanctions any ride you plan to attend—and exactly what their rules are.

Fortunately, each group publishes its own regularly revised rule book, spelling out all the details you'd need to know before entering a ride. Anyone planning to be active in distance riding should definitely have a membership in one or more of these organizations.

Awards

It's important to remember that Competitive rides are divided into different weight divisions (rider plus tack) and awards given to winners in each division. These divisions vary from one sanctioning group to another, so make sure you are familiar with the guidelines of the organization that sanctions the ride you are attending. Some rides are organized on the basis of "novice" or "open," taking into account the experience of the horse and/or rider.

Most rides have six placings within each division, as well as completion awards for all who finish. Awards may also be given for any or all of the following: best of breed, horsemanship, best trail horse, oldest and/or youngest rider, best horse-and-rider partnership, high-point family group, overall champion, and reserve champion.

Since Endurance and Competitive rides differ so much, they truly offer something for everyone. Louise Riedel, Secretary of the UMECRA, has ridden over 6,500 miles in Competitive and over 8,000 miles in Endurance, and she finds "equal but different challenges in both of these phases of distance riding." She also believes that "it takes a different type of horse to excel in each type of ride. My horse, Morazdac, is not a superior Endurance horse—he's too calm and laid-back and lacks that aggressive attitude that it takes to win in Endurance. These very traits are what make him a good Competitive horse."

23. Louise Riedel on her champion Arab, Morazdac. Secretary of the Upper Midwest Endurance and Competitive Riders Association (UMECRA), Ms. Riedel is also an AERC Hall of Famer. Photo: Louise Riedel

22. Left to right: Steve Bellavance, Valerie Kanavy, Robin Culver, and Web Coleman—all prizewinners at the Virginia 100-mile ride, 1984.

4 *Enduring Qualities*

How to Choose a Horse

It's fun to begin this sport in the company of an old friend, so if you are concerned that your present horse isn't good enough, don't worry. Almost any healthy, sound horse with a proper conditioning program can complete a distance ride. Perhaps he won't possess the special qualities that will make him a winner, but a fit-enough horse will almost certainly get the job done.

When I attended my first ride in 1977, I was riding my 16.2-hand Appaloosa gelding, Sunny Spots R. Many veteran riders told me to get another horse that was smaller, since smaller horses tend to do better in distance riding. "Get an Arab!" they said, because most of them thought that Sunny was too big and would never amount to anything. But he proved them all wrong, completing 4,410 miles, with two 100-mile wins and many Top 10 finishes. Tonkawaikah, another of my Appaloosa geldings, completed his first ride at 16 years and then finished the Race of Champions held in Wyoming's Big Horn Mountains in 1984 when he was 20! So perhaps you should give your present horse a chance before you rush out and buy a new one.

If you don't own a horse, then you will have the dilemma of what horse to buy and where to find him. I will try to give you a few pointers on what to look for in your prospect—qualities and talents that consistent finishers always seem to possess.

24. Faith Carr on the Arabian stallion, Flyer. He typifies the lighter body type commonly seen in distance horses. Photo: Terry Halladey

Breeds

The breed of the horse is not critical. Choose what you like. This sport is dominated by Arabians and part Arabians, but other breeds such as Morgans, Appaloosas, Tennessee Walkers, and many grade horses do very well. You will also see quarter horses, thoroughbreds, paints, mules, and pony breeds—anything goes. So if you have a favorite breed of horse, stick with it and try to find a suitable individual within that breed.

25. Bill Ansenberger on his 17-year-old standardbred gelding, Chief Simcoe. This team was the first ever to complete the Oregon 100 five times. *Photo: Terry Halladey*

26. Steve Bellavance on his quarter horse, Maybe Dallas Dawn, at the Vermont Stockhorse Association's 25-mile ride, 1985.

Age

Distance-riding competitions do not allow very young horses to compete. This is to protect their bodies from strain and concussion before they are fully grown. The AERC requires that Endurance horses be a minimum of 60 months from their actual date of birth in order to compete on rides of 50 miles or more; and Competitive organizations require a horse to be at least 60 months old to do 100 miles. Horses starting at 48 months are allowed on limited-distance rides of 25 to 40 miles. A horse without registration papers may be mouthed by the vet to determine its age.

Age is obviously an important consideration for the buyer. You may want to buy a youngster and gradually bring him along your own way, or you may wish to buy a horse that you can condition and compete with right away. It is important to remember that horses don't reach their prime until the age of eight, and distance horses will hold that prime until they are twelve or more. With proper conditioning and care they can compete far into their twenties.

27. Morgan mare Son's Siskiyou Doll, ridden by Larry Stephens, the 1980 AERC mileage champion. Photo: Nancy Cox

Physical Qualities

The horse *must* be sound. Any past problems or injuries, and how they were dealt with at the time, should be taken into consideration. Even minor problems will often magnify as you put miles on the horse, so the fewer bumps and lumps you have to start with, the better. He is going to get plenty more in this sport.

Look for balanced conformation. A horse whose rump is higher than his withers will carry more weight on his front end, leading to a greater chance of lameness. His neck should blend nicely into a long, sloping shoulder, which in turn will help him have a longer, freer stride. His girth area should be deep, allowing plenty of room for his heart and lungs; and his throatlatch area should be clean-looking to allow for good air flow. His top line should possess well-defined withers that will prevent your saddle from slipping forward or side to side. He should have a strong back that is not sensitive anywhere to your touch. If he has a well-sprung barrel (where the rib cage appears larger behind the girth) your saddle will not slip back when you ride uphill, thus avoiding the use of a breast collar, which can cause shoulder soreness, even when properly adjusted. His croup should be long and neither too flat nor too sloping, as both conditions limit the range of motion of his hind legs.

28. Ex-thoroughbred racehorse, Perkion, being ridden by Heidi Reeves—with 99½ miles to go!

29. Mules have been quite successful in Endurance riding. Frank "Mule Man" Bennett and Apache have completed 13 multiday rides. Apache has 6,280 miles to his credit, and Bennett has ridden over 13,000 miles. Here the team is shown riding across Blackrock Lake on the Applegate to Lassen multiday ride, 1985.
Photo: Frank Bennett

A horse's legs are extremely important, so check them over for any lumps or scars that may indicate he has had a previous problem (figs. 31–33). If possible, find out what caused these blemishes, because some may be only superficial and will not interfere with his soundness. I prefer a horse with heavier bone to one with fine bone because I feel he will have fewer leg problems. Some people consider heavy bone a sign of coarseness, but to me it is a sign of substance. It gives more strength to a horse's legs, unless, of course, this bone is so heavy that it qualifies him as a draft type—unsuitable for this sport. The legs of a distance horse must carry weight over extended time and distance and withstand prolonged concussion. Last, his hoofs must be large enough to support his body weight—they are his foundation. (See chapter 6 for additional information on legs and hoofs.)

Notice I did not mention his head, yet you see so many ads for horses starting off with "Beautiful head. . . ." I don't believe in "head hunting"—I cannot ride his head. While an attractive head is nice to look at, it is other features that make a horse usable.

30. Horses owned by the author and her family represent over 14,000 accumulated miles of Endurance rides. They are, left to right: Sunny Spots R, Tonkawaikah, Moka's Pat-A-Dott (all Appaloosas), and Chollima (an Arab). Photo: Karen Paulo

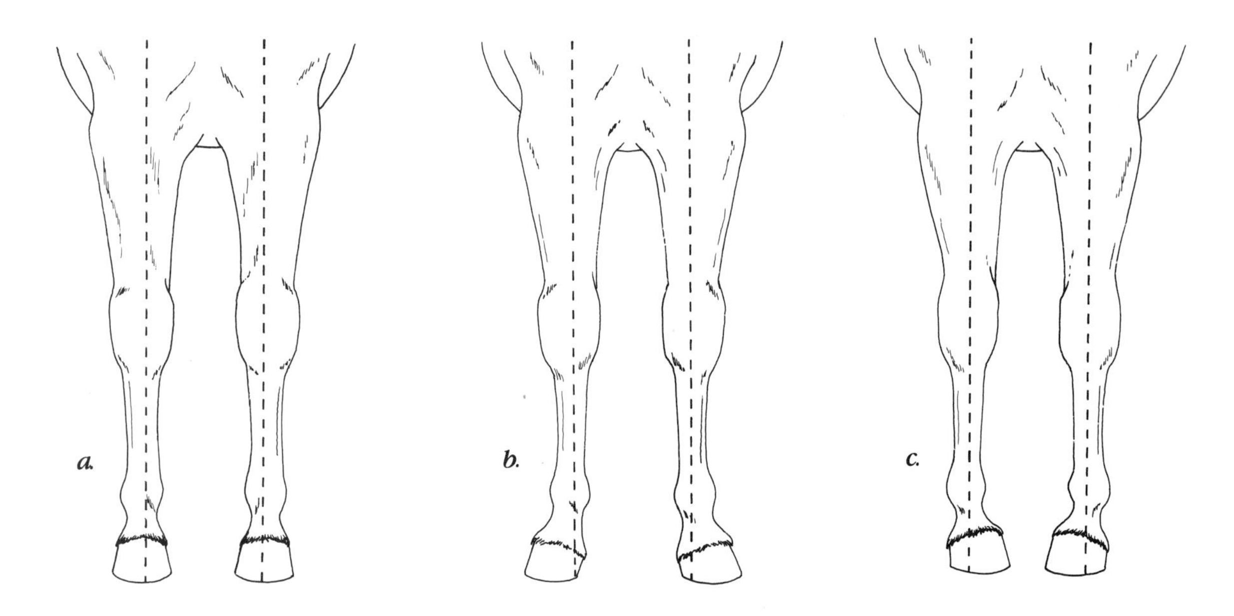

31. Front view of forelegs: a) correct alignment b) toeing out c) toeing in.
Drawings: Carol Wood

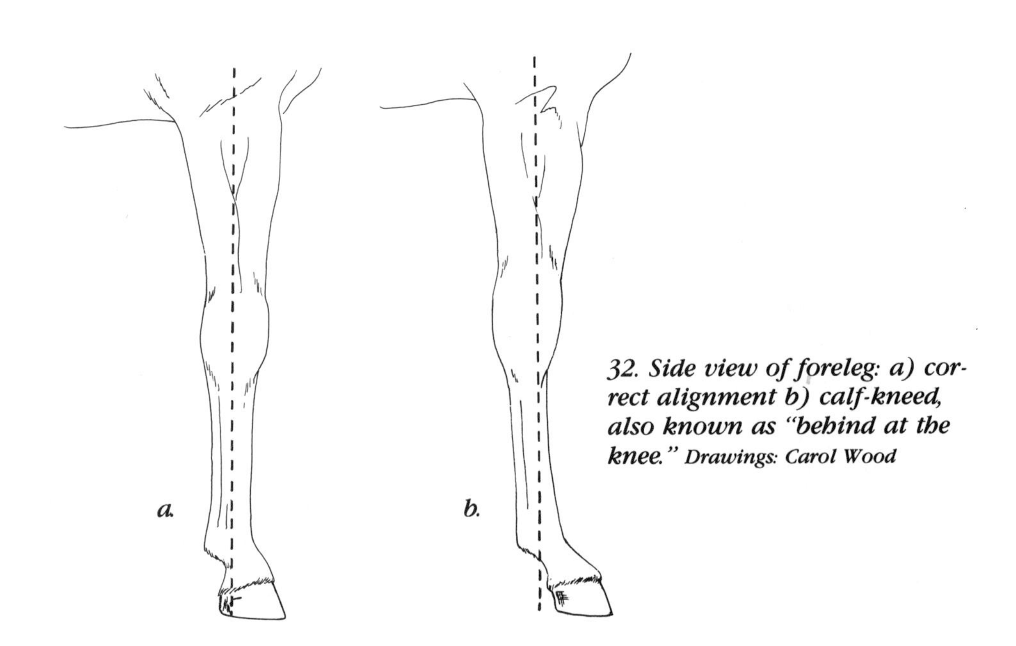

32. Side view of foreleg: a) correct alignment b) calf-kneed, also known as "behind at the knee." Drawings: Carol Wood

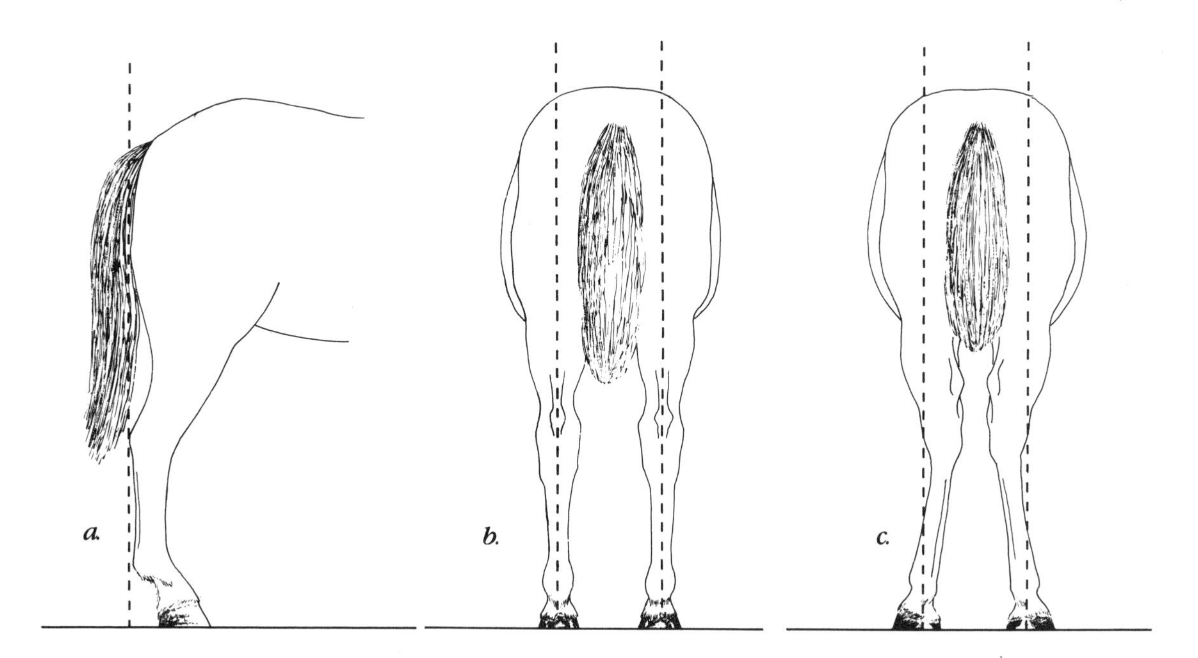

33. Hind legs: a) and b) correct alignment c) cow-hocked, with toes turned outward.
Drawings: Carol Wood

Now look at his overall appearance. A narrow horse resembles the shape of a radiator, providing more surface area in proportion to his weight (figs. 34–37). This allows him to throw off heat that builds up during work, making him more efficient, with faster recovery rates (see ch. 8). A wide-bodied horse can compete, too; however, he is squarer, and the thickness of his body doesn't allow heat to dissipate as easily—it builds up instead. Horses with highly developed surface-vein systems running all over their legs, shoulders, hips, and neck will tend to work cooler in general and also be better able to cool down when hot, because these surface veins are more exposed to air.

Look at his muscling. A horse with muscle that appears long, sinewy, and slight (like a deer)—typical slow-twitch muscle fiber—is naturally better able to perform endurance-type work. Conversely, a horse with thick, bunchy muscles (like a weightlifter)—fast-twitch muscles—is naturally better at speed work. You need the former type, if possible, for distance riding. (See chapter 9 for further explanation.)

34. Sunny Spots R is a narrow, streamlined horse with long, sinewy muscles and a "radiator" shape providing more surface area for more efficient cooling. Photo: Karen Paulo

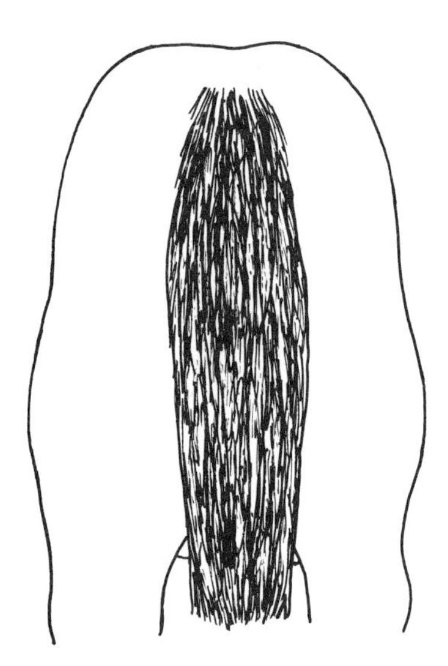

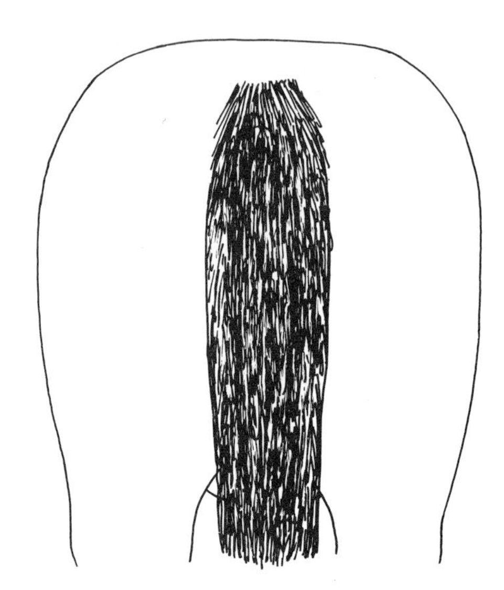

35. Rear-view diagrams of body types: a) radiator-shaped horse, best for heat dissipation b) wide, chunky horse dispels heat more slowly. Drawings: Carol Wood

36. & 37. Photos showing body types illustrated above. Photos: Mary Koefod and Mike Noble

Movement and Size

Watch how the horse moves. Is his stride free and easy? Is he an efficient mover? He should be. His legs should move straight with no hint of interference (fig. 38). They certainly should not swing about wildly! But, most important, his feet should land *flat* on the ground. It is often said that a horse with straight, clean legs who moves in a crooked way will have more leg problems than a naturally crooked-legged horse who moves straight and lands squarely. A horse that travels straight will also add more power to each stride (fig. 39).

Size is a matter of personal taste, although a small, narrow, wiry horse is usually considered the ideal type for distance riding. He has less bulk to carry around, and, as mentioned, he has a smaller body mass to cool. Larger horses can compete and even win, but the ones that do must have an extra-efficient cardiovascular system. You definitely need a horse that can carry your weight easily. In the horse-racing movie *Phar Lap* it was said, in effect, that too much weight can stop even a locomotive—and this is certainly true. Statistical data from the Race of Champions indicates that when a rider plus his tack weighs more than 23 percent of the horse's weight, he or she usually fails to finish.

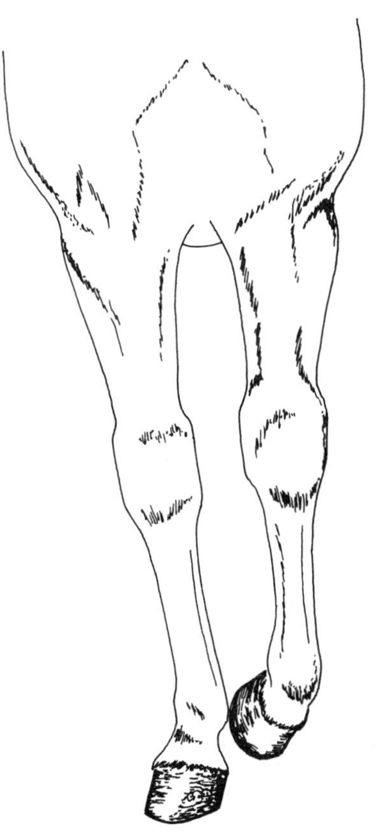

38. Interference—legs hitting because horse moves crookedly.
Drawing: Carol Wood

Testing the Horse

Be sure *you* ride the horse yourself. Apart from helping evaluate how much training he has had, and how much conditioning he is going to need, you will also find out if the two of you are compatible. Ride him for a while, then stop to adjust something and see if he is calm and quiet or if he behaves like a fool. He will not be a pleasure to ride if he fusses all the time and refuses to stand still. Is he responsive and easy to handle? Is he independent—not worried about going out alone?

39. Path of feet: a) a horse with normal movement b) a horse that toes out (splayed feet) swings inward while moving, causing interference c) a horse that toes in swings, or "paddles," outward, causing the joints to twist. Drawings: Carol Wood

Do you like his personality? After all, you are going to spend a lot of time together. Be sure to consider any idiosyncrasies; then decide if you have enough experience and patience to either correct or live with his quirks.

When you look for a horse, it's a good idea to take a stethoscope along. Three pulse readings at different times will give you an indication of his suitability for the sport. Take the horse's resting pulse before he has done any moving around (ideally, in his stall); later, take his pulse immediately upon dismounting after some significant exercise; and then take the pulse again ten minutes later to determine the rate of recovery. Many of today's top distance horses have a resting pulse of 28 to 32. Jennifer Cole DVM, distance rider and ride vet, tells me that studies have shown that a horse's resting pulse cannot be greatly lowered by conditioning. At most, it can only be lowered by several beats. (This is in contrast to human athletes, who can lower their pulse by 20 or more beats through conditioning.) Be sure to give extra consideration to a horse with a naturally low resting pulse.

Ask the current owner about the horse's experience. For instance, a racetrack reject may have mental and soundness problems that make him an unlikely candidate for this sport; however, if he was rejected solely for lack of speed, he may be ideal. Ask at what age he was broken, and what type and how much work he has done. Find out if he has had a regular worming schedule—lack of one may have caused permanent intestinal damage, limiting his tolerance for distance work. Ask if he has any shoeing difficulties and whether he has had his teeth floated (filed down with a rasp) and standard inoculations given regularly.

Vetting

When you find a horse that suits you, the next most important thing you can do is to have him examined by a veterinarian you trust and can talk with freely. The vet will be able to evaluate the horse's current state of health and tell you if he has the potential for doing what you want of him. This examination can be as extensive as you and the vet deem necessary. While the veterinarian obviously cannot guarantee permanent soundness he can go a long way toward alerting you to any *possible* problems you have not detected, or else calm your fears about some superficial injury you may have noticed. While Matthew Mackay-Smith DVM was vetting horses at the Race of Champions, he remarked that "each horse is like taking a pathology course—they all have lumps and bumps in every place possible." Remember that all horses have some faults; there is no such thing as the perfect horse.

How to Find a Prospect

If you are looking for an experienced distance horse rather than an untested individual, check the ads in distance-riding magazines, as well as in regional or local publications. Another way to find a proven horse is to ask a vet or someone in a feed store or tack shop if there are any distance riders in the area. They may well know about local horses for sale.

Bloodlines

We are now seeing the emergence of a new breed—the endurance horse. It is possible to find horses whose sire and/or dam competed in Endurance rides. The Endurance Horse Registry of America lists horses who have completed 300 miles in an elapsed year. Foals whose sires and dams are already EHRA-registered are automatically eligible for the EHRA registry. Some of the first registered foals are now coming of age and proving the inherited qualities of endurance, stamina, and soundness as they successfully travel the distance trails.

Previous Experience

If you are seriously considering the purchase of a proven horse, ask the current owner for a "performance record." If he or she doesn't have the information, contact whatever organization the horse competed in and ask for his record. I've known people who bought what they were *told* was a winning horse, only to find out later that the horse barely completed his one and only ride! Look at the written record closely and evaluate the consistency of his performances. If the horse has been pulled a lot from competition, find out why. Avoid purchasing a horse that was competed hard when he was only five years old. Ask questions of other people who may know or remember the horse.

Be as sure as possible that the horse is right for you before you buy it. Take your time to find that special individual who will be your partner and companion for years to come.

Part Two

Care and Feeding

5 *Fueling Up*

Feeding for Top Performance

Just as a car needs gas in its engine to create energy for motion, the horse requires nutrients in the muscles and bloodstream to fuel his motion. The energy in his system must sustain this motion for several hours at a time in competition. There is no specific formula, but we must supply the horse with the proper foodstuffs to give him the energy he needs for the task at hand.

40. Tom Goton and Kathy Ray offer their horses water from a mountain stream at the 1984 Race of Champions. A rider should never pass up an opportunity for water. Photo: Purina

Water

Every horse needs water on a regular basis, so be sure he always has plenty of good clean water all year round—even if this means, in the dead of winter, breaking the ice on the troughs several times a day. (A water heater for this purpose is ideal, because apart from keeping the trough ice-free, the horse doesn't have to waste energy unnecessarily heating up cold water in his stomach.) Water is needed even more by horses that are working and sweating: water is lost not only by sweat, but also through urine, and even with each breath he takes. The faster he inhales and exhales, the more water evaporates from his system. A dehydrated horse cannot digest his food properly, nor can he tolerate much exercise.

Hay and Grain

Most horsemen feed grain as a source of energy. The most commonly used grains are corn, oats, and barley, depending on what is available in your area. These grains average 10 percent protein and contain fat in the range of 2 percent to 5 percent. Commercial mixes, commonly used, run higher in their protein content—about 10 percent to 16 percent, but with the same 2 percent to 5 percent fat. All grains have a high phosphorous content but are low in fiber and calcium, so it is most important to feed your horse plenty of grass or hay as a fiber and calcium supplement.

Don't forget that the horse is a grazer by nature. He has a small stomach, and his system is designed for digesting grasses continuously over a 24-hour period. Yet many horses are kept in stalls and often fed large amounts of grain—perhaps 15 pounds—and small amounts of hay—say, 10 pounds—only twice daily. Many people do not realize that this practice stresses the horse's entire system, throwing off his natural levels of blood glucose. It can also foul the bacterial flora in his gut, leading to colic, which indicates a digestive upset in his system. A balanced diet should consist of 25 percent grain and 75 percent grass or hay. It is not a hard-and-fast rule, but most veterinarians agree that the grain percent should never exceed 50 percent of the horse's total ration. They also recommend that horses be fed their grain in small amounts in frequent installments. This is also the way you should feed hay, assuming your horse is not given free choice of when to forage (see p. 30).

Carbohydrates are the distance horse's primary source of energy, and they are commonly found in grain. Grain will also give him sufficient protein—he does not need high-protein supplements. Sarah Ralston DVM states: "While it is true that he will need more protein [than the horse involved in less demanding activities] this extra should not come from a higher percent of protein. The endurance horse will take in more feed, thus meeting his demands of more protein." Too much protein in the mature horse can cause many problems for him—excessive sweating, legs "stocking up" (becoming swollen or puffy), kidneys unable to function properly.

In providing ample amounts of fiber for your horse, make sure the hay is clean and free of mold and dust. Hay, like grain, varies in nutritional value. It is a good idea to take a sample of your hay to the County Extension agent or local agricultural representative for analysis. Good alfalfa hay is very rich in calcium and protein, often averaging 15 percent protein, with the best even exceeding 20 percent. Grass hays will usually vary between 6 percent and 10 percent. If you feed a hay too high in protein, you can run into a problem with excessive total protein in your horse's diet. Try to adjust all his foodstuffs so they average out to approximately 12 percent protein (10 percent digestible protein), which is considered ample for a mature horse.

Salt

Since grass (and therefore hay) is high in potassium but low in sodium, a salt lick or loose salt should always be available to your horse. Some people add salt to their horse's feed, but this is not advisable since horses will consume just what they need if given the free choice of loose or block salt.

Mineral and Vitamin Supplements

Your horse may also need some daily mineral supplements, especially if you fertilize your pastures. Most hay producers fertilize their fields and, while this improves the harvest yield, it can also diminish the crop's absorption of certain minerals. Have your hay analyzed to help you determine which mineral supplements may be needed. Some people give their horse a "mineral salt block" without realizing that this sort of block contains only a small percentage of minerals, which is often not enough. Look for the excellent mineral supplements produced by commercial feed companies.

41. This stallion's muscles have good definition and his coat glistens. However, some riders would consider him too lean. Hydaway's Prize Print, owned by Sandi Thomas, is a successful competitor and stud. This photo also shows the veins and arteries near his surface area—so important for quick cooling and fast recovery *(see p. 21).*

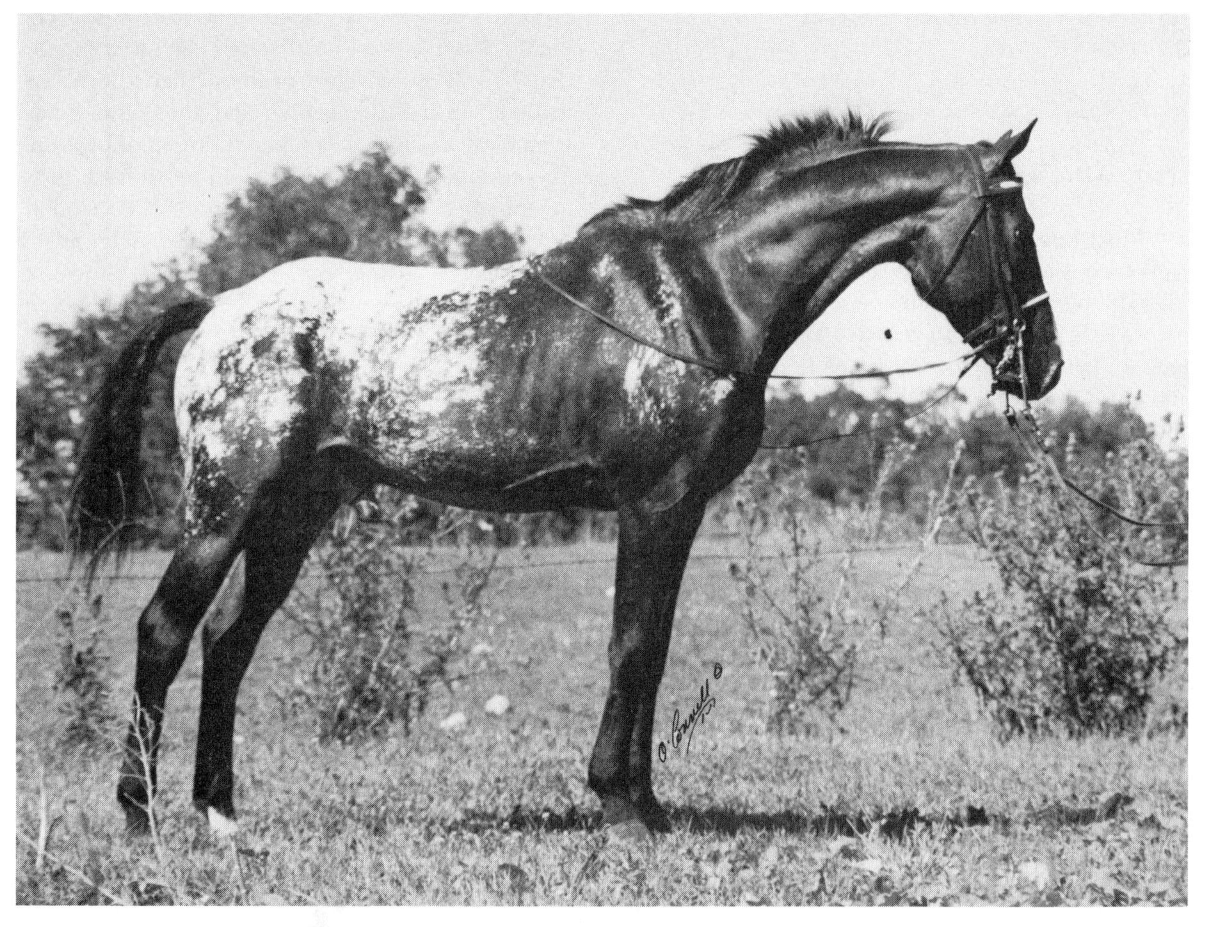

Daily vitamin supplements must also be considered. Good hay or pasture, and most commercial feeds will provide enough vitamins for the average horse. However, the horse that is working hard will usually need an additional source. There are many brands on the market. Read the labels and look for a product that will supply your horse with ample and balanced amounts of the B vitamins, as well as vitamins A, D, and E. Many vets advise that you stay away from supplements with too much vitamin A—more than 30,000 IU per ounce daily—and vitamin D—more than 3,000 IU daily. This is especially true if your horse is being pastured on green grass or rich alfalfa. All vets agree that you should give only one supplement to your horse at any given time, and be sure to feed it according to the directions. Just because a little vitamin supplement is good doesn't mean that a lot is better!

Studies have shown that selenium is a very important dietary trace element and is essential for absorption of vitamin E. Without this combination, your horse is prone to muscle weakness or tying up (see ch. 12). Since many regions of the United States are lacking in natural selenium, your horse may require selenium supplementation. Many commercial feed mixes add selenium; but it can also be administered by injection in a solution known as E-Se (also containing vitamin E). It has been determined that distance horses during competition utilize a great deal of selenium; their selenium blood level drops significantly after a ride. But the use of selenium can be tricky. While a horse that is low in selenium may develop a problem with his muscles, too much of it can be toxic. The best way to avoid the problem of too much or too little selenium is first to read the label on the vitamin supplement you are giving him and then ask your vet if this is the correct amount for your geographical area. (Note: A label that lists sodium selenite in the ingredients only, but not in the analysis, usually indicates a very low dosage of selenium.) You should also have your horse's blood tested for selenium occasionally. Since the selenium level drops after a tough competition, do this testing at least a week after such a ride. It is a good idea to consult your vet before supplementing your horse with selenium.

Fats and Cellulose—Other Energy Sources

In addition to carbohydrates and protein, your horse also ingests fat and cellulose from the grain and hay you feed him. Fat is the most efficient source of energy, carrying 2¼ times more energy than carbohydrates or proteins. Unlike humans, your horse does not produce fat-digesting enzymes that can be detected in the blood, nor does he have a gallbladder to store bile with which to digest fat. However, he can utilize small amounts of fat in the form of vegetable (corn or peanut) oil added to his grain. Many horses perform better and retain their weight better when given up to one cup of oil daily, but this practice must be introduced gradually. Since your horse's system is not designed to digest fat, too much at once will do more harm than good.

You should be aware that some commercial feeds designed for the athletic horse contain up to 14 percent fat, so if you are using one of these products it is better not to supplement his feed with oil. Too much fat in your horse's diet may cause metabolic problems—for example, tying up during distance rides, particularly in hot weather.

For simple-stomached animals, cellulose is often the indigestible part of plants. However, the horse's cecum and large colon contain bacteria that metabolize cellulose into a source of energy called volatile fatty acids.

How a Horse's Metabolism Works

Carbohydrates, protein, fats, and cellulose are broken down and absorbed through the intestinal walls and into the bloodstream. The horse stores these substances in the form of blood glucose, muscle glycogen, fat deposits, volatile fatty acids, and creatine phosphate. All of these chemicals are the fuel that is eventually broken down, or metabolized into energy for motion.

So how does the distance horse use all these fuels? According to Dane Frazier DVM, "As a horse starts to work at a slow speed it initially uses creatine phosphate as an energy source anaerobically* [without oxygen], not relying on the oxygenation of its muscle mass. This phase lasts for only a few to ten seconds. As exercise continues, and the horse supplies oxygen to its muscle mass, glycogen from the muscle and liver is converted to glucose and burned aerobically [with oxygen]. Free fatty acids and volatile fatty acids are mobilized from fat stores only in the presence of oxygen, yielding large amounts of ATP. This process can continue for hours, as long as the tissue can be oxygenated and an energy substrate [energy source] is available. *This is where distance horses do their work.*"

That may be more than you ever really cared to know about metabolism. However, it will help you understand what happens when you do slow speed work with a well-conditioned horse, which involves aerobic metabolism, as opposed to anaerobic metabolism that occurs when a horse goes at a rate so fast that his muscle tissues fail to get enough oxygen. Without enough oxygen, the horse then metabolizes glycogen anaerobically, which causes an accumulation of lactic acid in his muscles. The lactic acid creates increased fatigue and pain and ultimately prevents further work. When your horse is in this condition, he is known to be in *oxygen debt*. When your horse slows down enough to resume aerobic metabolism, his muscles will have enough oxygen then to metabolize the lactic acid and his pain will go away.

*For full discussion of aerobic/anaerobic distance-riding training, see chapter 9.

The Daily Regimen

Your feeding program is also very important. For example, my horses are fed only three to six pounds of grain per day (usually a sweet-feed mix of corn, oats, and barley—and I often add more corn for extra fat). The poundage will vary with the horses' workloads; the more they are ridden, the more they should get. It is a good idea to cut your horse's grain ration in half on the days he is not ridden (see Tying Up, ch. 12). I give my horses unlimited hay to make up for the small amount of grain ration. The hay is usually grass and alfalfa, sometimes oats and alfalfa. In addition, they receive a vitamin supplement in their grain and free access to a mineral mix that includes some salt. During conditioning and competition I also add a half pound of a 14 percent fat grain product to their feed. If you are giving over five pounds of grain per day, be sure to divide your feedings into three, and if you feed ten or more pounds, divide the feedings into at least four.

On the eve of a distance ride, I will give my horse enough hay so that he'll still have plenty left in the morning. This gives him sufficient fuel for the effort. I'll also feed him about a pound and a half of grain an hour or so before the ride. By day's end, your horse is going to be famished. He probably only managed to eat for a few minutes during the ride—a few mouthfuls of mash here, a pound of hay there, and maybe a few snatches of grass along the trail. But remember: although his appetite is probably enormous, his system is tired. Introduce food to him slowly, starting with grass, which is not only digested easily, but contains enough water to help rehydrate the horse. Bear in mind that too much of any food at once could cause a serious digestive problem, so give him only small amounts at a time of bran mash, grass, or soaked hay over lots of feedings. The objective is to feed him his regular ration, plus some extra feed, in order to speed his recuperation and combat weight loss during the first 24 hours after a ride.

Make sure that the total amount of grain you give him during this time does not exceed *twice* his normal daily ration. Rations can return to normal one day after the ride. However, if your horse has lost a great deal of weight, continue giving him some extra grain in frequent feedings until he starts to fill out. But don't forget to cut him back before you ride him again. When you do, I suggest you start out at no more than a walk and trot for the first few miles to avoid tying up.

When developing your feeding program, it is advisable to consult your vet. He will help you understand your horse's specific needs and problems. For instance, if your horse is having difficulties with his metabolism, your vet will suggest a blood test to reveal the source of these problems and will probably suggest that you add, reduce, or eliminate specific ingredients in your horse's diet.

Keep evaluating your horse's overall condition. If he is too fat, cut back his grain. As Kerry Ridgway DVM says, "You've got to remember something: This horse is to ride—you're not feeding it to eat it—it's to ride." Conversely, if the horse gets too thin, you are going to have to increase all his feed, especially grain. A horse that is too thin lacks the fat deposits that are necessary for all-day energy.

If your horse suddenly seems to require a lot more food in order to hold his weight, have him thoroughly checked by your vet. Poor teeth are often a cause of weight loss, since they prevent food from being properly digested. Internal parasites (worms) can also rob your horse of valuable nutrients. Contantly reexamine your feeding schedule and your conditioning practices.

A horse not receiving the right nutrients in the right amounts will often have a dull and rough coat, instead of a smooth and shiny one. Along with a rather bony appearance, he will usually have a little potbelly. The horse's eyes will lack sparkle, and he may exhibit a lazy attitude and a low tolerance for work (fig. 42). On the less obvious side, your horse may appear healthy but, during competition, will run out of gas after 35 to 40 miles. He may not have enough fat cells from which to draw energy; he may be eating a diet too rich in grain, which will foul up his glucose level; or he may simply need more feed before and during competition.

Dr. Ridgway observes that "it is difficult to tell

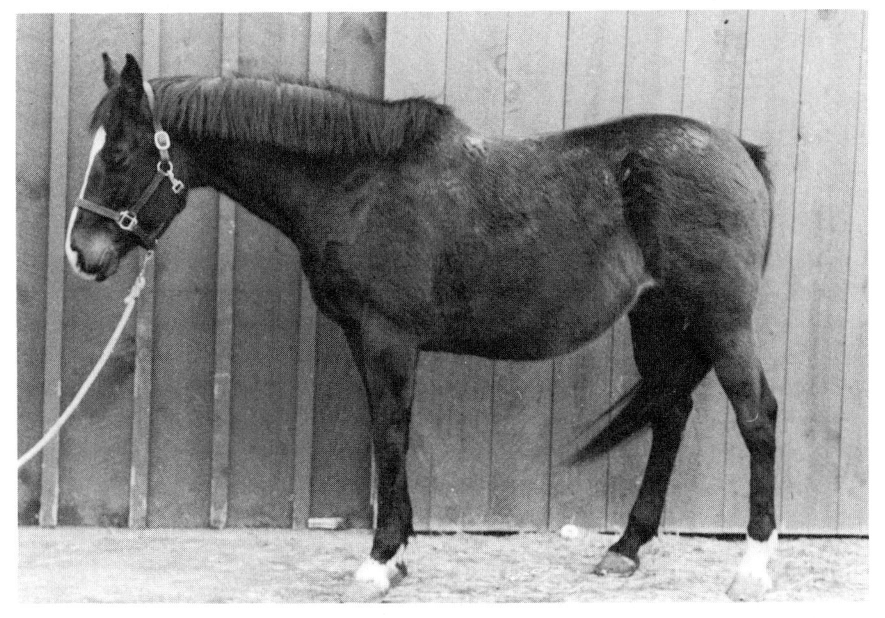

42. Poor nutrition is evident here—note the dull coat and potbelly.
Photo: Mike Noble

an overconditioned horse from a horse with malnutrition." If at any time during your conditioning program, or during a ride, your horse's performance begins to fade rather than improve, then it is time to step back and have a very good look at your whole feeding and conditioning program.

Your goal is to produce a healthy, sleek athlete, with a trace of fat over his ribs for reserve energy. He should glow from head to tail!

43. Preston is a six-year-old registered quarter horse. He's an excellent example of a strong, fit athlete whose coat glistens with health. Photo: Robin Culver

6 No Foot, No Horse
Hoof Care and Shoeing

The old adage "No foot, no horse" still applies today. It's true in all equestrian sports, but has special meaning when applied to distance horses.

A distance horse will need to be shod more often than the usual six to eight weeks for the average working horse. Since his hoof growth may not keep up with his frequent need for new shoes, he often develops cracks and chips from the farrier's nail holes. During a long season his hoofs may also become dry and brittle from heat created by abrasion and concussion. So when you begin this sport it's a good idea to have a horse with large round hoofs that are not already brittle or cracked (fig. 44). Hoofs should be larger at the bottom than at the coronary band (the top). The hoof's wall (outermost layer) should be healthy and thick so it can retain the nails that hold his shoes on. A healthy hoof has a large pliable frog (fig. 45).

44. Example of badly cracked, brittle hoof.
Photo: Mike Noble

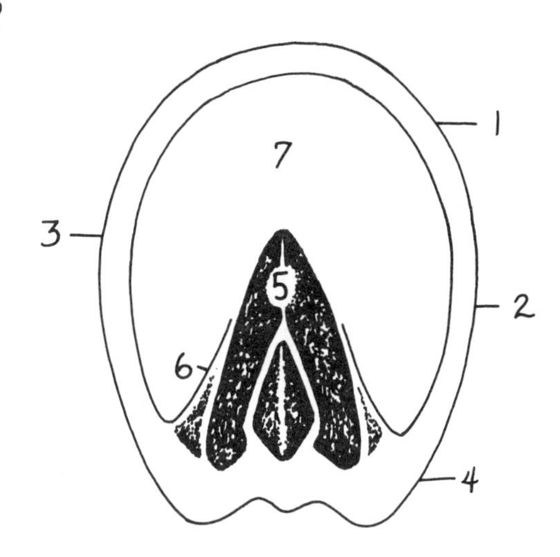

45. Diagram of bottom of hoof. Drawing: Carol Wood

1. *toe*
2. *quarter*
3. *bend of quarter*
4. *heel*
5. *frog*
6. *bar*
7. *sole*

Shoeing

One of the most important points to remember when you have your horse shod is that his feet must be balanced—that is, they should land flat and level on an even weight-bearing surface. Any imbalance will contribute to joint strain or lameness. If one side is higher than (lands before) the other, it will throw the bones in the leg out of alignment. Some horses do need slight adjustments in hoof balance if they interfere (i.e., forge and overreach—when the hind hoof, shod or unshod, occasionally hits the front hoof). This shoeing practice should be handled with great skill and restraint—doing just enough to prevent the problem.

The shoe must be very carefully shaped to fit the horse's foot, and the farrier should leave plenty of room for expansion in the quarters of the hoof. The shoe should be long enough to protect the heel, but not so long that it can catch on anything on the trail or be grabbed (stepped on) by another foot. The farrier must make sure the hoof is shod in a way that allows the straightest possible line from fetlock through pastern to hoof (fig. 46). Some people like to have the foot angle steep, with the heels high, supposing it takes strain off tendons and ligaments; but this also leads to increased strain in the joints. Others like to have the toe long and the heel short in order to lengthen the stride; but this is excessively tiring for the horse. Fatigue can lead to serious tendon and ligament injuries that may take months to heal. It's best not to go to any extreme, but rather to follow the horse's natural angles (fig. 47).

Most horses are shod according to their normal pastern angle, which is usually 50 to 55 degrees to the flat surface they are standing on. This angle is measured by a hoof gauge used by the farrier (fig. 48).

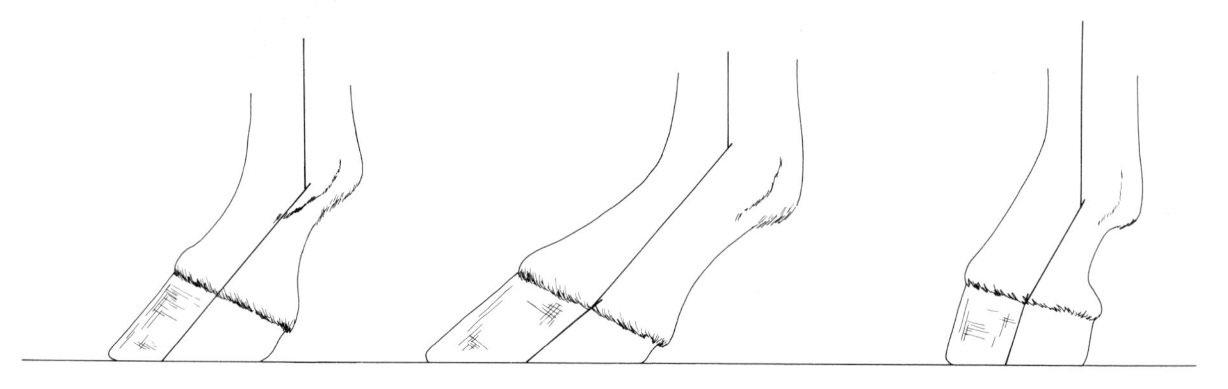

46. Left: correct hoof axis—hoof angle same as pastern. Center: incorrect—long toes, low heel. Right: incorrect—angle steep, high heel. Drawings: Carol Wood

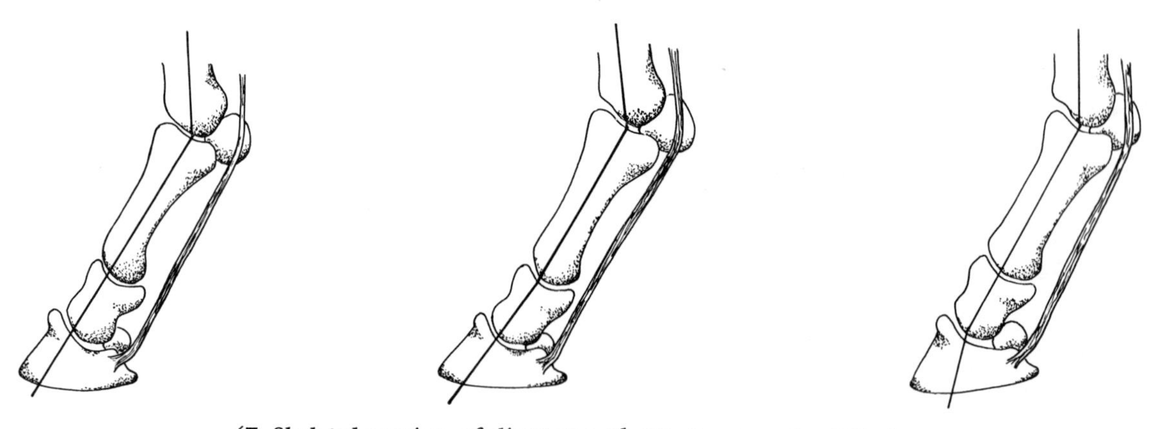

47. Skeletal version of diagrams above. Drawings: Carol Wood

48. Hoof angle being measured with a protractor. *Photo: Karen Paulo*

After shoeing, the hoofs should match. If one front hoof is shod at 49 degrees and the other is shod at 54 degrees, the horse is clearly going to have problems. (Imagine if you had to run around all day wearing one high heel and one sneaker!) However, this is a surprisingly common error. With many horses, the natural angle of the front hoofs differs slightly from that of the hind hoofs. This is normal—just so long as each *pair* is the same.

The most common shoeing faults are: improper trimming; failure to balance the hoof; too small a shoe; poor fit due to rotation or slipping of shoe during nailing; incorrect nailing. Any of these errors may lead to a number of problems, including, at the least, a faulty way of going and, at worst, serious lameness.

Shoes

There are many kinds of shoes available for the horse, and a number of them are experimental (figs. 49 and 50). Despite today's technological advances, good old steel shoes are still widely used and probably best for most horses in most situations. I tend to prefer "rim" shoes to regular shoes because the indentations at the toe and along the nail holes that form an inner and outer rim provide better traction. Also, for reasons unknown, they appear to wear better. Shoes with a wide web (wider than the normal ¾-inch shoe) will give the hoofs more weight-bearing surface as well as more protection from stones; but they also add more weight. The use of borium (flakes of an extra-hard metal welded onto the bottom of the shoe) increases the wear time of the shoe and prevents slipping, but may lead to leg problems, since it tends to grab the ground and is stressful to the leg joints.

There are many plastic shoes on the market that make lots of claims. But few distance riders I know are satisfied with them. They either don't last as long as metal, or the horse has trouble keeping his footing in grass or mud. The hoofs may also be more prone to break up, since the nails tend to move around more easily in a soft shoe.

Shoeing practices vary with the farrier and the horse. Some shoers will use only six nails, even though eight holes are available in most shoes. In this sport it is better to use all eight (unless there is a big chip or some other major weakness in the hoof wall near a nail hole). Horses with a poor-quality hoof wall in the heel may benefit from the added support of "egg-bar" shoes. With the egg-bar shoe the hoof doesn't contract and may even expand, assuming the farrier does his job properly.

Rolling the toes may work well for the horse that tends to travel short in front and needs an easier breakover (the moment in his stride when he lifts his foot off the ground). Rolling the toes also helps horses that interfere since it speeds up the front feet just enough to get them out of the way of the hind feet.

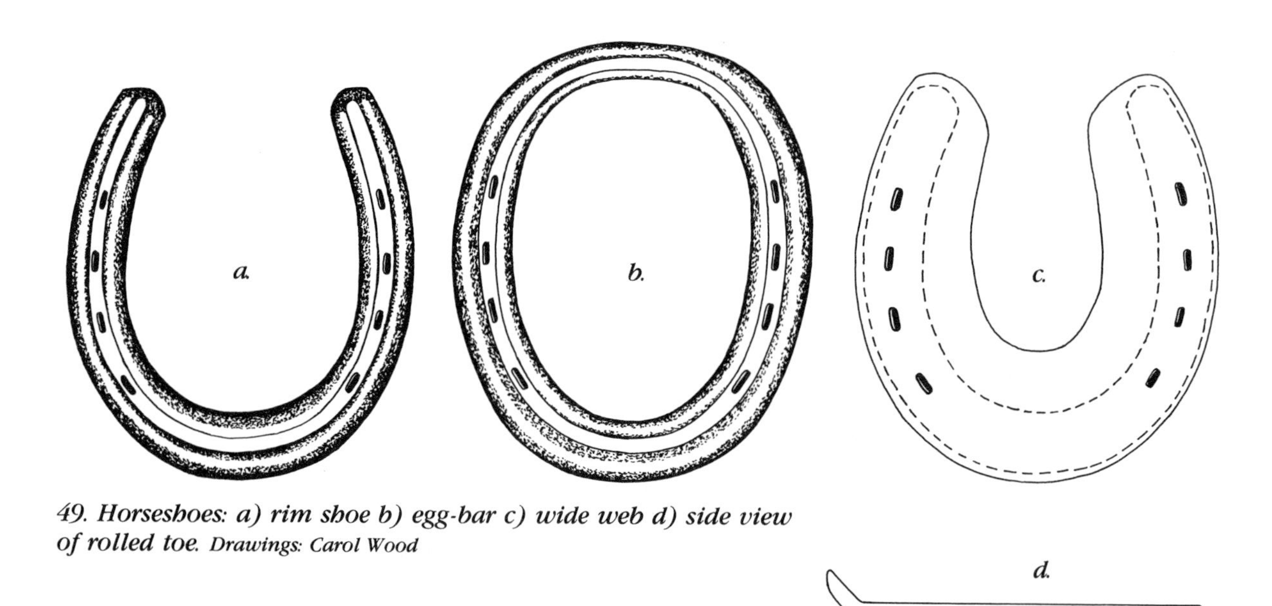

49. Horseshoes: a) rim shoe b) egg-bar c) wide web d) side view of rolled toe. Drawings: Carol Wood

50. Shoes and pads. Top row: rim shoe with rolled toe and full pad; Easy-boot; plastic (flex-step) shoe. Bottom row: Multi-Product regular shoe; MultiProduct rim shoe; Diamond rim shoe (much narrower, especially at the heel). Photo: Karen Paulo

If your horse is having problems with his feet or legs, and your farrier gives you several shoeing choices you are not sure about, then ask your vet for assistance. Sometimes an inexperienced farrier will start experimenting by changing angles or adding a "trailer" (one side of the shoe lengthened), either of which may injure your horse at some point if done incorrectly. Trust your instincts: if a shoeing method doesn't make complete sense to you, then ask questions until you get satisfactory answers.

Pads

The hoof pad (a protective layer between the shoe and hoof) has a very real place in distance riding, even though it has its drawbacks. (Some Competitive rides do not allow hoof pads at all.) One problem is that if used all the time, they tend to let the horse's foot get soft—and it is difficult to see what trouble might be brewing underneath the pad, such as thrush (see p. 72). Another problem is that a padded horse is rarely as surefooted as an unpadded horse, because he is less likely to pay attention to where he puts his feet. The advantage of pads is that they are very helpful to the horse when you are riding on rocky terrain. That is when I pad my horses. But I always remove the pads after the ride, before the horse's feet soften up. Some distance rides will actually advise you to pad your horses, but you should use your own judgment and determine for yourself whether an area is rockier than what your horse is used to. Ride managers often automatically list "pads advised" for the benefit of the few riders who complain about the smallest amount of rock on a trail.

Pads, like shoes, come in all varieties. Leather pads tend not to last long. Pads made from shoemakers' boot soles will hold up well, but the material is often very thick and difficult to work with. Another drawback is that its thickness adds length to a hoof plus unwelcome extra weight. Several horseshoe companies make good, durable, light plastic pads that even rocks can't destroy. And there are several varieties of hoof pads that are specially designed to absorb shock and concussion. They vary in material, durability, and in the way they are applied.

When you use pads, the space between the sole and the pad needs to be filled in order to keep debris out. The filler, or "packing," is traditionally made of oakum and pine tar, but this usually oozes its way out after only a few miles. A better packing is silicone caulking (the rubbery material used around bathtubs) that is squirted in with a caulking gun. After the silicone has been applied, duct tape is wrapped around the hoof to hold it in. Your horse should stand as quietly as possible on a level surface for about an hour to allow the silicone to set. The duct tape may be removed in a day or two.

Occasionally, as the hoof grows, some sand works its way in between the silicone and the sole. If too much gets in, it puts pressure on the sole and the horse will feel "ouchy." When this happens, and you'd rather not pull the pads, you can cut a small hole (½ to ¾ inch in diameter) in the pad, near the toe, and the sand will work its way out.

If your horse is bothered by concussion, and you don't want to pad him completely, you may consider using "rim pads." These are pads that fit under the shoe the same as standard pads, but the sole area is left open. They don't protect the horse from rocks; but they do help absorb and dissipate shock. They are helpful for the horse that is uncomfortable on hard surfaces or whose feet tend to break up from overuse.

Hoof Supplements and Dressings

The vitamin *biotin*, which you add to your horse's feed or administer by syringe, has proven very effective in improving hoof quality and also speeding up hoof growth. There are many brands available, so check with your vet, feed store, tack shop, or magazine ads for the kind and amount of this supplement best suited for your horse.

There are a number of hoof dressings available that frequently make misleading promises about their effectiveness. Basically, hoof dressings are sealants: they simply prevent moisture from escaping so that the hoof will not dry out and crack. It is important that such dressings be applied only to the top surface of the hoof—never the bottom—allowing water to penetrate the sole area and not escape through the hoof wall.

An easy way to help keep your horse's hoofs moist and healthy is to create a mud puddle around his watering trough by allowing the water to overflow each time you fill it.

Cyanoacrylate bonding products are designed to strengthen your horse's hoof wall. They are effective enough to enable some pleasure horses to go entirely unshod. They can also strengthen shod horses' cracked and peeling hoofs, especially around nail holes. A thin layer is applied to the hoof with a sponge; it cures, or dries, in sunlight (or with ultraviolet light) in about twenty seconds. The drawbacks are that it's a bit messy, and it requires an absolutely clean hoof wall. It is also tough on your fingers, but it's well worth it!

Shoeing Schedule

Horses vary in the amount of time they need between shoeing. It depends on their rate of hoof growth, and this is largely determined by age, feed, and activity. As mentioned earlier, six to eight weeks is a good average time span, though some horses can go longer. However, if you are competing regularly, hard shoes will probably wear out sooner. Try to organize your shoeing around your competing schedule. Make sure your horse is shod

51. Hoof wall being trimmed.
Photo: Karen Paulo

at least a week before your ride. If his feet were trimmed too much, the new nails might be too close to the soft wall of the hoof, which could cause him some pain. In addition, overtrimming may make him "sole sore." Allowing a week's time gives the horse's soles a chance to toughen enough to protect them from rocks on the trail. If your farrier regularly pares and trims the frog and sole down to tender tissue, ask him—nicely!—not to trim so much. He should cut away only the dead, rotten frog matter and remove enough around the frog to clean it out. He should also trim *only* enough of the sole to avoid any shoe pressure on it. (See figures 51 and 52.)

Shoeing Alternatives

"Easyboots" are a successful alternative to shoeing (fig. 50). Easyboots are durable, made out of a heavy polyurethane material, and come in several sizes. The boot slips over the hoof and clamps into place with a cable and hook. They work remarkably well and serve many purposes. First, they can be used instead of shoes. Second, their lightness and portability make them ideal in case your horse loses a shoe and you cannot get to a farrier quickly. Third, they can be slipped over the hoof and shoe for temporary protection (as an alternative to padding) when the trail becomes rocky. Finally, they can be removed when no longer needed. Easyboots are simple to use and available from most tack shops, horse catalogs, or farrier suppliers. Like pads, they are welcome on Endurance rides. Most Competitive rides ban them except as a temporary replacement for a shoe lost on the trail; when you find the farrier, you may replace the shoe and continue the ride without penalty.

Remember, your horse's feet are his foundation. They need regular and professional attention. But don't feel you must try out every new idea or product that comes along—just continue to do what's always worked best for your horse.

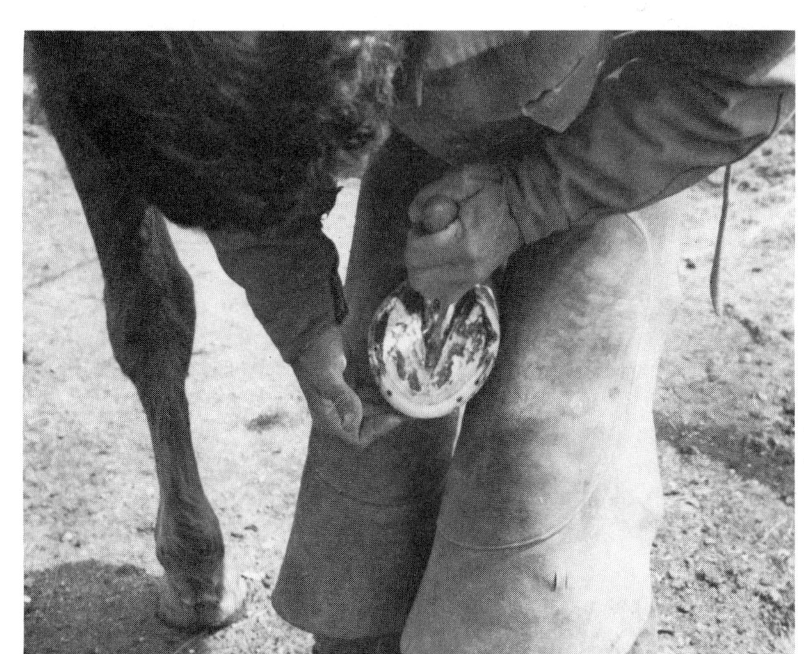

52. Dead tissue being removed from hoof. Photo: Karen Paulo

7 *Electrolytes*
How to Use These Valuable Supplements

Simple inorganic salts (electrolytes) are present in all animal cells and are necessary for every bodily function. A shortage of electrolytes can drastically alter the horse's performance. Dane Frazier DVM asserts, "In the extreme case, malfunction of electrolyte physiology can kill."

What's so precious about electrolytes? Electrolytes, salts found in the bodily fluids of all animals, are necessary for proper metabolic function. They determine the fluid balance within the horse's body, playing a key role in muscle control and relaxation. They are sweated out of the horse's body when the horse does any kind of hard work. When lost in significant quantities, they must be replaced if the horse is going to continue to perform at any level in distance competition. The electrolytes that are lost in the largest amounts are: sodium, potassium, chlorine, calcium, and magnesium. They all play a significant part in the horse's delicate fluid balance.

Sodium is responsible for the maintenance of blood volume; if the horse's blood volume is low, so is his potential for exercise. *Potassium* is vital to muscles, especially the heart; without potassium, the muscles weaken. *Chlorine* balances the sodium and potassium. *Calcium* is very important for muscle and nerve control; a calcium deficiency is often the cause of "synchronous diaphragmatic flutters," commonly known as "thumps" (see p. 68). *Magnesium* is also needed for muscle and nerve control; without it the muscles fail to contract and relax properly, hindering locomotion and possibly inducing thumps.

Fortunately, replenishing these valuable fluid elements is easy, for there are many excellent electrolyte preparations on the market. These products, however, vary in their ingredients, so be sure to read the labels carefully. Virtually all of them contain sodium chloride and potassium chloride. Most will carry forms of calcium such as calcium lactate, calcium gluconate, or calcium carbonate. But you may have to look hard for the product that contains magnesium; when you find it, be sure that the source is *not* magnesium sulfate; instead look for magnesium chloride or magnesium oxide. (Unlike the other two, magnesium sulfate does not get absorbed from the intestinal tract directly into the bloodstream, so it never reaches the cells where it is most needed.) A few commercial electrolyte powders or pastes also supply cobalt, copper, manganese, zinc, and selenium. Nearly all have dextrose as a base, making the taste more palatable.

"An economical electrolyte supplement may be achieved," points out Dane Frazier, "by adding two parts 'Lite salt' [half sodium chloride and half potassium chloride], which is available from most any supermarket, with one part ground limestone [calcium carbonate]." Dr. Frazier also recommends the addition of magnesium oxide. Ask your vet or feed store where you can buy these substances. Since availability varies according to the area you live in, you may have to contact a vitamin manufacturer to find these items.

Dr. Frazier recommends that horses be supplemented with electrolytes during training, competition, and also after the event as part of the recovery process. Other vets feel that the horse needs electrolytes only during competition, and some vets think a horse doesn't need them at all. However, studies have shown that distance horses under stress and sweating heavily—especially when performing in heat—benefit from the use of

53. Darolyn Butler administering electrolytes to her horse Thunder Road, using a syringe. Photo: Howard Hartman

electrolytes. They suffer less stress and and fatigue, and dehydration is minimal. Electrolytes also can prevent metabolic disorders such as thumps, colic, tying up, and exhaustion syndrome (see ch. 12).

Electrolytes cannot be stored in the horse's body, but large quantities exist in intestinal contents. They are normally passed out in sweat and urine fairly quickly. There is no reason to give the horse electrolytes more than a day before a ride, when he is just working lightly. Using a worming syringe, I usually give my horses electrolytes at every vet check during a ride; then one hour after the ride is over. Two and four hours later, I continue the electrolytes with small feedings of mash; and again with their feed the next morning. This is not a hard-and-fast formula, but simply what I have found works for me in my part of the country (the northwestern United States). Generally speaking, electrolytes should be used when the weather is hot and humid and where there is plenty of water for the horse to drink on the trail. They are not needed when the weather is cool or when your horse is only sweating lightly.

If *at any time* your horse stops drinking due to illness or fatigue, electrolytes will only worsen his condition, thereby dehydrating him more. Do not give electrolytes under these circumstances. Get a vet immediately.

The easiest way to administer electrolytes is to mix an ounce or two of electrolyte powder in a small portion of wet bran mash, regular grain, or whatever feed your horse likes best. Another method is to mix one or two ounces of the powder with water in a *clean* worming syringe and squirt it into the horse's mouth (fig. 53). His mouth should be free of any hay or grain, since he could too easily spit the preparation out. Riders have been known to mix electrolytes with apple sauce, karo syrup, honey, molasses, and even cake frosting—all with good results. You can also dredge a wet carrot in electrolyte powder and feed it to your horse.

Part Three

Conditioning

8 *Reading Your Horse*
How to Check His Vital Signs

Knowing how to evaluate your horse's condition is essential. His welfare is in your hands. It is your responsibility to know when he has had too much work and when you need to call for assistance. By paying attention to your horse's vital signs, as well as his attitude and impulsion, you can *read* your horse like a book.

Pulse

A horse with poor pulse recoveries is probably not just simply tired, but could be experiencing *fatigue* or *metabolic* problems that may require veterinary attention (see ch. 12). It is therefore very important for you to know how to take his pulse. The easiest way is with a heart monitor, which you can use in or out of the saddle. Heart monitors are expensive, but definitely worth their cost. (See chapter 10 for a full discussion of heart monitors.) A cheaper, more practical instrument is the stethoscope, which can be purchased from your vet or any medical outlet. When you take your horse's pulse with a stethoscope, place it behind the left elbow, listen closely, and adjust the position of the instrument until you get the clearest sound. You should hear a resounding *lub-dub*. Using a watch with a second hand and counting each *lub-dub* sound as one beat (not two), count for 15 seconds. Multiply this count by four, and you will get the number of beats per minute (bpm). If, for example, you count 12 beats in a 15-second period, your horse has a pulse rate of 48 bpm. Counting for less than 15 seconds is likely to produce an inaccurate reading.

You can also take your horse's pulse with your fingertips by seeking out the arteries under his jaw, inside his knee, under his tail about five inches from the top, or inside his pastern (fig. 54). Once the pulse is found, count beats as described above. If your horse moves around, it may be difficult to obtain an accurate reading using this method.

The resting pulse of your horse should be recorded daily so that you can learn what is normal for him. Be sure the count is taken in a familiar environment when he is calm and undisturbed. The normal resting pulse is usually between 32 and 44, depending on the horse and his condition. A lower resting pulse is usually found in well-conditioned horses, some of whom may even have pulse rates in the upper 20s.

Your horse's pulse should drop rapidly when he is slowed from a lope or trot down to a walk. In a vet check during competition, his pulse should drop to 60 within 10 minutes of arrival; and you should aim for this same pulse rate when you do a mock vet check during conditioning. If his pulse wanders up and down and doesn't stabilize easily, *fatigue* is probably setting in (see ch. 12).

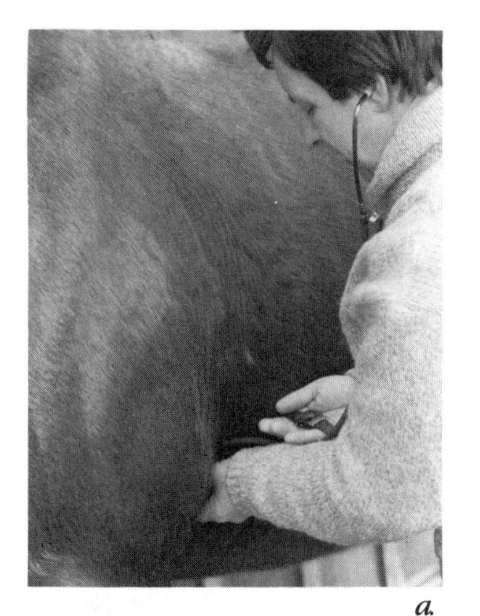

a.

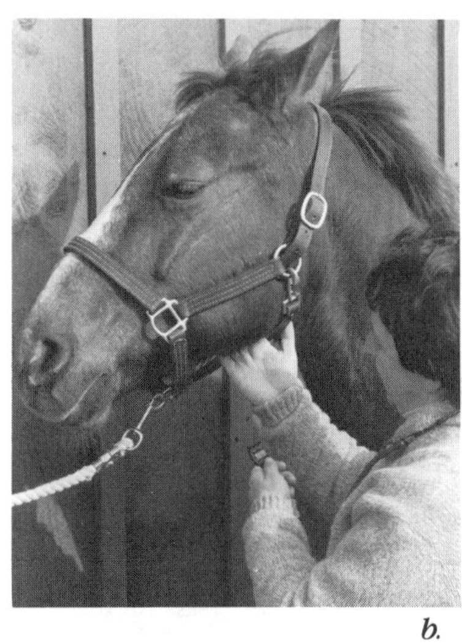

b.

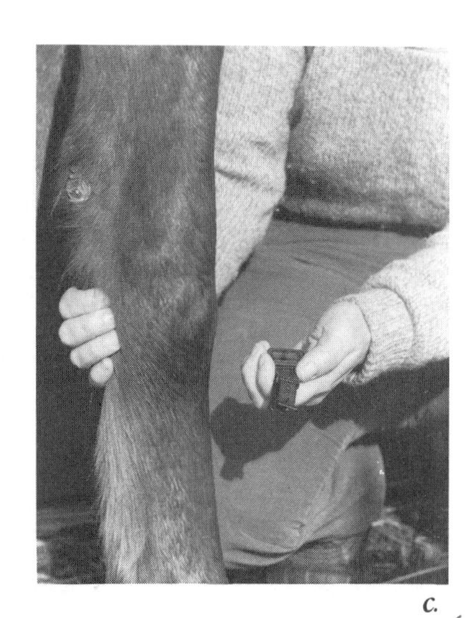

c.

d.

e.

54. Taking the horse's pulse: a) behind left elbow b) under the jaw c) inside the knee d) under the tail e) inside the pastern.
Photos: Mike Noble

Respiration

Respiration is another sign that is easily monitored. A horse's average resting respiration rate is between 8 and 20 breaths per minute. With hard exercise, it can skyrocket to over 100. If the horse is hot he will take rapid shallow breaths in order to dissipate the heat. This is normal and will be interspersed with large deep breaths to satisfy his need for oxygen. The only time for concern is when the horse's respiration becomes labored, irregular, or when it *remains* higher than his pulse rate.

The most accurate way to find your horse's respiration rate is to place your hand on his side, near the flank. Then slide your hand along his side, stopping where you can most easily feel him expand with each breath. The sliding motion prevents you from alarming or tickling your horse, which could happen if you placed your hand against his lower side too suddenly (fig. 55). Count each in-and-out as one (not two). Count for 15 seconds and again multiply by four to get your minute count. A very fit horse takes long, slow breaths; you may have to count for the whole 60 seconds to accurately determine his resting respiration rate.

There are other, less accurate, methods of taking the horse's respiration. Some riders will simply watch the motion of his flanks, or his nostrils, counting the number of in-and-outs for a minute. Others will place their hand up to the horse's nose, counting the blows of hot air that meet their hand. Since most horses will tend to sniff your hand, this method of reading may not reflect the true respiration rate.

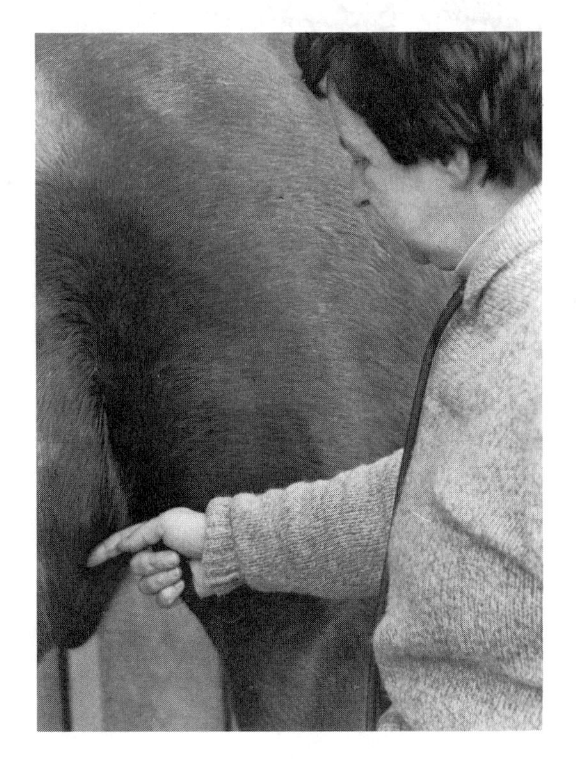

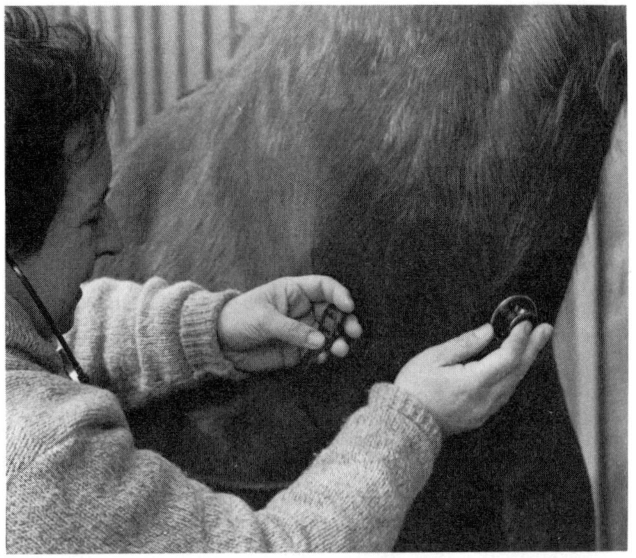

55. Left: pointing to area where respiration is measured or observed. Above: the windpipe—another area where respiration can be measured with a stethoscope. Photos: Mike Noble

Dehydration

In addition to pulse and respiration, there are other indicators of your horse's condition that should be monitored regularly. It is important to check his hydration. A dehydrated horse simply cannot function and can be threatened by a metabolic disorder (see ch. 12). In order to check your horse's hydration, take a pinch of skin on his neck, or point of shoulder, then let it go. His skin is normally very elastic and will snap back into place like a rubberband. But if your horse is dehydrated, his skin fold will stay up at first, then sink very slowly back into place. Count the seconds it takes for the skin to fall back. If it stays up for over three seconds, you'll know your horse is quite dehydrated (fig. 56). He needs to be offered water and should not be ridden until his condition improves.

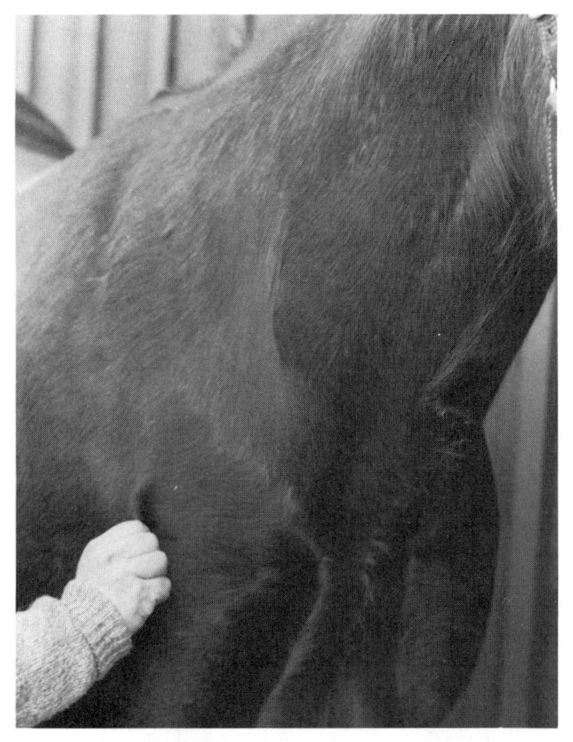

56. Skin-pinch test for dehydration at point of shoulder. Photo: Mike Noble

Mucous Membranes and CRT

Your horse's mucous membranes (gums and inner eyelids) reveal a great deal about his condition. Both should be light pink. If gums are muddy or blue, it indicates a lack of oxygen due to fatigue or even worse, shock (see ch. 12). When the inner eyelids become red, it is an indication of blood congestion, still another sign of fatigue (fig. 57).

His *capillary refill time* (CRT) is another means of evaluating tiredness and dehydration. Place your thumb firmly against your horse's gum for two seconds, then remove it. In a normal, healthy horse, the body fluids will rush back into place in one or two seconds, returning all color to the whitish area that was left by your thumb pressure. A horse low in body fluids will have a slow CRT—three seconds or more (fig. 58).

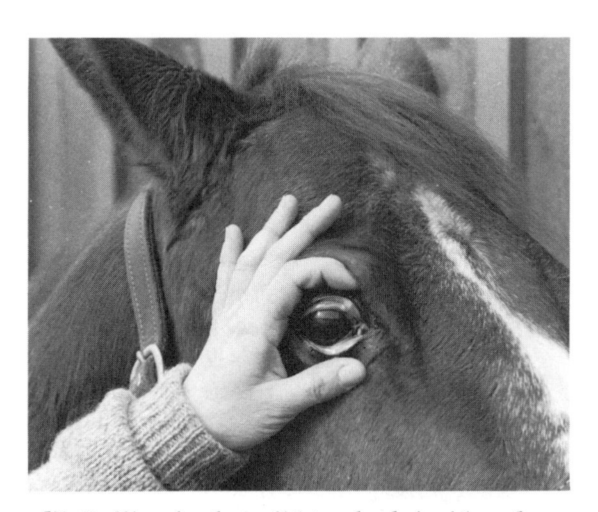

57. Rolling back eyelid to check inside color. Photo: Mike Noble

58. CRT: left, pressing down on horse's gum for two seconds; right, white spot on gum is observed to time the return of normal color. Photos: Mike Noble

Sweat

A hot horse normally sweats as a natural means of cooling itself. If your horse is hot but not sweating, chances are he is, or will become, dehydrated—so always be alert to this symptom. He should sweat clean, clear liquid. The sweat should not be yellow, white, or sticky—signs that his system is not working properly to cool him and that you need to take action, such as cooling him with water or supplementing him with electrolytes.

Smell

A healthy horse doesn't smell bad, even when your nose is right next to his skin. If your horse's skin or sweat smell unpleasant, he is probably ill. Abnormal-smelling urine may indicate he has a problem with his kidneys, and foul-smelling feces can be the result of problems with his intestinal bacteria. Bad breath also indicates a stomach problem, though it could be caused by a rotting tooth.

Gut Sounds

Gut sounds are also a measure of your horse's well-being. A healthy, resting individual will have lots of bubbling and gurgling noises that can be easily heard through a stethoscope or just by placing your ear against the horse's flank (fig. 59). If a horse is overstressed, these sounds may be absent, because much of his blood supply is diverted to his brain, heart, and lungs, where it is needed more at that moment. If this happens, the horse will have no hunger and will often have colic (see ch. 12). It is a sign that your horse needs rest; you may also let him have a few nibbles of a wet feed or grass until he recovers. It is important not to overfeed a horse who has no gut sounds.

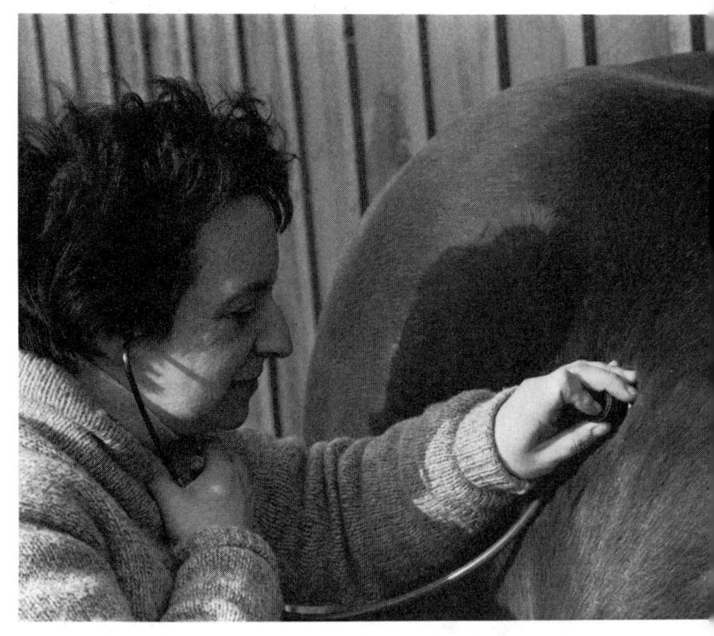

59. Listening for gut sounds. *Photo: Mike Noble*

Stride

Riders who know how to read their horses can often detect subtle changes by paying attention to the rhythm and length of their stride. Unevenness and a shortened stride can signal muscle fatigue, the onset of lameness, or tying up. (Do not make this observation when your horse is picking his way over rocky terrain, where he is very likely to be uneven.) Any changes in his impulsion or strength within his stride may also indicate fatigue. Sometimes this is stiffness that can be remedied by changing your pace—if you've been trotting, a brief canter can actually limber up the horse since he'll be using different muscles. If your horse is still stiff after this short canter, then it is advisable to get off and walk him.

Urine and Feces

Distance riders are a rare equestrian group because they are so highly concerned with the quality and quantity of their horses' urine and feces. While it may appear strange to see a rider watching a horse urinate and saying "Looks good!" the fact is, the rider is simply evaluating the horse's condition. On a ride of 50 to 100 miles in hot weather, the horse's urine will often become a stronger yellow as it becomes more concentrated. This is normal. But orange, or worse yet brown, or else very *little* urine may also signal the following: dehydration, fatigue, tying up—or all three (see ch. 12). Urine that continues to be clear yellow and plentiful assures a rider that this horse is not being unduly stressed.

The horse's feces should not become watery, nor should they contain mucus; these symptoms usually indicate tiredness and stress. On the other hand, if the feces are very hard and dry, your horse is probably not taking in enough water.

By reading your horse well, you can evaluate all the data that his body is giving you and decide how he should be trained and ridden. There are countless ways to monitor your horse—these will come with experience. I have mentioned only the more common methods. Eventually you should come to know your horse as well as you know yourself!

9 *Endurance First, Speed Second*

Conditioning Your Horse

The safest way to condition a horse is to make physical demands on each of his various bodily systems and then allow them to rebuild before subjecting them to further stress or aggravation. You cannot condition him by just taking him out and running him into the ground; the process must be done slowly and carefully if you aim to build him into a strong and durable athlete. A program that is too severe will break down one or more of his physical systems. Conditioning the distance horse is a lengthy and strenuous process—there are no "three-week wonders" in this sport!

Studies have shown that it takes as long as three years for a horse's *entire* body to reach its ultimate level of fitness. His muscles and cardiovascular system will improve the fastest—usually within six months. At this point your horse will often appear very fit. But beware! Many riders have pushed their horses harder than they should at this stage, causing lameness; even if the horse *looks* fit, his tendons, ligaments, and bones are not ready yet. A horse's bones may take up to two years to be fully conditioned for distance riding, and his tendons and ligaments usually require three years or more to reach their maximum strength. If you want to build up a horse that will last for thousands of miles of competition and remain sound, then you must strive to have the horse's body as fit as possible. Trotting mile after mile should become second nature for any distance horse.

Aerobic and Anaerobic Exercise

Before discussing conditioning programs, I would like to elaborate on the two types of exercise—aerobic and anaerobic—that are involved in any program and the three types of muscles.

In *aerobic* exercise, oxygen intake and consumption are the same; the horse never goes into oxygen debt. Aerobic fitness exercise is achieved with lots of walking and trotting and is the basic type of conditioning. It is usually referred to as "long, slow distance" (LSD). With this exercise approach, distance is gradually and continually increased, but speed is not. This kind of conditioning provides the foundation of strength that you will continue to build on. If it is omitted from your horse's conditioning program, there is a good chance he will eventually be troubled by lameness or some other illness.

In *anaerobic* exercise, your horse uses up more oxygen than he takes in. This happens in speed work and sprints, where the horse goes into oxygen debt and is forced to huff and puff to get enough air to continue. This type of exercise should come much later in your program. If used wisely it will strengthen your horse, but if not it can lead to the horse's breaking down. You must build endurance *before* introducing speed. (For discussion of aerobic and anaerobic fitness, see chapter 10.)

60. Speedy, a very fit horse, eager and ready to go the day before the 1986 Race of Champions, Colorado. *Photo: John Di Pietra*

The horse's body contains three types of muscle: *smooth*, found mostly in internal organs; *skeletal*, used for bodily movement; and *cardiac*, found in the heart. Conditioning affects only cardiac and skeletal muscles, making them more efficient and improving their blood supply. It also allows the heart to perform more effectively. Skeletal muscles comprise both endurance (slow-twitch) and sprint (fast-twitch) fibers. The slow-twitch muscles can sustain motion for hours, while the fast-twitch muscles afford quick bursts of speed. These fiber types are differentiated by their ability to use oxygen—slow twitch burning fats and stored glycogen aerobically, the other having only moderate ability to use oxygen. Training aerobically increases the capacity of slow-twitch fibers to use oxygen; anaerobic training develops the speed fibers.

Conditioning Program

Please note that the conditioning methods that follow are intended as *guidelines* only. All horses are individuals and should be treated as such. There are no hard-and-fast rules, so feel free to modify these suggestions to fit your horse's capabilities.

Three-Year-Old Horses

I do not recommend riding a three-year-old. The risk of injury to a horse this young is too great, and concussion and strain on joints, tendons, and ligaments at this age may ruin the horse for the future. It pays to let your youngster have an extra year of development. However, if you must ride your three-year-old, then do gentle exercise and *never* stress him. Start out at a walk and slowly add a bit of trotting. Stick to this LSD exercise—no cantering or galloping. Build up to rides of 3 to 5 miles, depending upon your horse's opportunity to condition *himself* outdoors by running with other horses. Don't ride a youngster of this age in the ring for any length of time (it's boring work, and cornering is hard on his legs), just head for the trail in the company of an older horse. Always keep an eye on his legs for the smallest signs of swelling and/or heat, and if these occur stop riding him completely until several weeks after the symptoms have disappeared.

Four-Year-Olds

I like to start working with a distance horse when he is four. By that time he has usually lost a lot of the silliness of immaturity, his attention span is longer, and he is also strong enough to be ridden a bit farther. After he is going comfortably and is used to being ridden regularly, you can start a conditioning program.

Stick to LSD exercise, which will condition his soft tissue (muscles, tendons, ligaments, heart, lungs, and circulatory system) without stressing his bones. Riding him every other day works best, with turnout and free exercise on the off days. Begin with walking rides of about five miles and work in short trots on the flat and uphill after two weeks. *Gradually*, at a rate of about two miles each week, increase the distance to ten miles. When he is doing this comfortably, choose one day each week for a longer ride; increase this day's mileage slowly so that by late fall, before you rest him over the winter, you are doing around 25 miles, preferably over varied terrain. At this point the ride should be two-thirds trotting. Keep your average speed down to 6 to 8 miles per hour. As your horse gets closer to five years old, you can occasionally allow him a gentle canter uphill (easier on his legs than downhill canters, which should still be avoided at this stage) for about a quarter mile. Don't overdo it; he may want to do more, but you must remind him that you know more than he does.

As mentioned earlier, horses that are 48 months old may be ridden on 25- to 35-mile novice Endurance and Competitive rides. However, I do not recommend it, nor do many other veteran distance riders. Too often, young horses are burned out by an overanxious rider wanting to come in first. If you use the ride as a learning experience for the youngster, it can be useful. But don't let yourself get caught up in the competition.

Five-Year-Olds

A five-year-old, conditioned correctly, should be able to cover more miles at a slightly faster speed than a younger horse. You must remember, though, that if he has not been properly conditioned previously, he will need to be started and trained just like a four-year-old. But it's still a good idea to stay mostly with LSD work, miles of trotting, and very little cantering.

Six Years and Older

A horse six years or older can physically tolerate more work. After you have carefully advanced him to weekly rides of 25 miles over varied terrain—and he is doing this easily—you can begin to work his legs harder. His bones, tendons, and ligaments (which have received relatively minor stress to this point) are now ready for more strengthening. A good gallop of about a half mile on a gradual uphill will make new demands of his body and will strengthen it in many valuable ways. Work this into one of your shorter rides of 8 to 10 miles. After a few weeks, if all is going well, you can add one more short gallop into that same workout, so that you're doing two half-mile gallops.

Hill Work

If there are hills around you, by all means use them. Five miles of slow hill work will do far more good than ten miles of trotting on the flat. Your horse will learn how to rate himself; his muscles and cardiovascular system will build up easily with less strain on his legs; and he will learn to use his rear end efficiently on hills. Since most distance rides are in fact hilly or mountainous, training on hills can be a big advantage. Horses of all ages and stages of conditioning will benefit from this type of work (fig. 61).

Further Conditioning

After three or four months of this type of conditioning, a typical weekly schedule for a horse six years or older, aiming toward an Endurance ride, would be: one weekly workout of 25 to 30 miles over varied terrain at an average speed of 7 to 10 miles per hour; and two or three rides of 8 to 10 miles with one of them including two half-mile gallops.

If you are aiming toward Competitive events, your training should be geared to speeds of 5 to 7 miles per hour, which is what you will need in that type of ride. You won't have to train as many miles per day, since entry-level Competitive rides are only 25 to 35 miles long. A weekly schedule should include one ride of 20 miles at an average speed of 5 to 7 miles per hour, and two or three rides of 6 to 8 miles, plus one or more gallops.

61. All horses benefit from conditioning work on hills. Photo: Purina

At this point, the Endurance horse should be ready for his first 50-mile ride, which is sanctioned by the AERC and many breed registries (see appendix II). There are 25-mile Endurance competitions, but I prefer to start out with a 50-mile ride. Your horse may become too accustomed to going just the 25-mile distance and might be reluctant to head out for an additional 25 miles, particularly if you are competing on a trail with loops that return to camp in the middle of the ride.

Many horses and riders have failed when their first effort has been a 100-mile ride, so it is a good idea to complete a few 50-milers before tackling the longer distance. If your horse handles the 50-mile distance with no ill effects, he should be ready for a longer ride. After several 50-mile outings, he will also have gained invaluable experience. (See chapter 23 for discussion of advanced conditioning for a 100-mile ride.)

Resting Your Horse After Competitions

After a 50-mile ride, I like to give my horse at least three days of complete rest, turning him out in the field where he can exercise. If it is the horse's *first* ride experience he may need an entire week off. Even an experienced campaigner may require a full week off after a very tough or particularly fast, stressful 50. When I do resume conditioning, I take it easy, riding about eight miles, trotting about three quarters of the distance. I evaluate how strong the horse feels. If he still feels tired, I may shorten the ride to five miles and do less trotting and more walking. If the horse is strong and raring to go, I'll let him gallop a hill or two.

The needs of a first-year horse will differ from those of the seasoned, experienced horse, because the latter is fitter, stronger, and better developed. The average first-year horse should not be allowed to compete weekly, especially if he is only five or six years old. He will lack the superior fitness and strength that is required to compete week after week. A first-year horse ideally should only be competed monthly. He needs more time to bounce back after his first few rides. As he gains in strength and fitness, he will recover more quickly and perhaps by the end of the season he can compete every two to three weeks.

The veteran horse with at least three years' experience can often compete weekly or on multiday events. The first-year horse's entire system would not be able to cope with the demands put on it by such a rigorous ride schedule.

➡ Always be aware of even the most subtle signs of overwork in your horse, and be willing to back off and rest him whenever he needs it.

Training Along the Trail

During your training rides, hold simulated vet checks. Allow your horse some time to stand around and eat a bit of grass. Check his pulse and get a feel for how long it takes him to recover. Sponge him down if the weather is warm. If you are riding in a group, ask each person to check *another* rider's horse. This not only provides an objective measurement, it also lets a horse get used to other people handling him—which can be traumatic for some individuals who are unaccustomed to strangers.

While it is important for a distance horse to be conditioned alone, and to get him used to going down the trail on his own (since this often happens during a long ride), it is equally important to get him accustomed to riding with other horses. Juggle your position with your friends' so that sometimes you are in the front of the group, sometimes in the middle getting used to horses all around, and sometimes in the back. A horse that is not used to the company of others tends to waste a lot of energy worrying about them (fig. 62).

*62. **Opposite:** It's important to get your horse accustomed to training with others so that he doesn't get excited and waste precious energy at a competition. Photo: Charles Barieau*

The Horse's Mental Attitude

Don't overlook your horse's mental attitude. He should move happily down the trail under his own impulsion, without the rider needing a whip or spurs. If he shows any change in attitude, check to make sure he is not ill or that he possibly has a nutritional deficiency. Confinement creates neuroses in many horses, so allow them lots of turnout and free exercise with other horses as often as possible.

Layoffs

Many Endurance and Competitive riders let their horses rest during the cold and icy months. If you choose to turn your horse out for the winter—or lay him off for any other reason, such as an injury—you should be prepared, when you bring him back into work, to spend about two months of LSD training as a base for further conditioning. Luckily, a horse does not lose condition as quickly as a human does. In fact, he regains his previous level of condition relatively fast. After the two months of LSD work, and if you are sure the horse is legged up, you can carefully advance him to the desired level of training. If he has been laid up due to injury, this process may take longer. Remember always to monitor his pulse following a workout and look carefully for any signs of overexertion.

Horses over Fifteen Years of Age

Whatever age your horse is, if he has not had previous distance conditioning, you must still build the foundations with LSD work. An older horse—15 years or more—still possesses the potential for distance work, though his speed may not be great. Such individuals will thrive on LSD work and, in fact, often need less conditioning than a younger horse. When I was riding my old gelding, Tonkawaikah (fig. 63), in his late teens and early twenties, he really loved the miles of trotting, but the speed work tired him. One of his favorite exercises was ponying (fig. 64). I would pony him halfway around a loop of trail and then turn him

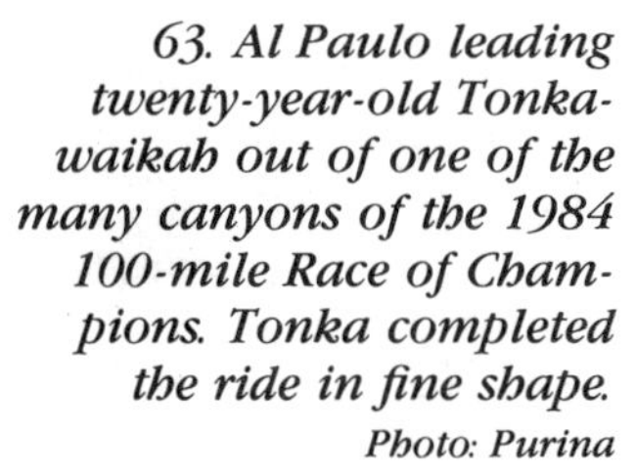

63. Al Paulo leading twenty-year-old Tonkawaikah out of one of the many canyons of the 1984 100-mile Race of Champions. Tonka completed the ride in fine shape.
Photo: Purina

loose and let him head for home at his own pace—which was usually faster than mine. I would watch him from a distance and he'd go cross-country on his favorite shortcut, trotting the hills and cantering the flats. One day when I had been out ponying him, my husband, Al, was still at home and he observed Tonkawaikah alone, beating the path at a rapid trot. A short distance from the house, the horse slowed down on his own and walked in cool—just as he always did when we rode him!

As you can tell by now, there are many different aspects of conditioning—and a great deal to remember. I would now like to emphasize what I feel are the most important guidelines.

• Be certain your horse is sound, healthy, parasite-free, and on an optimal diet for energy production and weight retention.

• Don't *condition* daily; three or four days a week are sufficient. Muscles require 48 to 72 hours to heal and develop into stronger tissue. So vary the types of work during the week to stress different parts of your horse's body. This means that you don't have to work hard every day. Schedule light days, and days off, each week.

• Increase work and stress levels very *gradually*.

• Examine your horse each morning at feeding time. Check him for puffy legs, tenderness, and heat in the joints. Stiffness, lack of appetite or alertness, a dull rough coat, and an abnormal attitude are all common signs of overuse.

• Record your horse's pulse daily. Learn what his normal readings are. An elevated pulse could indicate impending illness or lameness. Record his pulse when you dismount, and then within 10 and 30 minutes to determine his recovery rates. A horse that fails to reach 60 or less bpm within 30 minutes has been ridden too hard; adjust your training program accordingly.

• Take time to warm up before workouts and cool down after them. The horse that is "rode hard, brought in hot, and put up wet" will seldom last.

• Never ride hard or fast downhill. If you do, you risk seriously injuring your horse from the concussion to his front end.

A well-planned conditioning program—together with good feeding and care—will give you a solid horse to compete with and to enjoy for many years. It takes a long time to build a champion. But when people marvel at your *great* horse, it will be worth all your time and effort!

64. Ponying is an excellent timesaver when you are conditioning more than one horse. It is also a good method of training the young horse and getting him used to unfamiliar sights and sounds. Here Al Paulo, on Dusty Desperado, ponies Chollima in Oregon. Photo: Karen Paulo

10 *The Heart as a Gauge of Fitness*

How to Use a Heart Monitor

By now you should understand how important it is to know your horse's normal resting pulse rates and be able to evaluate his pulse recovery rates. The big question is, what pulse rate is the horse recovering *from*? Was he 160 bpm at the top of that last hill? Or 196 bpm? A rider can learn a lot of things with a stethoscope, but determining your horse's *working* pulse is not one of them. The horse's heart rate plummets the second you slow him from a gallop to a walk. It drops so fast that by the time you stop the horse, dismount, get out your stethoscope, place it on him, and start counting, the pulse has already dropped *at least* 30 beats. Of course, you can save time by feeling the pulse with your hand placed beneath the girth, or your fingers placed on a major artery. But a rider has to be very skilled to find the right spot quickly.

If you want to have a completely accurate picture of your horse's condition at all times, an on-board heart monitor is a necessity. It is not cheap, however—prices range from $400 to $1,000. But if you compare these prices to the cost of replacing your horse, or having to pay extra vet bills due to lameness from overtraining, the monitor then seems more affordable.

Some people shy away from heart monitors. Many longtime racehorse trainers scoff at those who use them, saying, "A real horseman doesn't need a gadget to tell him about his horse. I know when my horses are tired and when they're fit." Maybe so. But do you suppose they know exactly how hard that horse is really working? It's doubtful. No one should fear or resent a device that enables the horse's body to "talk" to you. Such an instrument is a learning tool, teaching us more about our horses than we knew before. This increases our awareness and in the long run improves our horsemanship.

How the Heart Monitor Works

There are different kinds of heart monitors. They all consist of a small box (the transmitter), plus two cables with electrodes at their ends. Some heart monitors have small electrodes that attach to the skin of the neck and shoulder. These often require clipping those areas of the horse, the use of electrode gel, and replacement of the electrodes each time the device is used. Other monitors have larger electrodes—one placed under the saddle and the other under the girth—and you need only wet the hide in these areas to conduct the electrical impulse of the heartbeat (figs. 65 and 66). Still others have electrodes built into the saddle pad, with the transmitter box built into the saddle. The *type* of monitor you choose, however, is not as important as its accuracy. Be sure that you are buying a heart monitor that has been made specifically for horses. It must be accurate at ranges from 25 to 280 bpm. Some human heart monitors have been modified for equine use, but they are often inaccurate.

In order for the heart monitor to function at its best, you must know what is normal for your horse. So saddle up with it and record your horse's heart rates at various gaits and various speeds within the gaits. Every horse is different. For example, I have one horse that walks with a 56-bpm pulse, trots the flat at an eight-mile-per-hour pace with an 80-bpm average, trots slight uphills at 110 bpm, and does 150 bpm on steep slopes. After a half-mile uphill gallop, he's usually 143 bpm at the top, dropping to 72 after a minute of walking. A more experienced horse of mine—a veteran campaigner—works at an average of ten beats less per minute than the first horse. By knowing and recording each horse's working pulse rates, you can

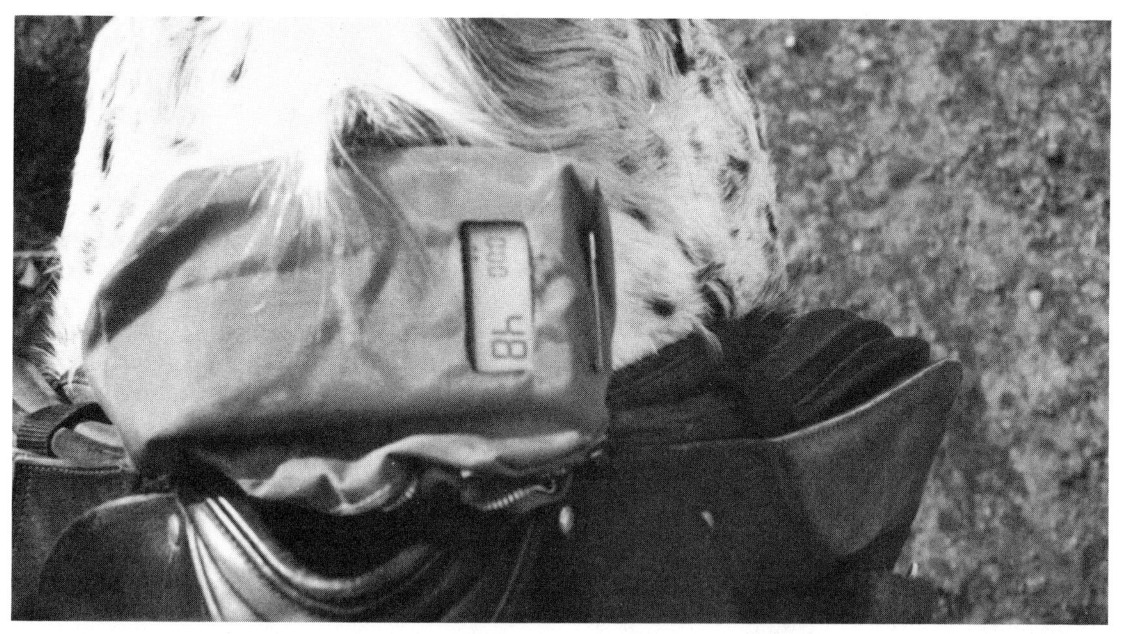

65. Rider's-eye view of a heart monitor in a Velcro pouch that fastens to the saddle and allows the rider to dismount and lead the horse, unencumbered by cables and straps. The readout is quite visible and is easier to see in this position than if the monitor is carried on rider's arm or thigh. Photo: Karen Paulo

recognize the relative progress in his fitness—because these rates will lower in time, and his recovery will get faster.

Aerobic and Anaerobic Fitness

When conditioning for distance, the heart monitor takes all the guessing out of when the horse is working aerobically or anaerobically. On long, easy gallops, you can maintain the horse's speed within aerobic ranges. The heart rates can tell you when he has had enough, which will prevent fatigue and overtraining. Studies have shown that the best aerobic training is done at approximately 130 to 140 bpm. It's a good idea to learn how fast your horse has to travel to obtain this optimal heart rate—that is, when the cardiovascular and the muscle systems work efficiently yet are stressed enough to cause true conditioning.

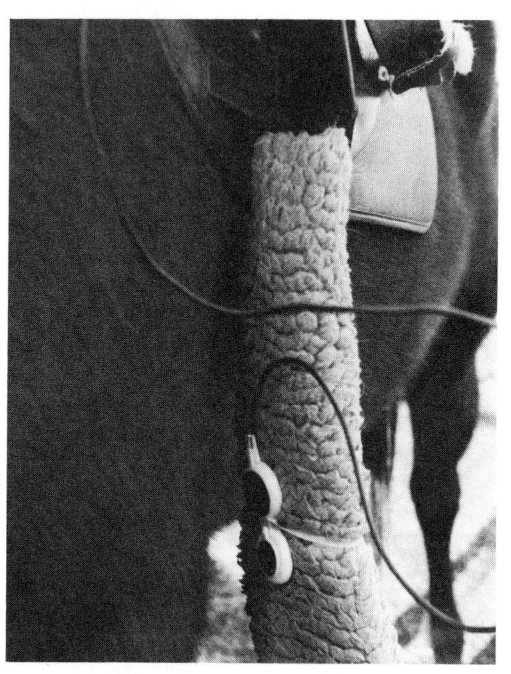

66. An electrode placed between girth and horse. Here, it is held in place by a rubber band to prevent slipping and thereby ensure accurate readings. Photo: Karen Paulo

The heart monitor shows you precisely when your horse is creeping over that aerobic threshold into the anaerobic zone.

We often think that one has to ride fast for work to be anaerobic. Not true. A horse's pulse can reach 160 to 180 bpm by trotting a mile uphill, or even when walking up a very steep grade. Speed is not the only factor in determining how hard a horse works—indeed, many horses will have a lower heart rate at a slow canter than they have at a fast trot. The slope and footing also have a great deal to do with it.

➘ Distance conditioning usually becomes anaerobic at 150 to 180 bpm, depending upon the individual horse's physical makeup, athletic ability, and fitness level. When these rates are exceeded, a buildup of lactic acid occurs, and fatigue begins to take over. Fatigue is what we must avoid, since it is the prime cause of lameness and illness (see ch. 12). The rider needs to be able to recognize the combination of pace, terrain, and conditions that bring his horse to anaerobic function. And learning the speed at which your horse's heart works most efficiently is an essential part of pacing him correctly (see also chapters 6 and 9).

Many monitors have a High and a Low setting which can be adjusted to your horse's fitness level. For example, if you want him to maintain a pace somewhere between 100 and 140 bpm, set your Low at 99 and your High at 141, and the heart monitor will beep when these levels are reached. This enables you to feel and sense your horse, rather than watch the monitor all the time. As the horse gains in fitness, he will be able to move faster within those parameters. For instance, he may trot an 8-mile-per-hour pace at 120 bpm in the early stages of conditioning; two months later, he may trot 10 miles per hour at 120 bpm. In later stages of conditioning, you may need to use either more speed or steeper hills to push the horse over 160 bpm to further his physical fitness. Short anaerobic workouts of about a half mile at 180–200 bpm (never *over* 200 bpm) will allow the horse's body to adjust to, then rid itself of, lactic acid—provided that ample recovery time is allowed.

Other Uses for the Heart Monitor

When under severe physical or emotional stress, most horses have an elevated heart rate. In this situation, the heart monitor is extremely useful, since it can signal oncoming lameness when the condition is still quite subtle and might otherwise go unnoticed. I remember when one of my horses trotted at 136 bpm, where he would normally be about 100. When walked, his pulse was at 78 bpm, and never dropped into the 50s, his usual walking rate. I knew something was wrong, so I dismounted and walked home. Two days later, the horse was "off" in the left front. But, thanks to the monitor, that condition was short-lived. Had I continued working him as normal, the lameness would surely have been more severe.

Elevated heart rates can also signal other impending illnesses—again, in the early stages when the physical signs are often too subtle for most riders to notice. On the other hand, some horses experience *lower*-than-normal pulse rates before they become ill. Just be aware of any readings that are not within your horse's normal range.

According to a heart monitor manual, some *average* heart-rate readings for horses are as follows:

Walking 4 mph	*80 bpm*
Trotting 8 mph	*120 bpm*
Trotting 10 mph	*140 bpm*
Cantering/galloping 12 mph	*160 bpm*

One warning regarding the heart monitor: Don't let it become a crutch. Don't rely on it so much that you ignore all other signs and signals that the horse is sending you. The heart monitor may be a valuable aid in training and evaluating your horse, but it shouldn't be your only aid. Always look at your horse's overall appearance. Evaluate his well-being and disposition. No tool or machine should ever replace the rapport between a horse and rider—it should only serve to improve the communication and understanding.

11 *Make Your Horse Last*
Warming Up and Cooling Down When Conditioning or at a Ride

There are many ways to ruin your horse's potential career in distance riding. The most common ways are failure to follow good warm-up and cool-down procedures.

Warming Up

Too many riders expect their horse to go out and give his best performance totally "cold," without first preparing him for the task ahead. This lack of consideration can be a major factor in the cause of injuries—usually muscle and tendon strains. If your horse has been stabled or tied all night, or has just come out of a trailer, his muscles are going to be tight and stiff. There will probably be some congestion in his joints—waste and by-products that appear as stocking-up due to lack of circulation while standing. By walking your horse around, and by manipulating his muscles and joints by hand, you will bring about better circulation—which will allow more blood and oxygen into those stiff areas. This enables his muscles and joints to perform better and with less stress in the ride ahead.

Preride Exercise

At an Endurance competition, your options for preride exercise are open. Some riders will warm up their horse around camp for 15 minutes or so before the ride starts. Some will also stretch their horse's muscles by picking up one leg at a time and pulling it forward and back, slightly working his joints with mild rotation (fig. 67). If you do this, be careful not to force the rotating motion against any resisting muscles. Be gentle. At Competitive rides, particularly multiday rides, preride exercise is limited to a 10- or 15-minute walk in hand. This makes the rider's manual work on the horse's legs and muscles all the more important.

67. Warm up your horse by pulling one leg at a time with gentle rotation of the joints.
Photo: Al Paulo

Cooling Down

It is just as important to give your horse similar attention and consideration after a ride is over. I firmly believe that a rider begins to prepare his horse for the next distance competition when he crosses the finish line of the last one. Poor care at this point can cause a number of problems that may or may not show up right away. One horse may become colicky within a very short time; another horse's postride problems may snowball into bigger ones later on.

If you have ridden 25 to 50 miles at a fairly easy pace—5 to 7 miles per hour—and crossed the finish line in the same manner, your horse should require very little cooling down. He will probably finish with a pulse of 60 bpm. In a very short time, all his bodily functions will have returned to normal. After a few drinks of water, a little sponging on the neck, and a bit of grass or hay, he will be resting happily.

68. If the horse becomes hot in cold weather, throw a blanket (or cooler) over him, saddle and all, and loosen the girth. After a few minutes, you can remove the saddle.
Photo: Al Paulo

Dealing with the Hot Horse

For a hot horse who has been ridden hard and is sweating, steamy, and breathing heavily, more attention is required. He should be walked about slowly—still saddled, but with his cinch or girth loosened. He should be allowed 12 to 15 swallows of water every few minutes. If the weather is cold or windy, you should place a wool cooler over him and his saddle to protect his muscles from a sudden chill (fig. 68). On milder days, a fishnet cooler will keep the horse's body temperature high enough to get him dry without chilling him. On a day too warm for a complete cover, it's still a good idea to place a cooler behind the saddle. This allows him to dissipate accumulated heat without chilling his major locomotive muscles (fig. 69).

This is a good time to give your horse electrolytes—if needed. But since it is too soon to feed him any grain, you should administer the electrolytes by syringe.

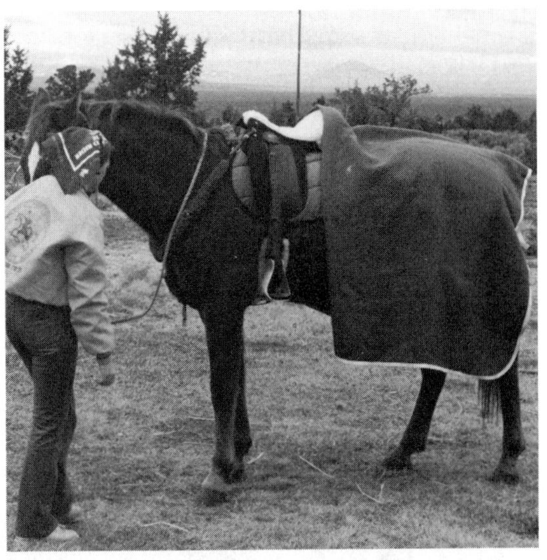

69. As you unsaddle, fold the blanket back so that the loin and hips don't get chilled. Then pull the blanket forward again.
Photo: Al Paulo

Walking the Horse

You may be wondering why you need to walk a horse that has just gone 50 or 100 miles. The horse's muscles act as auxiliary blood pumps moving the blood and waste materials out of his muscles and back toward his heart. When a hot horse is allowed to stand, that blood tends to pool as the circulation slows down. If the waste materials are allowed to remain in the area, the end result is muscle soreness, stiffness, and filling of his joints. A mile of walking will do more good for his recovery than a pint of the best liniment.

Walking is extremely beneficial to your horse's entire system—not just his legs. The only time you should *not* walk a horse after a ride is when he is showing signs of exhaustion (see ch. 12). As a normal practice, I like to remove the saddle about ten minutes after the ride. If the weather is cold, I still leave the cooler on the horse's loins and hips. At this time most horses will have cooled down enough so that it's all right for them to stand still while their legs, head, and neck are sponged with cool or tepid water.

Bathing the Horse

On occasion, I have seen some horses soaked from head to hoof with *cold* water and with no obvious ill effects. But I have also seen many horses develop problems from this approach. As a rule, it is better to wait at least an hour before *complete* bathing—and then only if the weather is hot and sunny or if your water has been warmed up. Otherwise, simply take a damp sponge and clean off dirt, salt, and sweat from the horse's body.

70. Linda Petrequin cools her Morgan gelding, Salty's Blaze, at the end of the Trask River ride, near Portland, Oregon. Photo: Dorothy Petrequin

Pulse and Respiration

It is a wise practice to monitor your horse's pulse and respiration when cooling down after a ride. If he doesn't recover at his normal rate, take his temperature. A horse whose temperature is higher than 103° (most horses work at 101° to 103°) will require a lot more cooling down with water on his head, neck, legs, and especially on the large arteries of his inner thighs and belly. If his temperature is normal, but his recovery rates are still abnormal, monitor him carefully.

When applied to the large veins and skin vessels, water cools the blood, which in turn cools his body overall. Warning: very cold water over the thick muscles will constrict their blood vessels and actually inhibit cooling. If at any time your horse appears uncomfortable and exhibits signs of colic, he should be walked slowly, kept warm, and never allowed to roll. If his symptoms do not disappear very soon it is best to summon a veterinarian.

Feeding, Grooming, and Leg Care

Once my horse's vital signs return to normal and he is thoroughly cool, I like to walk him about and let him nibble some grass. At this point, most horses like to have a good roll in the dirt to relax themselves. They get to scratch all those itchy places! My gelding, Moka's Pat-A-Dott, alias Speedy, a veteran who competes in Endurance rides, likes time to relax and eat and not be bothered. He has made it quite clear to me that he wants to be left alone at this time. So I either let him munch grass or eat hay in his corral. I also give him a few handfuls of grain, a cup of bran, and electrolytes, all moistened with water (see ch. 7). Feeding him a small amount at this time does not cause any digestive upset. After an hour or two alone, he welcomes a vigorous brushing and a good leg-soaking in a creek, if available (fig. 71). Brushing cleans the grit and sweat from his hair, as well as massaging his muscles. The creek removes any filling from his legs, and massages them as well.

When his legs are dry, I rub them with liniment to relieve any potential soreness or stiffness. I massage his legs until the liniment has dried, then slosh on some more and apply leg wraps. Read the label carefully on the liniment to make sure you can *rub* it into your horse's legs, rather than simply apply it. Also, be sure that the liniment is safe to bandage over. When I wrap his legs, I use fat-leg quilts under the bandages to cushion his legs in case I wrap them unevenly or too tightly. The material I use is known as "track bandage" (made of knitted material); you can buy these with Velcro ends, which are most convenient. Heavy flannel is also perfectly good for bandaging, and can be secured with masking tape (figs. 72–74).

After all this is done, your horse is well taken care of. Now it's your turn to grab a cold, refreshing drink and plop yourself into your chair.

71. A good soaking helps remove any filling in the horse's legs. *Photo: Charles Barieau*

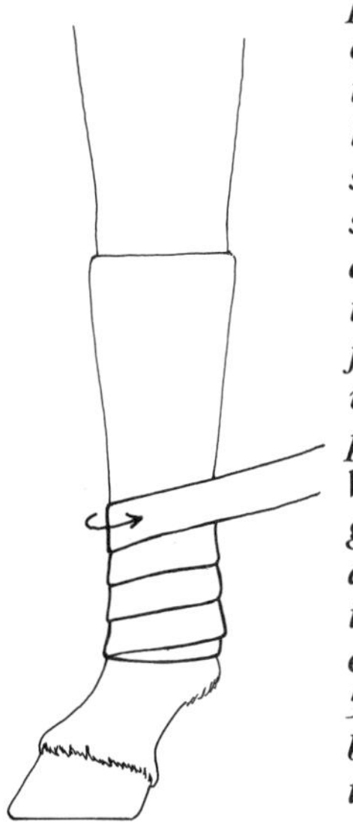

72. The standing bandage: Holding the leg quilt in place, start applying bandage over quilt at the bottom of the leg—near the fetlock area—on the inside. Be careful not to start the wrap on a tendon or an injury. Wind the bandage around front of leg, pulling toward the back (never pull bandage around back of leg; it puts dangerous pressure on tendons). Keeping the tension snug, overlap each turn by about 50%. Wrap should not be wrinkled or too tight. Drawing: Carol Wood

73. The spider wrap is used for bandaging injured knees or hocks. Use a sturdy fabric (such as muslin) approximately 12" × 16". Cut the tying segments 6" to 8" long. Drawing: Carol Wood

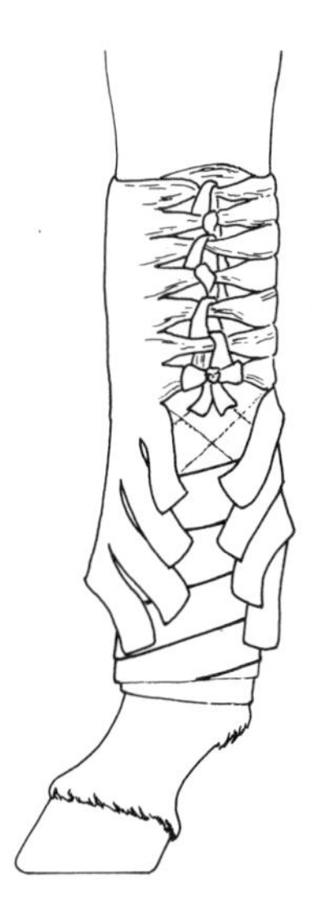

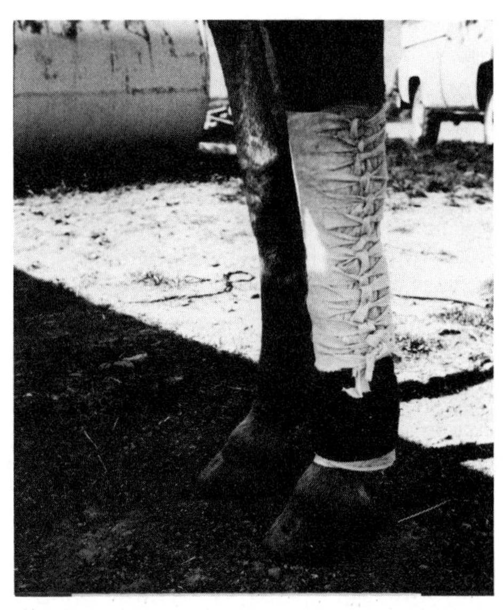

74. The spider wrap: To prevent the spider wrap from sliding down, first put on an ordinary standing bandage (fig. 72). Then wrap a lightweight leg quilt around the knee or hock and apply spider wrap, starting at the top. Connect each pair of tying segments with a bow and tuck any loose ends under the next pair of tied segments. Finish off the wrap with a bow or a knot you can easily undo.
Drawing: Carol Wood. Photos: Karen Paulo

Part Four
Health

12 *Troubleshooting*
How to Detect and Deal with Problems in the Horse

Most horses may experience some difficulties during competition, if not during the conditioning that precedes competition. These troubles may be caused by you, or they may be beyond your control—it doesn't matter. What is important is that you learn the signs of impending problems and know how to deal with them.

Tiredness

Tiredness is the most common problem of horses in this sport. Signs of tiredness are often overlooked or misunderstood. It is your job as the rider to fully know your horse's normal attitudes and behavior. As he gets tired he will show a change in attitude: he will become less willing to keep up the pace and less responsive to your aids. His gaits will lose impulsion.

It is all right for your horse to get tired during his more strenuous efforts, whether in conditioning or toward the end of a competition. A certain amount of tiredness at the end of the day is a good thing, because it tells you that your horse was tested. But he should not become tired in the middle of a regular workout or early in competition. This is a sure sign either that something is wrong with him or that you have asked him to do more than he is ready for.

Remember that your horse's heart rate should return to 60 bpm or less within ten minutes of the end of an exercise (see ch. 8). A tired horse that has been pushed too hard will have a slower recovery time. Another clue is that he may require more time than usual to cool down. And sometimes, after you think he is cool and you put him away, he may break out into a second sweat and need further cooling. If your horse hasn't exhibited these particular signs of tiredness, he may well do so through a lack of appetite—another common symptom of overexertion.

It is important to recognize these signs. When you encounter any of them, you must allow your horse sufficient time to rest. If the symptoms show up at home, give your horse a day off. If you don't take prompt action when you see these signs, he will progress from tiredness to acute fatigue.

Acute Fatigue

Acute fatigue is normally seen only during competition and can be deadly. It is hard for an acutely fatigued horse to continue, even after a rest. The horse will show intensified forms of all the tiredness symptoms discussed earlier. His gait becomes plodding and his springy step disappears as his muscles and tendons lose their elasticity. He seems to strain with each step and may also stumble. If you dismount and take his pulse, you will notice that it lacks the resounding character of his normal heartbeat. His pulse may wander up and down, and even the slightest further movement may shoot it into the 100s. The muscles of his shoulders and haunches will shake with tremors.

Exhaustion

You must stay off your horse when he is in this condition and send for help, or lead him slowly toward the next checkpoint. If you act sensibly, he should recover. But if you ask him to continue, he will begin to wander mentally and will lose all awareness of his surroundings. Exhaustion will now set in, with a risk of permanent damage or even death. When he is exhausted, the horse's pulse will race wildly and his gums will turn a bluish or muddy color for lack of blood. (His blood, with its life-sustaining oxygen, is now diverted to the most important parts of his body—the heart and brain.) He will also be severely dehydrated and suffer from a lack of electrolytes. He may assume a rigid sawhorse stance, or he may collapse. Death is almost certain without immediate veterinary help.

Cumulative/Progressive Fatigue

There is a different form of fatigue, one that is more difficult to recognize as such because the horse doesn't necessarily appear to be tired. It is often caused by pushing him a bit too much during distance rides or workouts. This is known as cumulative, or progressive, fatigue—not as immediately threatening as acute fatigue. It will often be the cause of lameness, such as strained ligaments and tendons due to tired muscles. Look for tenderness or thickening (inflammation) in your horse's legs. If these signs go unnoticed, the area will overload and break. Picture a rubber band that is repeatedly stretched beyond its capacity: it develops holes, ripples, and weaknesses, till it finally snaps! So do tendons and ligaments.

Cumulative fatigue may also be manifested in your horse's digestive system in the form of colic. It prevents him from assimilating his feed properly; this can lead to malnutrition. You may also notice that his hoofs are becoming brittle and cracked and are unable to hold his shoes. The nail clinches will often rise up like a row of shiny buttons within two to three weeks of shoeing. Further signs of hoof problems caused by this type of fatigue are corns, sole tenderness, and laminitis. Any or all of these breakdowns in his system can lead to acute fatigue, described earlier. Many cases of acute fatigue are caused by the overlooked symptoms of cumulative fatigue.

Cumulative/progressive fatigue can be avoided by proper conditioning, sound riding practices, and good feed. Most important, it can be avoided by paying close attention to those first subtle signs of tiredness.

Dehydration

Dehydration is one of the most common medical problems in distance-riding competition. It may actually originate from poor training or conditioning practices, then show up later in competition. Dehydration frequently occurs because a well-meaning rider is too rigorous in restricting his horse's water intake. While it is a good practice to restrain your horse from drinking too much at one time, you nevertheless should not leave a water stop until he has had his fill. In other words, allow him a few sips of water, walk him around, let him nibble some grass for a few minutes, and then offer him water again. Electrolytes (see ch. 7) will help keep a horse's vital systems working normally and will encourage him to drink water.

Never pass up water in a competition, since it could be many miles before you get another opportunity. It's a good idea to train your horse to drink anywhere and often. You can do this by offering him water at every accessible spot when you are conditioning him.

Test your horse for dehydration before it becomes a serious problem (see ch. 8). It is extremely important to know when he is becoming dehydrated, because this condition often develops into many of the other, more serious problems dealt with in this chapter.

Hyperthermia

Hyperthermia (high temperature) occurs most often in horses competing in humid or hot climates. As the horse works, his body is normally cooled by the evaporation of his sweat. In humid weather the sweat doesn't evaporate; and in hot, dry weather it may evaporate too fast. In both cases, the horse is not getting cooled properly by sweat. The horse has another cooling mechanism that consists of his small surface blood vessels dilating as a means of bringing more blood up to his skin, where it can cool more easily—but to achieve this his heart has to pump harder. If these two cooling systems fail or are insufficient, and as work continues in hot or humid conditions, your horse will begin to pant, taking many shallow breaths in an effort to dissipate heat. If panting doesn't help, his temperature may climb to 104° or more. If you still ask him to continue, this hyperthermic condition could develop into exhaustion and he may also go into shock (see page 67).

Horses can collapse and die from heat exhaustion, so it is most important to cool your horse at the first signs of hyperthermia. The recommended procedure is to apply *tepid* (never cold) water all over his body; make sure he is protected from the sun; and, if there is access to ice, place an ice pack on his head. When his temperature has dropped to 103°, stop any further drastic cooling efforts since you may cause him to go into shock. Continue to apply the usual cooling procedures (see ch. 11) until his temperature is normal. You should be aware that laminitis may occur as a result of hyperthermia, so consult your veterinarian for the latest preventive procedures.

75. Shade, sponging, and wet towels go a long way toward cooling the overheated horse. Photo: Karen Paulo

Acute Laminitis/Founder

Acute laminitis, or founder, is a condition in which the sensitive laminae of the hoof break down. It can cause irreversible foot damage if not treated within 16 hours of the onset of the symptoms—after which the coffin bone may have severely rotated. You can recognize a horse with laminitis by the way he stands: his front feet will be far ahead of him, and his rear feet well under him; his back will be arched in a vain effort to remove weight from his sore feet; there will be a strong digital pulse felt on his pastern. If all four feet are affected, he may lie down and refuse to get up. He may also sweat profusely and have muscle tremors. When you examine his hoof, you will find it extremely tender. This is due to decreased arterial blood supply and possible rotation of the coffin bone. If this condition exists his hoof may become separated from the sensitive laminae.

Laminitis is often not diagnosed as a fatigue-related problem because the most frequent cause is a sudden change of feed—for instance, a different type of grain or too much lush grass. However, it *can* be caused by cumulative fatigue or hyperthermia. Horses may also founder from any of the following: working too many miles on hard surfaces at a fast pace; drinking too much cold water when they are hot; becoming stressed due to overwork; being allowed to get too fat; taking incorrectly dosed medications.

Call your vet at the first sign of laminitis. It's a real medical emergency.

Shock

Shock is a failure of the horse's circulatory system. It can be caused by fatigue, severe blood loss, trauma, heat exhaustion, laminitis, colic, or a reaction to an injection. A horse starts to go into shock because so many blood vessels dilate all at once that his blood volume becomes insufficient to fill up his entire circulatory system. This leads to low blood pressure, causing inadequate blood supply to the less vital organs. His body responds by reducing blood flow to the less vital organs so that more blood can flow to his brain, heart, and lungs. If this natural defense is successful, your horse may survive with the *immediate* help of a vet. Otherwise, shock becomes irreversible and the horse will die. Even your vet may not be able to save his life if the condition has gone on for more than an hour.

You can detect early signs of shock by checking your horse's CRT (see p. 49) to see if it is more than two-to-three seconds. Other early signs are cool, pale mucous membranes in his eyelids, a weakened or thready pulse, lowered body temperature, and increased respiration and pulse rates.

Tying Up

Tying up can develop early in a ride—within the first few miles—or it can come on later as fatigue sets in. An early indication that your horse is tying up is when his stride gets shorter, especially behind. Despite the fact that he is moving his legs, he appears not to be really going forward. This begins subtly and becomes more obvious as the condition worsens. The horse often shows his pain by looking at his rear end. He tends to sweat profusely, toss his head, and breathe with difficulty. His muscles quiver and feel cold when you touch them, because circulation is lost as he deteriorates. Next, his rump muscles will swell and become rock hard as they cramp up. If you continue riding, your horse will eventually come to a screeching halt and be unable to move at all. If he urinates, his urine will be dark orange or coffee-colored.

Azoturia is a form of tying up commonly seen early in a ride. It happens when a horse, having been fed a very rich diet while being rested (usually before a competition, though it can happen at home) is worked too suddenly. In order to avoid azoturia, cut your horse's grain ration in half on days that you don't ride him, and allow him as much free exercise as possible on his days off.

Tying up may also be caused by nervous tension, physical stress, trauma, or by starting a distance ride at too fast a pace, not allowing your horse's muscles to warm up properly. I've seen horses tie up on rides that have steep climbs, or climbs with loose footing, within two or three miles of the start. These horses' muscles were not yet ready for the extra effort demanded of them. Still another cause of tying up is riding your horse too soon after he has been trucked a long distance and confined in a small space. Finally, tying up can happen if you dump very cold water all over your horse's rear-end muscles when he is hot.

A recommended remedy for the early signs of tying up is to cover your horse's rump muscles with a blanket; massage these muscles and keep them warm. Do not force the horse to move unless he is *willing* to walk—walking may be very beneficial in this situation. If he exhibits some of the more extreme symptoms described above, such as quivering, sweating profusely, breathing with difficulty, and unwillingness to move, call a vet immediately. Cover and keep him warm; do not move him while waiting for the vet to arrive. Try to keep him on his feet. Veterinary assistance is essential in preventing permanent damage to your horse's hind legs and muscles.

Colic

Colic (abdominal pain) often occurs during a ride. It is most commonly caused by a rider who allows his hot, thirsty horse to drink too much cold water at a given time. It also can happen at the end of a ride, when a careless rider gives his horse too much water and/or food *too soon*. A horse's digestive system doesn't work properly when he is tired.

A colicky horse will show signs of pain—sweating, kicking at his belly, or wanting to roll. If you examine his belly area, you can actually see that it is tight and cramped up.

If your horse exhibits signs of colic while you are on the trail, get off immediately and walk him slowly. If he doesn't improve, lead him to the closest source of help. *Never* allow him to lie down and roll, since this may well cause more serious complications—such as a twisted intestine, which is usually fatal. Keep him walking unless he is willing to stand quietly before a vet arrives to treat him.

With any luck, you may find that your horse is okay after walking him for a while. If you are in competition, be sure to tell the next vet you see what has happened and ask him to check out your horse before continuing. You don't want to risk finding yourself five miles farther down the trail with an even sicker horse.

Thumps

Thumps (synchronous diaphragmatic flutters) are involuntary contractions of the diaphragm, best observed when your horse is standing still. You will see a ticking or thumping action in your horse's flanks in rhythm with his heart rate. In severe cases this thumping can actually be heard, and your horse can literally collapse. It is generally thought that thumps are caused by respiratory fatigue, in which the diaphragm tires and as a result develops involuntary contractions that coordinate with his heart rate. Sometimes thumps are caused by respiratory fatigue coupled with an electrolyte imbalance—especially from a lack of calcium, potassium, and magnesium. If this condition is detected early, lots of rest and electrolytes will help your horse to recover.

3 *The Lame Horse*
How to Identify the Signs

Every rider should know how to recognize and evaluate a lame horse. You must not only know what to *look* for, but also develop a *feel* for any subtle changes in your horse's stride that could indicate impending lameness.

Recognizing Lameness

The severity of lameness depends on its cause and what area of the horse's body is affected. A horse that is "slightly off" is harder to diagnose than a horse that is obviously lame. Mild lameness may quickly advance to a crippling condition if you continue to ride him without properly evaluating and dealing with the problem.

When you watch a lame horse in motion, he will step lightly on the sore leg and his head will rise simultaneously in an effort to take weight off that leg. As he bears weight on his sound leg (whether front or rear), he will place more weight on it than on the affected leg. If a foreleg, his head will then move down—giving him a bobbing action. When trotted in a circle, a horse will normally carry more weight on his inside legs than his outside legs, so if he is "ouchy" on his left front, for instance, while being trotted to the left, his limping and bobbing motion will increase. A lame horse will often show his symptoms sooner when being trotted in a circle than he will on the straight.

Hind-leg lameness is more difficult to discern, because the rear of the horse supports much less weight than the front. Riders are often fooled by rear-leg lameness. If a horse feels pain in his right hind leg, for example, he usually transfers the weight from this leg onto his sound "diagonal." He will therefore *appear* lame on the *left* front, leading the rider to believe that this is where the problem lies. You may also notice (if you stand behind

76. Vets and scorer, checking for soundness, watching a rider jogging her horse out on a paved strip. Photo: Mike Noble

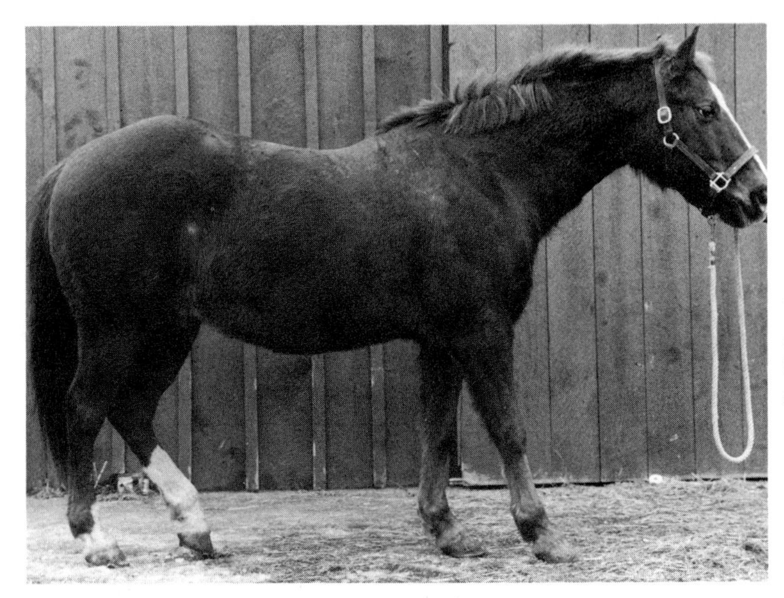

77. Horse is pointing right front leg and resting left hind, both being indications of discomfort and/or lameness. Photo: Mike Noble

him) that one hip remains higher than the other because of his efforts to keep weight off the sore leg. Note: there is less head bobbing in rear lameness; the head is lowered, not raised, when weight is placed on the sore limb.

Lameness is most easily detected and felt when you stand in the stirrups at a trot. This is because you are then able to feel your horse's stride more sensitively than when you post—and also because most lameness is simply more easily perceived at a trot. Your horse's stride will lose its normal smoothness, creating a bumpy effect as he favors his sore leg and tries to keep weight off it.

A horse's stance can also help you spot lameness. If the lameness is in a front limb, your horse will often "point" his sore leg by placing it farther forward than the other—thus removing weight from the hurting leg. If both front legs are sore, he will usually stand with his rear legs well under him in an effort to remove the weight from his front. With rear-leg lameness, your horse may rest the sore leg by holding it out a bit to the side or by cocking his foot underneath him (fig. 77). He may also find a place to stand with his front downhill, thus taking weight off his hind legs.

In order to determine exactly where your horse is lame on the affected leg, inspect it with your hand, searching for heat, swelling, and wounds. Also check his hoof for heat, or a pulse in the side of his pastern—either of which would suggest a problem in his foot. Watch for discomfort in his reaction as you carefully explore his leg and manipulate each joint. When you reach a sore spot, his head may jerk up and he will probably try to pull the sore leg away from you.

Causes of Lameness

There are many sources of common lameness—most found in the lower leg (knee and hock downward). These include stone bruises and abscesses in the hoof; laminitis; injuries to tendons, ligaments, and bone in the cannon-bone area (between knee and fetlock); and sprains and bumps almost anywhere. Shoulder and stifle injuries can also cause lameness, so be sure to explore these areas if you fail to find the problem lower down. If your horse is only slightly off, perhaps all he needs is rest and massage. If he doesn't improve in a day or two, contact your vet. If your horse is very lame, get your vet to make a diagnosis as soon as possible. A horse with severe tendon and ligament injuries has a much better chance of full recovery if properly treated as soon as you notice the problem.

If your horse becomes lame while you are on the trail, you alone will have to determine where he hurts and the severity of the injury. The terrain that you have just traveled through should offer some clues. Stone bruises are suspect if the area is rocky and if your horse is not wearing pads; slippery clay or mud can cause strained joints and pulled muscles; and deep sand may lead to a tendon or suspensory-ligament injury. In addition, your horse can hurt one or both hind legs as he lunges and slips while going up or down a steep or rocky incline.

Whenever you feel your horse may be lame, you should lead him home gently, or, at an Endurance competition, into the next vet check. Sometimes, if you're lucky, he will "walk out" of his lameness in a few minutes. Perhaps he just came down on a rock the wrong way, or hit his leg on a stump or with another leg. Maybe he developed a cramped muscle, or simply stepped wrong. In cases like these, he will probably be okay to ride again slowly, but you must keep a close eye on the situation—if the lameness persists or recurs, get him home or to a vet. On a distance ride, the vet will advise you whether to pull him from the competition or perhaps continue only at a walk. Often a vet will allow a slightly off horse to continue if he just has a stone bruise; but he will usually pull a horse that has a tendon or joint injury.

Most vets at a ride evaluate the type and degree of lameness and grade it, which determines whether your horse will be allowed to continue. After the finish, his soundness is judged for *placing* awards in Competitive rides, and for *completion* or *best condition* awards in Endurance rides. Most vets use the classifications set by the American Association of Equine Practitioners (AAEP), which are as follows:

Grade 1. Difficult to observe. Not consistently apparent regardless of circumstances (e.g., weight carrying, circling, inclines, hard surface, etc.).

Grade 2. Difficult to observe at a walk or trotting a straight line; consistently apparent under certain circumstances (e.g., weight carrying, circling, inclines, hard surface, etc.).

Grade 3. Consistently observable at a trot under all circumstances.

Grade 4. Obvious lameness; marked nodding, hitchy or shortened stride.

Grade 5. Minimal weight bearing in motion and/or at rest; inability to move.

78. Vetting at a Competitive ride: left, checking for filling; right, checking for heat. Photo: Mike Noble

Some types of lameness may not appear while you are riding, but will show up later when your horse has been in the vet check for ten minutes or more. Strained muscles often appear at this time while the horse is cooling down and stiffening.

Proper management is usually the best protection against lameness—but occasionally, no matter what we do, it happens anyway. Your best chance to avoid serious, crippling lameness resulting from a minor injury is to detect and treat the problem as early as possible. If your horse seems to recover miraculously—all at once—from being lame, don't immediately assume that he is completely well. If you climb right on him and continue to ride, the problem may not only recur, but it may be even worse than before.

In general, be sure to give your horse ample time off to recover and heal from any kind of lameness. One rule of thumb: allow the same amount of rest time that it took for the limp to disappear. For example, if on the seventh day of his lameness, his signs—e.g., soreness, swelling, and heat—finally disappear, then give your horse at least seven days more "sound" rest before you ride him again. Any lameness in the upper leg is notoriously slow to heal, and may require longer rest time. Injuries that are not given enough time to heal can lead to chronic lameness—sometimes ruining your horse's future as a distance athlete.

*Common **HOOF** Ailments Causing Lameness in Distance Horses*

Abscess: A collection of pus surrounded by inflamed tissue, often caused by severe bruising.

Contracted Heels: A narrowing of the heels and the frog, often due to poor shoeing and trimming.

Corns: Bruises most often found near the bars of the hoof (at the heel), often due to improper shoeing, leaving the shoes on too long, and/or allowing the hoof wall to grow over the edge of the shoe.

Gravel: An infection of the hoof, usually the result of sand or gravel particles that have become embedded in the hoof. The ensuing infection causes lameness that, unrelieved, continues until the pus exits the hoof at the coronary band.

Laminitis: Failure of the sensitive laminae of the hoof, with possible internal and irreversible damage. In distance horses this is most often caused by running too hard on unforgiving surfaces.

Navicular Disease: An inflammatory condition affecting the surfaces of the navicular bone; erosion of the bone and irritation of the tendon that passes over it. Often caused by faulty conformation, poor shoeing, or overuse.

Stone Bruise: A bruise, or bruises, on the sole of the hoof caused by hard work on rocks or on gravel roads. Recognized as tender areas on the hoof sole.

Thrush: A degenerative condition of the frog and surrounding tissues. Sign is a tarlike, smelly discharge. Most often caused by unsanitary conditions, poor shoeing practices, and failure to clean the hoofs regularly.

Common **LEG** *Ailments Causing Lameness in Distance Horses*

Arthritis: Swelling, stiffness, and pain in a joint, often due to a blow that caused calcification of the joint. Common arthritic conditions are: *osselets*, calcifications and/or abnormal bone growths in the fetlock joint, caused by trauma and resulting in limited flexion or mobility; *ringbone*, a new bone growth that occurs on the first, second, or third phalanges (bones of the pastern and hoof). Causes of ringbone are poor conformation (particularly steep shoulders and/or pasterns), crooked legs, severe strain to the joint capsule, or poor shoeing. Arthritis can affect virtually any joint in the horse.

Bowed Tendons: Also called *tendinitis*, it is fiber damage of the deep flexor tendon or the superficial flexor tendon. Bowed tendon is the result of repeated severe strain, causing some fibers to rupture, and is most commonly found in the forelegs. Conformational weaknesses and poor shoeing may contribute to the condition. A bowed tendon requires months of rest—possibly a year or more—for it to heal completely. Returning the horse to work too soon makes the condition chronic and the horse unsound.

Curb: A thickening of the plantar ligament at the back of the hock. In distance horses the most common cause is overextension of the hock, too much steep-hill work, or working in deep sand.

Splints: Abnormal or new bone growth on or around the splint bones. Splints are commonly the result of trauma or a direct blow to the leg. Very high splints near the carpal bone interfere with joint motion and may cause prolonged lameness. Lower splints usually cause temporary lameness.

Suspensory Ligament Injury: A strain or sprain to the suspensory ligament. This injury, which can be as serious as bowed tendons, causes heat, swelling, and pain anywhere along the leg behind the cannon bone.

Windpuffs: Unsightly bumps (swellings) near the top of the fetlock. They often appear after overexertion and may never go away, though constant wrapping or poulticing will reduce them temporarily. While windpuffs do not usually cause lameness, they can signal other impending lameness problems. With some horses, conformation predisposes them to this condition.

14 *Keeping Your Horse Sound*
Preventing and Managing Lameness

Endurance horses' feet and legs take a lot of pounding on all types of surfaces. With sensible riding and good care, the healthy, normal horse has thousands of miles in him. Less-than-perfect legs and hoofs will predispose him to many more disorders than the well-built animal. Even so, preventive daily care can and will avoid a lot of problems.

Hoof Lameness

It is most important to pay close attention to the condition of a horse's hoofs. Daily picking, and keeping the horse in a clean environment, will go far in preventing thrush (see p. 72). Lameness resulting from thrush can be treated by soaking the hoof in a hot-water-and-Epsom-salts solution for 20 minutes twice daily, and by squirting the area with a drying agent such as a prepared thrush medication or household bleach.

Lameness may also result from a poorly placed horseshoe nail. Pus pockets can form, causing heat in the hoof; this requires opening the abscess, soaking the hoof in Epsom salts and hot water, and possibly giving antibiotic injections (only on a vet's say-so) to fight the infection.

Leg Lameness

Leg problems are most commonly caused by strains of the tendons and ligaments. Since the horse's legs are stressed by each workout or ride, it is important to pay close daily attention to them. If you see any signs of stress—heat or swelling—hose the leg with cold water (fig. 79); if you have a creek or stream nearby, stand your horse in it for 20 to 30 minutes.

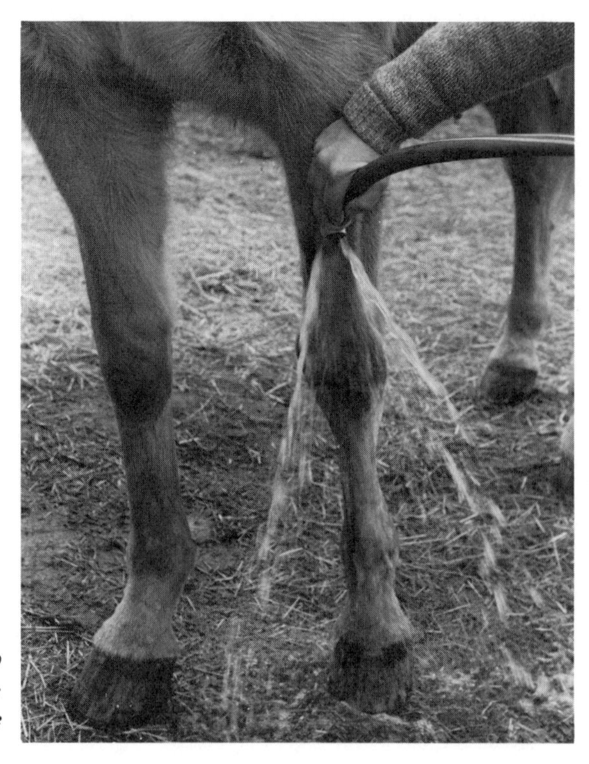

79. Applying cold water therapy with a hose to stimulate circulation. Photo: Mike Noble

Massage

It is useful to hand-massage your horse's legs to increase circulation. Notice that if you massage your own ankle, it soon becomes red. This is due to increased circulation, which brings more blood into the area. The blood removes waste products caused by stress and introduces fresh oxygen and nutrients to the tired tissue. All this helps to prevent swelling, filling, and stiffness.

Massage is time-consuming, but it's easy. Simply squirt a bit of liniment or rubbing alcohol on the legs and rub it into the ankle and tendons with the palms of your hands. I use a circular motion to better stimulate the blood flow. I prefer liniment to alcohol because my hands slide more easily. In addition, liniment further increases circulation by dilating the blood vessels. I rub until the liniment is totally dry, which usually takes about five minutes per leg. Caution: when you use a liniment be sure to read the directions, since some formulas will irritate the leg and possibly blister the skin when rubbed in (fig. 80).

Note: When you massage a horse's body, as opposed to his legs, use the heel of your hand instead of the palm. Exert enough pressure to keep your hand still on the skin; this allows the skin to move over the muscles, providing a deeper massage.

80. Massaging the horse's legs to increase circulation and promote healing. Photo: Karen Paulo

Medication with Leg Wraps

Leg wrapping may be useful in both preventive care and in helping the already lame horse (see p. 62). What medication you use under the wrap is up to you; it often depends on what is available in your area. Just be sure not to wrap over a liniment that should be left exposed to the air. Read the directions. If you use a medication that contains benzocaine, be sure to stop using it several days before any competition; if a horse licks it, it will enter his system—and benzocaine is a prohibited drug in all distance rides.

Mud Packs

Some horsemen choose to mix their own leg potions. One of the most common ingredients is fresh mud, if available—any clay-type mud will do. Mix a pound of this mud with ¼ cup of Epson salts and ¼ cup of apple-cider vinegar. Apply the mud pack to the leg and cover with a bandage. Be sure to make the wrap tight, since some mixes contract as they dry and cause the wrap to fall down. Leave it on for 12 to 24 hours. As the mud dries, heat and puffiness are drawn from the leg, removing congestion. Mud also works incredibly well as hoof-packing, to help hoofs cool out following a tough ride.

The mud pack is one of the oldest remedies known to horsemen; it is still in wide use around racetracks today. Most horse-supply stores sell a dry mix that horsemen can simply add water to, if they haven't got the right natural mud around.

Hydrotherapy

Probably the best therapy for all lameness is cold water massage. You can apply it with a hose or find it in a running stream or creek (fig. 81). The running water cools and massages the legs. If, in addition, you hand-massage the legs with a liniment when you're finished hosing, you should get very good results.

Standing a horse in a turbulator (whirlpool bath) is also very effective. I remember strolling down racetrack shed rows when I was young and seeing bad-legged horses standing in their own private whirlpools. The horses were invariably relaxed and sleepy-eyed as the whirling water seemed to massage all their troubles away! It may take some coaxing and patience to accustom the horse to the turbulator at first, but he will quickly learn to love it because it feels so good on those aching legs.

Ice Therapy

Cold therapy is very useful during the first 24 hours following injury or stress. *Icing* is the most effective method, and some tack shops sell ready-made ice boots. You can also use your horse's regular shipping boots. Put them on his legs loosely at the top and snugly at the bottom, then fill them repeatedly with ice water.

There are also leg wraps made especially for cold therapy. Some you simply wet and freeze; they remain flexible while frozen, making them easy to use. Other wraps contain a cooling gel that must be refrigerated in order to work. The problem with these is that the gel too readily attracts dust and dirt—and since they are not washable their usefulness is often short-lived. Finally, there are wraps that feature a pouch of liquid that you freeze. The frozen pouch is placed into a pocket of the leg wrap, which is then wound around the leg; these are totally reusable.

Heat Therapy

Heat therapy is useful for injuries older than 48 hours and for infections. Some veterinarians like to use alternating hot and cold soaks for laminitis. In addition to soaking in hot Epsom salts solution, you can also buy hot wraps similar to the cold ones discussed just above. Instead of freezing the removable pouch, you boil it and then put it in the pocket of the leg wrap. Some heat wraps come equipped with a chemically active pack that heats itself when it is massaged.

Any serious injuries should, of course, be referred to a vet for proper treatment. And if your horse has a problem that requires extensive therapy, you may wish to invest in one of the newer, specialized therapeutic machines available. These products are numerous and new models show up constantly—so the best way to find and choose one is through your veterinarian or university vet school. Some schools have a variety of these units that you can use on your own horse; taking your horse to a university for treatment may be more thorough and less costly than buying and using the equipment yourself.

81. Leg-soaking in an active stream is excellent natural therapy because the water both cools and massages the horse's legs. Photo: Karen Paulo

Part Five

Equipment

15 *Ride Comfortably and Safely*

Clothes and Tack for Rider and Horse

There are no adequate words to describe the feeling you get from riding your horse along the trail through beautiful wilderness. There are also no words to describe the dreadful feeling you have when you find a large girth- or cinch-sore or raw area on your horse's back; no words to describe the feeling you get when your pants scrape the skin off your leg, or when your shoes or boots rub a blister on your foot. Obviously, in order to really have fun with this sport, one must be sinfully comfortable! "Impossible," you may say. "How can I be comfortable perched on a trotting horse for fifty miles?" Well, the fact is that you can't be at all comfortable unless you have done everything possible before the ride—not only in choosing your clothes, but also in preparing your horse's tack and other gear to take with you on the trail. So I will divide this chapter into three sections: clothes, tack, and gear.

82. Typical clothes for a hot-weather ride: Lycra tights with cotton shorts and socks over them; loose cotton T-shirt with halter top underneath, allowing rider to remove shirt, dip it in water, and put it on again to keep cool. Photo: Ted Brown

Clothes

It was once thought that after spending enough time in the saddle, great calluses would form on your skin to protect you from future discomfort. While this may be true to some extent, generally it is a myth; there are other alternatives that are better than self-torture!

Some of us start out with a pair of broken-in blue jeans (new jeans are too stiff), an old T-shirt, our usual underwear, and shoes or boots. These items may seem comfortable enough in the beginning, but as the miles pass by the friction between clothing and skin begins to take its toll, creating a number of unanticipated sores. Additionally, your feet may burn or become numb and even your underwear may cause great discomfort.

This is where the process of experimentation and selection begins. Look around at the experienced riders. Yes, they may look a little eccentric in their dress; but if you ask them, you'll soon find out they are very comfortable. Some competitors wear long johns or panty hose under their jeans or britches so that the friction is fabric-to-fabric, not fabric-to-skin. But on the longer rides, these items often stretch and bunch, creating small wrinkles that rub and chafe your skin. They are also very hot in summertime. As for the jeans themselves, the best are clearly those with *single* seams

83. Riding tights made of cotton Lycra or Coolmax (a material that draws moisture away from skin) combine the stretchiness of runner's tights with an inset of ultrasuede to prevent sliding around the saddle. *Photo: Frank Pryor, Phelan's Equestrian Catalog*

84. Muscle T's (left) can be worn by both men and women, though women usually wear riding bras (right) underneath. *Photo: Frank Pryor, Phelan's Equestrian Catalog*

on the insides of the legs—much more comfortable than the bulky double-stitched inseams.

A good warm-weather combination consists of jogging shorts, leotards or tights, tall socks, and a light cotton top (fig. 82). For cool weather use fleecy sweatpants and a sweatshirt, with outer clothing in several layers. If you don't like sweatpants (they can stretch and become baggy when wet), try jeans over shiny exercise pants made of nylon/spandex, which offer good nonfriction protection under any outer garment. For wet weather, you will need lightweight rain gear or any oil-treated cloth jacket. Be sure these don't fly or flop around—they might snag on something along the trail or scare your horse.

Basic clothing for all temperatures comprises long sleeves for brush or wooded trails and for sun protection; a helmet (see below); cotton underwear and socks that fit snugly. A cotton shirt that can be soaked in water along the trail will help keep you cool on very hot days.

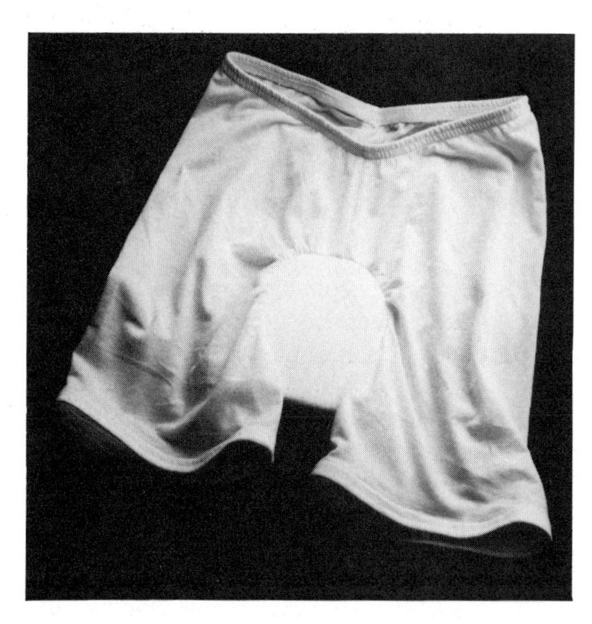

85. Seamless, padded-crotch underwear is designed to eliminate chafing and hot spots often caused by outer clothing. Photo: Frank Pryor, Phelan's Equestrian Catalog

Footwear

Footwear is very important. Jogging or aerobic shoes (without the big knobby soles that may numb your feet) are most popular because they are comfortable for walking, running, and riding. However, if you use this type of shoe, you must be careful to ride with only your toe in the stirrup. Never shove your foot too deep into the stirrup, since it might slide all the way through—a dangerous situation. If you can walk and run comfortably in boots with good heels, then wear them, because they are the safest for riding in general. Many riders wear shoes or boots that are at least a half size too large, since feet tend to swell during the course of a long ride due to the pressure caused by standing and posting in the stirrups. Children (who usually do little groundwork) should wear only boots, in the interest of safety.

There are still some tough, traditional riders around who haven't converted to more comfortable lightweight garments. Some wear just jeans and boots, and a few wear English riding breeches

86. Half-chaps prevent leg rubs while providing comfort and warmth. They also protect the rider's pants from the horse's sweat. Note, too, the comfortable, well-padded Hi-Tec riding shoes. Photo: Frank Pryor, Phelan's Equestrian Catalog

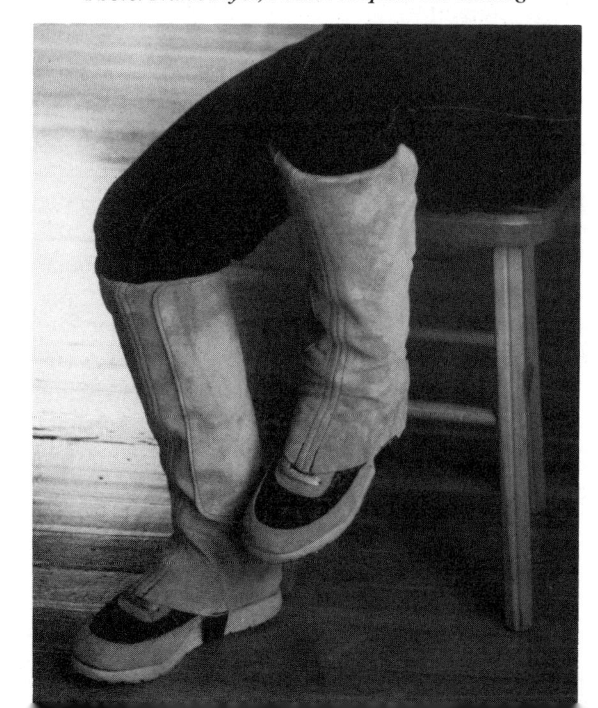

and conventional riding boots. But the important thing to remember about this sport is that it's okay to wear whatever you want, just so long as you are comfortable.

Helmets

Helmets are becoming very popular, since more and more riders now realize the dangers of the sport and the threat of serious head injuries. Helmets specially designed for riding can be found at most tack shops or may be ordered through equestrian catalogs. Some of these have been officially approved by the American Society of Testing Materials (ASTM). While no helmet can protect you at all times from every type of head injury, it is probably wise to purchase one of the ASTM-endorsed helmets, since they are generally of superior quality.

Some distance riders use bicycle helmets, but it is my personal opinion that they don't offer adequate protection. However, they are light, ventilated, offer some protection, are easy to find and buy—and they are better than no helmet at all.

Be sure that your helmet fits snugly, without moving around on your head. If it is too tight, it may give you a headache; so you'll have to find a happy medium. The chin strap should be used at all times to secure the helmet in the correct position. If the helmet has a peak or bill, it should flex easily or break off upon impact. This is to prevent injuries such as a broken nose—or worse, broken neck—that may occur when a helmet has a hard peak. If your helmet is ventilated like the bicycle helmets, the vents should not weaken the overall structure, nor should they be large enough to allow rocks to enter upon impact. The inner padding should be a high-density foam that will absorb the shock of solid impact. If you do crash, check your helmet thoroughly for any cracks or sign of weakness afterward, because a damaged helmet is of virtually no value and must be replaced.

Tack

Saddles

There is no question that the most important part of your tack is the saddle. When I first began with this sport in 1977, there were very few saddles on the market designed specifically for distance riding. Riders would often cut down a Western saddle (remove the horn and any unnecessary skirts and flaps), or ride a McClellan cavalry saddle or an English saddle. Today the possibilities have multiplied, because in addition to the many lightweight Endurance saddles available, there is now the Australian stock saddle—which is fairly light and offers more security than all the other saddles. The best place to see the widest variety of saddles is at a distance ride. Most riders will let you sit in their saddle and will be happy to answer questions.

When choosing a saddle, you must think of how it fits both you and your horse. It must be right for your particular seat. If it is too small you will be unable to move around in it. If it is too big you will move around excessively, causing friction and a hot or chafed behind.

Choose the saddle that not only helps you balance correctly but, most important, fits your horse's back. If it doesn't fit the horse properly, even minor discomfort may show up subtly in the form of a shortened or choppy stride. One way to try different fits is to borrow some of your friends' saddles; another way is to ask your tack shop if you can try some out before purchasing.

The saddle should have two to three inches of clearance above the horse's withers to avoid pressure or pinching. It should also not interfere with the horse's shoulder motion; nor should any weight be allowed on the horse's loins or spine. The gullet of the saddle (the air channel from pommel to cantle in the center) should be wide and high enough to keep any pressure off the horse's spine and to allow cool air to circulate down his back.

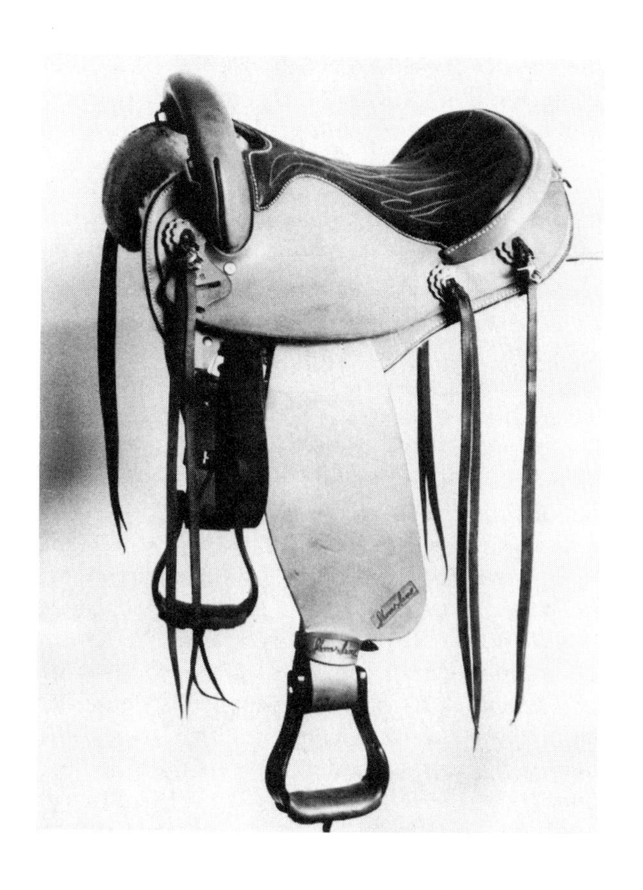

87. ***Above left:*** *The Sharon Saare Saddle is a popular Western-style saddle specially designed for Endurance riders. It has adjustable rigging, high-wither clearance, and weighs about 24 pounds.* *Photo: Sharon Saare*

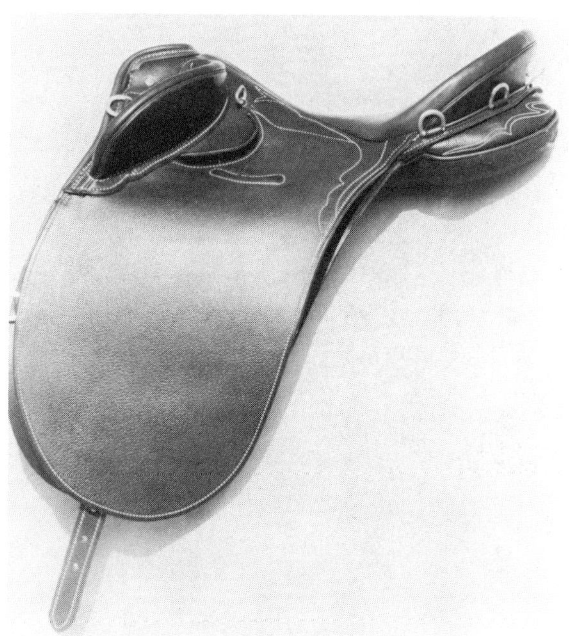

88. ***Left:*** *A typical Australian Endurance saddle—the Suprema National Warwick.* *Photo: Australian Riding Traditions*

89. ***Above:*** *Campbell's Paragon Endurance saddle has wide panels for proper weight distribution, large flaps for rider comfort, a padded seat, and a raised cantle for added security. It is popular with many men because it is available in larger sizes. The Paragon is manufactured in leather or synthetic material.* *Photo: Midwest Saddlery Co.*

A good way of testing how the saddle fits your horse is to look closely at his back after you have worked him. It should be evenly wet, with no dry spots (except possibly down his spine, assuming your saddle has a good air channel). Dry spots indicate that the sweat glands are no longer able to produce sweat, owing to unwanted pressure points on the saddle. There should be no rubbed or hairless areas; his hide should be smooth; it shouldn't be sensitive when touched; and there shouldn't be any lumps or bumps that arise from pressure points (fig. 90). Most of the time these bumps show up on either side of the withers, under the stirrup bars, and in the cantle area. To pinpoint pressure points, turn your saddle upside down. With a Western saddle, the fleece over the pressure points will be more compressed and more worn than the rest of the fleece. With an English saddle, the panel areas (weight-bearing surfaces on the underside of the saddle) will be more worn, and the leather darker and possibly lumpy. Still another way to detect pressure points is to apply talcum powder to your horse's back. Gently lower the saddle onto his back, and then carefully lift it off. The powder should be evenly distributed on the saddle. If it is not, it shows that your saddle doesn't fit this horse properly and you are going to have to restuff it or replace it.

Some saddles have panels that conform to a horse's back. These saddles have a design feature in which the bars of the tree are hinged, so that it self-adjusts to fit virtually any width of horse. The panels of the saddle you choose must also be large enough to distribute *your* weight evenly. Small, narrow panels are usually inadequate. This is especially true if a rider is heavy. A good rule of thumb is to allow a maximum of one and a half pounds per square inch on the weight-bearing surface of your saddle. A lower weight ratio is even better. Take, for example, the Brown's Ortho-Flex Performance Saddle, which allows even less than one pound per square inch. Len and Lisa Brown conceived and designed this special saddle while on a 3,000-mile pack trip (fig. 91). They found that large flexible skirts were necessary to distribute all the weight they were carrying (their own plus their equipment) in order to keep their horses sound.

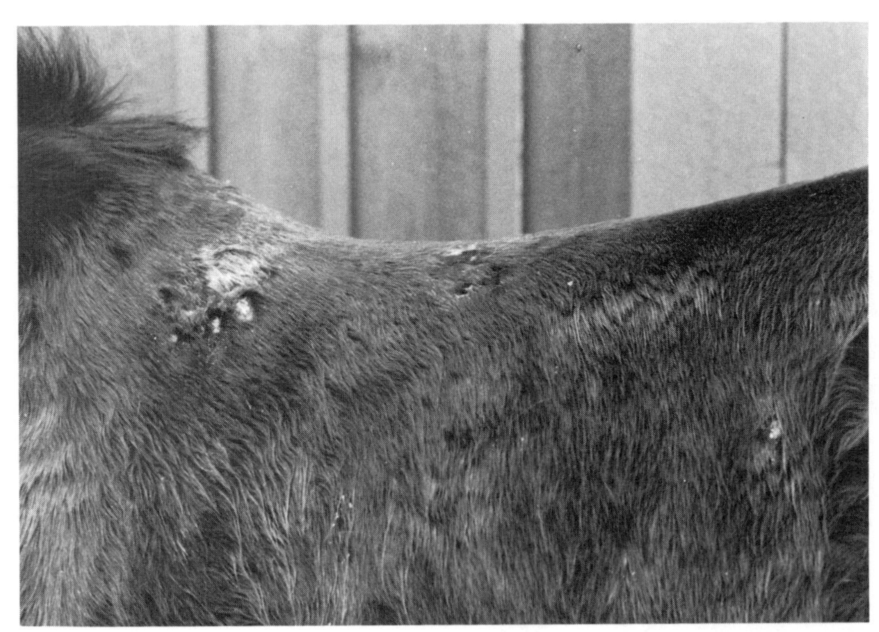

90. An example of damage to a horse's back caused by a poorly fitting saddle. Photo: Mike Noble

The weight of your saddle is another important consideration. It has been established at racetracks that an extra pound will slow a horse by one-fifth of a second over a distance of a mile. Imagine what a few extra pounds can mean over 50 or 100 miles! Endurance, McClellan, English, and Australian saddles can all be purchased in various weights from about 14 pounds up. Western saddles tend to weigh more. You can also buy saddles that weigh as little as six pounds. These are made of the same material that revolutionized running shoes—cool, lightweight, durable, space-age nylon, with well-stuffed, cushioned panels that distribute the rider's weight adequately (figs. 92 and 93). If you can find a lightweight saddle that fits you and your horse comfortably, and distributes your weight efficiently, then you will have an advantage. However, it is better to have a slightly heavier saddle in order to get one that fits both of you perfectly. It's certainly no advantage to have a light saddle with a sore horse or sore rider!

91. Brown's Ortho-Flex Performance Saddle. The large skirts distribute the rider's weight well and allow the saddle to fit almost any horse. Photo: Karen Paulo

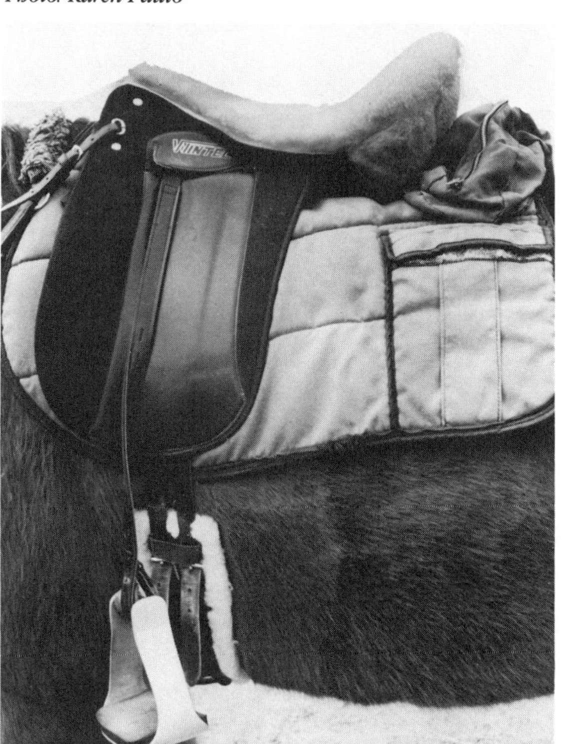

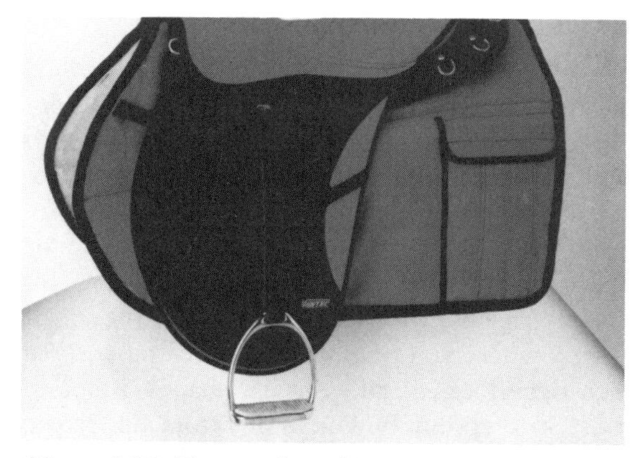

92. and 93. Two styles of super-lightweight (about 7 pounds), completely washable Wintec saddles, both made with synthetic suede, nylon fabric, and tough, molded plastic trees. ***Left:*** *a dressage model with Webbers, Western-style Endurance stirrup, woolen "seat saver," trail pocket saddle pad, and cantle bag.* Photo: Karen Paulo ***Above:*** *Endurance model with English-style stirrups.* Photo: Frank Pryor, Phelan's Equestrian Catalog

94. The Stoddard saddle, a modified McClellan saddle, is designed to fit most Arab-type horses. Note saddle pad sticking up through slot in saddle. Also there is an Easyboot fastened to the saddle back. Photo: Karen Paulo

A word of caution: most McClellan saddles do not fit many Arabian or Arab-type horses because the tree is too narrow and usually digs into the horse's back on each side of the withers. Newer Endurance-designed saddles, (modified McClellans) have been designed to fit most Arabian horses (fig. 94).

Saddle Rigging

With any Western or McClellan-type saddle, the rigging is very important. It needs to be positioned so that the cinch will not interfere with your horse's armpits and elbows. The rigging's location also determines how well the cinch prevents the saddle from slipping side to side or tipping forward or back. Some saddles have adjustable rigging, allowing you to place the cinch exactly where you want it; this is preferable since such rigging can fit all sizes and shapes of horses and also keep any bulkiness out from under the rider's calf (figs. 95 and 96).

An English-type saddle has three billets (the straps that attach the girth to the saddle). If your saddle slips forward, use the front two billets for your girth attachment. If it slides back, use the rear two. In general, it is preferable to use the outside two billets for greatest stability.

95. The rigging design of the Brown's saddle allows the girth to be placed in almost any position. Note that there is no bulk under the rider's leg. Photo: Karen Paulo

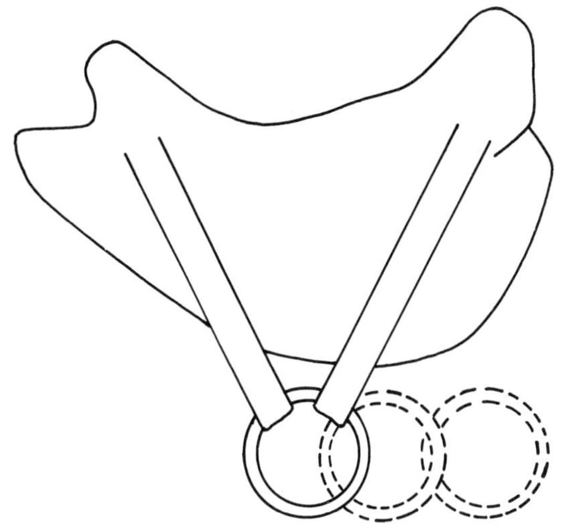

96. A rigging in the 7/8 position is most common in Western show saddles, placing the girth forward into the elbow—not desirable for Endurance efforts. The 5/8, or center, position is preferred and is now available on many Western and McClellan-style saddles. Drawing: Carol Wood

Stirrups

The stirrups or irons that you use can make a big difference to your comfort (fig. 97). If you ride English, you may find that traditional narrow irons put your feet to sleep, even with the addition of a rubber pad. Being metal, they are also heavy. The wider tread on a Western stirrup is more comfortable; it can be adapted to the English stirrup leather by shortening the neck bolt. You can also purchase wider stirrups specially designed for extra comfort, with large, heavily padded treads; or you can make your own tread with scraps of Kodel (synthetic fleece) or foam held in place by duct tape. This gives your foot excellent cushioning for the long rides.

Children should always use tapaderos (leather hoods on the front of Western stirrups), or if using an English (or English-type) saddle, a safety stirrup. Adults may wish to take the same safety precaution; there are a number of excellent safety stirrups available in larger sizes.

Stirrup Leathers

Comfort is also determined by the length of your stirrup leathers. If they are too long, your inner thighs will ache, and if they are too short, your knees will hurt. By trial and error, you must find the length that suits you best. Stirrup leathers that pinch are easily corrected by covering them with fleece halter-tubing that secures with Velcro. A fairly recent invention, known as "Webbers," was introduced by Wintec with their innovative, lightweight, synthetic saddles. Webbers help the pinching problem by using a synthetic leather with a loop at the top for placing over the stirrup bar. The bottom of the synthetic leather loops through the slot in your stirrup and is secured to the rest of the strap by means of a flat buckle near the stirrup itself. This eliminates the buckle bulge where a conventional leather is hooked into the stirrup bar near the front of the thigh (see figs. 92 and 93).

97. The spring stirrup absorbs concussion, allowing the rider to trot or canter for long periods of time. It saves the rider's knees and ankles and provides a safe getaway in the event of a spill. There is also less muscle fatigue, less back discomfort, and more energy left at the end of a ride. Photo: Karen Paulo

Cinches and Girths

Cinches and girths are available in a variety of materials. The fleece-lined, nylon-web types are very popular. They are durable, washable, and available for both English and Western saddles. Some Western cinches can be purchased with an elastic end, similar to English girths; these are desirable because they make it easier for the horse to breathe. Synthetic- or wool-fleece girth covers placed over traditional string cinches or girths give excellent protection from rubbing and chafing. Also, they are easy to change and wash.

98. Commonly used cinches and girths: top, Western Kodel-lined cinch; middle, cotton fabric foam-filled dressage girth; bottom, Woolback dressage girth with elastic on one end (body is made of heavy nylon). Photo: Karen Paulo

Saddle Pads

Saddle pads protect the horse from the saddle. If horses were perfectly designed, you wouldn't need a saddle pad. However, their shapes vary and change, and saddles don't always fit the same way; so the saddle pad comes to the rescue. However, the use of a saddle pad should *never* compensate for a poor-fitting saddle. Pads made of wool or synthetic fleece are widely used, their durability and washability being a definite advantage (fig. 91). Wool is favored because it allows less slipping and keeps the horse's back cooler than do synthetics. Navaho rugs may be used as a bottom pad. They absorb moisture and concussion well, but they can wrinkle and they become heavy when wet. Felt pads offer superior absorption of sweat and concussion, but the problem here is that they are almost impossible to keep clean. However, if you have a horse with a back problem, felt pads are your best bet—and worth the inconvenience.

Foam-rubber pads that resemble egg crates are popular, as are closed-cell foam pads (fig. 99). Both are used for shock absorption. Pads constructed of woven-latex rubber offer superb protection with very little bulk. Their unique construction allows for air circulation and for the horse's sweat to run off; the latex also seems to grip the horse's hide, so that the pad stays put. These pads can be easily hosed or machine washed. You can also use a "trail pocket saddle pad," which is discussed later in this chapter.

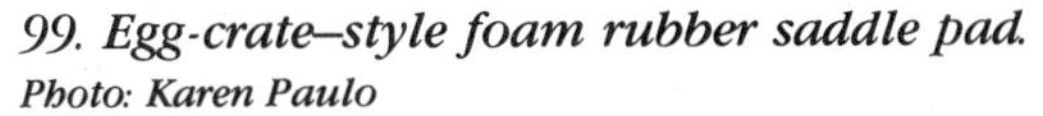

99. Egg-crate–style foam rubber saddle pad. Photo: Karen Paulo

Bridles

The bridle should fit your horse comfortably, with a loose brow band that does not pinch his ears and with cheek pieces that do not touch his eyes or the surrounding areas. The throatlatch should be loose enough so that a couple of fingers can be inserted between it and your horse's jaw; otherwise, he may not get enough air. Nylon tack is most popular, because salt and sweat tend to rot leather easily. (Sponging your bridled horse's head doesn't do much for the leather, either.) The horse's bit should be large enough not to pinch his mouth, but not so large that it slides around causing sores. Any kind of bit is acceptable, providing it gives you adequate control while interfering as little as possible with your horse. A hackamore (bridle without a bit) is ideal because it allows your horse to eat and drink easily—but use it only if it gives you proper control over the horse (fig. 100). My husband's Arab, Chollima, dislikes the scissor effect of a hackamore, so Al rides him only with a halter for the last half of a 100-miler or in the later days of a multiday ride, when he is not so fresh. A combination halter/bridle is also ideal. Remove the bit and your horse has a halter on at the checkpoints, enabling him to eat and drink more easily, as well as be tied up. When you're ready to ride again, just reinsert the bit (fig. 101).

You can also get nylon tack that reflects light in the dark—useful any time you have to ride at night. (See chapter 24 for more about riding in the dark.)

*100. **Above:** A flat-noseband hackamore, having no bit, allows the horse to eat and drink easily on the trail. This type of noseband doesn't pinch off air or form a lump on the nose, unlike certain round nosebands. Photo: Karen Paulo*

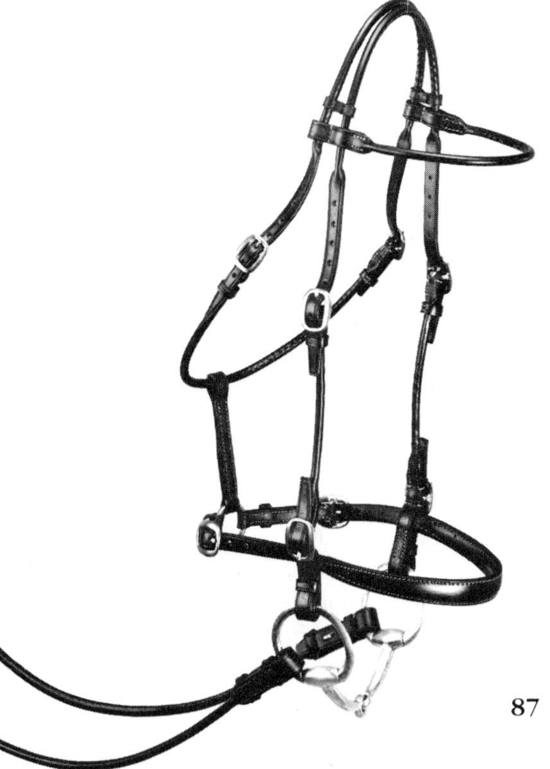

*101. **Right:** EPIC Multi-Bridle allows the horse to be tied securely with the halter section—dropping the bit for feeding and watering. Photo: Phelan's Equestrian Catalog*

Reins

Use reins that feel comfortable in your hands. Some riders prefer round reins made of braided nylon or converted from lead ropes. Others prefer nylon or leather roping reins or split reins. You may also use English-style reins of leather, rubber, web, or braided material. My husband, Al, braids our reins from parachute cord; they are roping reins that snap on the bit and have a built-in tailing line or lead line on the left side, so you never have to unsnap a rein or pull reins over the horse's head—a great timesaver (see fig. 63). Some horses have thin skin and their necks can be rubbed bald by reins during a long ride. If this happens, try different types of rein material until you find the least abrasive rein.

Leg Protection

If your horse interferes (see p. 33) and needs leg protection, be sure to use "interference boots" that don't cover up any more leg than necessary. (Reminder: boots are allowed only in Endurance rides and not in sanctioned Competitive rides.) The boots must be lightweight, flexible, and not binding on the tendons. I recommend the neoprene type (a dense but thin foam rubber covered with a thin knit fabric) with a leather patch and Velcro fasteners. Vinyl-Equilon latex-lined boots are acceptable as well. If your horse wears a hole in his boots, it can be mended with silicon shoe-repair material (available in most sporting-goods stores)—much cheaper than buying new interference boots.

Breast Collars and Cruppers

Don't use unnecessary equipment—just what your horse needs. Breast collars are often a cause of shoulder lameness, according to Matthew Mackay-Smith DVM. If you must use a breast collar, get the "Y" shape, since it allows greater freedom of movement. Cruppers are needed only if your saddle continually slides forward on your horse's neck. If this happens when you are using a breast collar, be sure it is not the breast collar pulling the saddle forward.

BioThane Tack

Nylon tack has become extremely popular because of its durability. But there is a new material called BioThane that is virtually indestructible (fig. 102). Stronger than nylon, it doesn't shrink, stretch, rub the horse, or need cleaning; and it remains flexible even in freezing weather. It works beautifully as latigo straps, stirrup leathers, and cinches or girths (providing it is covered in fleece). Several manufacturers produce BioThane bridles, breast collars, and harnesses in many different colors.

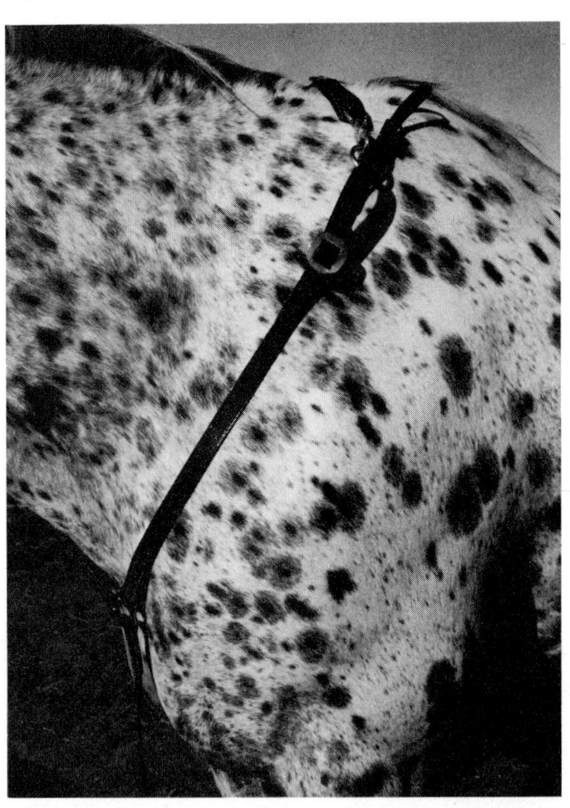

102. BioThane English-style breast collar with snap at withers for easy removal. Photo: *Karen Paulo*

Gear

When you set off on a distance ride, you will need to carry a number of items with you. In an Endurance ride you won't find *anything* to eat or drink between vet checks, while most Competitive rides provide some form of refreshment along the way. Endurance riders should thus be prepared to take along some water, juice, fruit, and a snack—as well as some carrots for the horse. In Endurance competition, riders are really on their own and may never see a soul except at checkpoints.

All distance riders should carry a stethoscope, sponge, string, hoofpick, an Easyboot, electrolytes, a pocket knife, and a vinyl or canvas folding bucket.

Buckets

There are occasions when your horse is thirsty and the only available source of water is inaccessible—perhaps because of a steep bank, a bog, or rocks. That's why it's advisable to have string and a folding bucket. Knot the string to the handle, flatten the bucket, and tie it to your saddle. You can then cast the bucket into the water source and slowly pull it up by the string, letting it fill itself. Because this type of bucket is often too narrow for the horse to reach the bottom, it may be necessary to collapse it as your horse is drinking, so that he gets the last drops. Most folding buckets are available in a handy 2½-gallon size from sporting-goods outlets (fig. 103).

Sponges and Water Bottles

You must always take a sponge along for cooling down the horse. Many riders attach some string to the sponge so they can dunk it into any available water they find. In this way they can cool their horses quickly without getting off (fig. 104).

Water bottles with holders that fasten to your equipment or your belt are a must in all hot-weather rides.

Carrying Equipment

All the items listed above must be carried somewhere. A "trail pocket saddle pad" works superbly with an English, Endurance, McClellan, or Australian saddle. The underside of the pad is made of wool or Kodel fleece; the top is made of durable cordura nylon; and in between is a half inch of polyester fiberfill. Moreover, it is equipped on each side with a large pocket and flap that is secured with Velcro, so that all your items are easily accessible. Another advantage of this saddle pad is that it doesn't bounce around like other carrying equipment—which means it is not cumbersome to you or your horse (figs. 92 and 93).

103. Collapsible 2½-gallon vinyl bucket is ideal for carrying along on a ride. Photo: Karen Paulo

104. Ideal use of a sponge to pick up water from a creek on the trail. The rider here is Brian Weaver on Annaleah Moonbeam; they were first-place winners at the 1987 Race of Champions. Photo: Howard Hartman

Cantle (or "banana") bags are also useful (fig. 92). Choose one that is lightweight, washable, and made of a durable fabric. Be sure you have a solid, safe means of attaching it to your saddle, lest you lose the whole cargo trotting down the trail! I once had to ride with a naugahyde cantle bag under my arms for several miles when the puny stitching around the tying-rings tore out.

"Fanny packs," worn on your belt, are also handy. They usually have one zippered pocket in the back or else several pockets all the way around the belt piece. Those with several pockets are preferable, since they don't bounce around as much. Also, it is better to compartmentalize your items in order to find them quickly.

It is important to clean all your equipment, particularly your tack, regularly. As you clean, pay close attention to condition. Look for cracks or tears in your latigo straps, billet straps, stirrup leathers, reins, and girths or cinches. If the bolt in the neck of your Western-style stirrups is cracking, you should replace it; and check your English-style stirrups for any weaknesses in the metal. Evaluate what needs to be repaired or replaced long before an actual ride, so that you are not forced to use equipment that might lead to a dangerous situation. Your life could depend on it.

Safety and comfort can make the difference between a fun ride and a hazardous ride. Wear whatever you feel will make you and your horse most comfortable—so that you both enjoy the miles ahead.

Part Six

Rider Preparation

6 *Getting Fit to Ride*

How to Condition Yourself and Handle Stress

Distance riding is a high-stress sport, even though we do it for fun. Of course, not everyone believes it's fun to go out and ride 100 miles through the wilderness—on some occasions in the cold and rain. Your back aches, your feet are numb, and you worry for hours, over many miles, about your horse's condition and whether you are on the right trail. These physical and mental pressures create stress, which is the price we sometimes pay to enjoy ourselves and to become one with our horses.

My goal here is to help you reduce this stress. Unfortunately, many distance riders are very tough and persevering individuals who are superb at denial! They deny that the sport is stressful; they "tough out" the discomfort and pain. They are so good at denial that they don't even permit themselves to think about physical strain or mental anxiety. They even deny that distance riding can be dangerous, because they are so sure they'll never have a spill and get injured.

Some of the greatest bodily stresses are sore bones, cramped muscles, an aching back, and painful feet. Fact is, if you're tired, you cannot function properly—and as a result may even hinder your horse's motion. However, if you take the time to condition your own body, making it fit for all-day riding, much of the soreness and stress can be avoided.

Suggested Exercises

Getting fit isn't easy for most of us. We never seem to have enough time to exercise ourselves in addition to our horses. Personally, I hate to exercise on my own and would much rather just ride. But since I know that I must be reasonably fit, I've learned some effective shortcuts that can be worked right into a riding schedule. One is to dismount and jog the last mile home, leading your horse in. Not only is this excellent exercise for you, but it brings your horse in cool and dry. It also teaches him to jog beside you—something that comes in handy during Endurance competition.

Another good practice is to ride to the bottom of a big hill, dismount, and walk or run up it, leading your horse. This is excellent for your cardiovascular system as well as your leg muscles. Sometimes I even leave my horse tied to a tree at the bottom of the hill and jog up and down it on my own. After this exercise, my weary and wobbly body really appreciates the ride home.

Walking, jogging, aerobics, or dance-exercise classes are all good for conditioning—as is bicycling. Indoor cycling machines are very handy, especially in bad weather. There is also a wide variety of home-exercise equipment available, as well as a number of very effective exercise and aerobics videos.

Swimming is another useful form of exercise, since it involves nearly every muscle in the body. While it is great for conditioning your muscles, it doesn't benefit your cardiovascular system as much as other aerobic exercises (unless you swim extremely hard). Nevertheless, swimming does not pound your bones the way running does, so is therefore kinder to your body while building up your muscles.

Whatever form of exercise you choose, it is most important to concentrate on strengthening the abdominal muscles, which are instrumental in alleviating back pain caused by riding long distances.

Riders sometimes go to great lengths and expense to lighten the load of the tack and equipment that their horse must carry. Yet they tend to forget the ten-or-so extra pounds on their own bodies that they could and should get rid of. A practical exercise program *and* a sensible diet will take the pounds off safely, and will certainly make your horse's life easier.

Remember to start slowly and easily—don't overdo it. Working yourself to exhaustion will not get you fit; it may just make you sick.

105. "Sometimes you eat a lot of dirt." The author and Sunny Spots R coming in sixth at the Mt. Burney 50. Photo: Hughes

106. Endurance rider Marty Jensen runs marathons to keep in top condition. Photo: Karen Paulo

Stress and Energy

There are other stressful riding conditions that can be dealt with sensibly. In cold weather, dress in layers to give you extra protection. Wearing sunglasses or having a sun visor on your cap or helmet cover will protect your eyes. Sunglasses also keep dust and sand out of your eyes. Drinking plenty of fluids, especially water, before and during competition, will help eliminate dehydration and fatigue. For an additional electrolyte boost, you can add about ½ teaspoon of concentrated lemon juice to each pint of water. Avoid drinks containing caffeine or alcohol. And eat nourishing food (not junk food) to help keep your energy level up.

Psychologist Les Carr has done a lot of research and observation on the psychological aspects of distance riding. A successful veteran Endurance rider, he states that "rider stress takes away from enjoying the pleasure of endurance riding. And most important, rider stress interferes with focusing one's energies upon the care and maintenance of the horse. . . . A stressed-out rider increases the probability of finishing with a stressed-out horse."

Through exercise, proper nutrition, and at times the judicial use of aspirin or ibuprofen, one can lessen both the pain and anxiety that a rider endures. Most important, your own fitness is the key to reducing all physical and mental pressures.

17 *Good Form for Good Results*

How Dressage Can Help

When many riders think of dressage, they are instantly turned off. They have an image of prissy equestrians performing in a ring. However, the basic principles of dressage can help almost any horse on the distance trail.

Position—General

It is always important for you to ride *with* your horse, not just *on* him. If your sitting position and motion are always ahead of the horse, anticipating his every move, he will waste a lot of energy because you are throwing him off balance. And the same thing will happen if your seat is always behind the horse. Some saddles can make you lose balance, so you should try other types of saddles to help solve this problem (see ch. 15). If it is not the saddle, then you may be well advised to invest in a few riding lessons. Don't be ashamed—you are simply trying to improve yourself and your horse's performance.

You should look at photographs—or even better, videos—of your riding technique, and observe your position on the horse. Two common faults are frequently seen on the trail. First, there are riders who lean forward at the waist and stick their behinds far out behind them—a common problem

107. Dina Rojek riding Windy Ridge Iris. Both horse and rider are well balanced. *Photo: Mike Noble*

with women riders. Second, there is the "Hoss Cartwright" style of flopping elbows, body laid back, with feet planted forward up to the horse's shoulder—a position men often assume. Moderate versions of these styles are okay, but done in the extreme as they often are, they interfere with the horse's motion.

Ideally, you should always be balanced over your horse's center of gravity, which is located directly behind his withers. Weight that is directly over the center of gravity is carried much more easily than weight behind or in front of that critical balance point.

To start correcting your seat and position, sit in your saddle while your horse is standing still. Sit up straight, and then imagine a vertical line running from the top of your head through your shoulder to your hip, ending at your heel. Often, the upper body will seem to be in line, but the leg and foot are too far forward. This can put your whole body out of line—usually behind your horse's center of gravity. A good test is to glance down without moving the rest of your body. You should be able to see only the tips of your toes poking out beyond your knees. If you can see more of your foot, then you must move your whole leg back. Start to practice your new position at the halt, and gradually apply it to a walk, trot, and canter. It is frustrating to break old habits, but the rewards can be very worthwhile.

108. Suzanne Hayes trotting on CM Surriah. Rider is balanced over the horse's center of gravity, allowing him to move efficiently. This team was overall winner and Best Conditioned after completing the six-day 310-mile Lost Wagon Train ride, 1986. Photo: Terry Halladey

Position at the Trot

After you're able to maintain the correct position at the walk, try working at the trot. If you post at the trot, use your legs to lift and lower your body. Legs that are carried properly—not swung to and fro with each stride—enable you to post with an up-and-down, rather than a back-and-forth motion. Don't allow your horse's gait to *throw* you up and down, but rather maintain a balanced position. Once you are truly balanced and posting with your horse's natural rhythm, you can actually influence his stride. If you post high in the upward swing, his stride will lengthen; and if you reduce your posting, his stride will shorten. Regularly change the diagonals you post on. This means that when you rise at the trot, and your horse's left shoulder comes up and swings forward at the same time, you are on the left diagonal. If you then skip a beat (by sitting or standing in the saddle) you will switch yourself onto the right diagonal. Many horses and riders have a favorite diagonal—usually because the rider tends to post on the most comfortable one. Unfortunately, this may lead to the overuse of all the muscles on one side of your horse. Both diagonals should, ideally, be ridden equally. So when you begin to post on the alternative diagonal, you may be uncomfortable at first

109. Nina Warren on Amir Nezraff (AERC Hall of Fame horse, 1988). Note excellent balance at the canter. Photo: Bob Kretchek

and perhaps even think your horse is lame. But persevere—and as you and your horse get stronger on that diagonal, his stride will become much smoother.

If you stand at the trot, try to ride in complete balance and be aware of your body's position. When you are in this "floating" stance, your body may tend to bend at the waist, leaving your bottom stuck out behind. This certainly doesn't help your horse in any way; and it is also hard on your own knees and lower back. Make sure you ride with your heels down to help your body stay aligned. This will also keep weight off your toes, which often fall asleep or burn over long distances.

Position at the Canter

At the canter, many good riders stand in their stirrups, bringing their bodies slightly forward as the horse's center of balance moves forward. Riders with weak legs tend to rely on their reins to hold them in position. This, obviously, is very hard on the horse's mouth and should be avoided at all costs. If you *sit* at the canter, keep your legs directly under you so that your body is balanced. You can increase or decrease your horse's stride if you sit properly. Too many riders have their feet out in front of them, putting all their weight on their behinds, rather than distributing it between seatbones, legs, and feet. You may see these riders bouncing merrily down the trail, but this very bouncing will ultimately damage a horse's lower-back muscles. When these muscles are sore, flexion is hindered and your horse is unable to use his hindquarters properly. When you ride heavily on the horse's back, you are shortening his stride and lessening the power of his hindquarters. So be sure to ride in a balanced position at all times. Finally, get your horse to switch his canter lead occasionally, so that he doesn't overwork one set of muscles. Some horses do this automatically.

Leg Aids

Few distance horses and even fewer distance riders know how to apply leg aids properly. They can be very useful on narrow trails and may even save you a bruised knee from a collision with a tree or post. Leg aids are easy to learn and use. Basically, you teach your horse to move *away* from your leg pressure. For instance, as you apply pressure with your right leg, your horse's rear should move slightly to the left. When the aid is applied in conjunction with your right rein (which controls the horse's forehand), you will bend the horse's body around a turn or a tree. This will help you to make cleaner and smoother maneuvers down winding and tight trails.

110. Ninety-nine miles out, the author is seen here in a poor position—too far forward, feet sticking out, and toes down. Photo: Ken Carlson

Hands

It's very important for your hands to be sensitive to your horse's mouth. Hard and unyielding hands on the reins may cause your horse to toss his head and lose sensitivity in his mouth—which will eventually hamper one of your major means of communication. Rough, jerky hand movements will frighten him, perhaps making him blow up, or even worse, run off. Your hands must be quiet and held low, reins barely touching his neck or mane; he should be given subtle cues for turns or stops, not abrupt yanks. You should guide your horse along quietly, without breaking his concentration.

Impulsion

Balancing the horse with the right combination of hands, legs, and seat will keep him working well from his hindquarters. This improves his impulsion. The horse whose stride is strung out is often uncoordinated and heavy in front. This may cause front-end lameness. To collect your horse, you must squeeze gently with your calves and sit *down*—not back—to drive your horse's rear end under him. At the same time, you should gather his front end by using a light contact with his mouth to prevent his back from hollowing. Your horse should then be able to bring his head down, round his body, and stride freely—which will give him more power and efficiency.

Don't overdo it. You are not looking for a show-ring image. Your goal is to ride *with* your horse, enabling him to perform in an efficient and energy-saving manner. That's the lesson that dressage can teach the distance rider and horse.

Part Seven

Going on a Ride

18 *On the Road*

Trailering Your Horse

Traveling from competition to competition, your horse can undergo a great deal of stress. A little planning will go a long way toward making his travels more pleasant and less energy-draining.

The Horse Trailer

On the road, your horse's accommodation is the horse trailer. It should be roomy enough for him to stand comfortably and long enough for him to stretch in order to urinate. If he can't urinate, he may become ill. He will also get stiff and sore if he has to stand hunched up in too small a space. The horse should have some room between his chest and the trailer's front partition, and also a bit of room behind him—although many horses like to "sit" on the tail chain or the tailgate. Trailers that position the horse at a 45-degree angle to the road (known as "slant loaders") usually provide the horse with more room.

The divider between horses in any trailer can be a solid partition or it may be a simple bar; the latter allows them to spread their feet for better balance. A solid partition will keep horses from stepping on each other, but I have seen some individuals who hate it and who travel much better with only a bar divider. Partitions that can be removed are very useful during loading.

Check the floorboards of your trailer by pulling the trailer mats out or by crawling under the trailer. You must be sure they are not beginning to rot and weaken; if they give way, your horse could easily fall through. Finally, it's a good idea to hose the floorboards periodically to dilute the urine and manure that have soaked into the wood.

111. Broken-down horse trailer—the result of not checking lug nuts and bearings before the trip. Photo: Karen Paulo

Tying Your Horse

If you use crosstie straps to secure your horse's head, they should have a quick release, or "panic" snap where they attach to the horse's halter (fig. 112). Be sure that you know how the snaps work; and oil them regularly to keep them in good working order. If, instead of crossties, you simply tie your lead inside the trailer, tie it where you can reach it safely and readily in an emergency. Use a safety knot that you can release quickly. But, just in case, always carry a sharp knife to cut the horse loose in case your knot jams or the quick releases don't work.

Blankets

If the weather is cool and your trailer is semi-open, your horse may need a blanket. Use a blanket material that breathes, such as cotton or wool, so that he doesn't overheat. If it is raining while you are traveling, water often gets sucked into the trailer and your horse will need some protection. Here, a blanket made of a material that breathes yet is truly waterproof (Gore-Tex or the like) is ideal. Trailers that are completely closed will, of course, keep a horse warm and dry—but it's generally a good idea to open one or more vents to prevent the trailer from becoming too hot and also to provide fresh air.

Tail-wraps

A tail-wrap will shield the tail of the horse who likes to rub it on the back of the trailer. Velcro fasteners are useful. Wraps made of neoprene (a synthetic rubber) stay on better than others; however, they have the disadvantage of causing the tail to sweat and become uncomfortable on long trips. I suggest using the neoprene bandages because they offer the best protection. After you remove the wrap, you can easily sponge any sweat off the tail. A little sweat is a lot better than a rubbed-out sore tail.

112. Lead lines with different snaps: left, quick release, or "panic" snap; center and right, regular fittings. Photo: Frank Pryor, Phelan's Equestrian Catalog

Boots

Your horse should be fitted with a good pair of shipping boots to protect the lower leg and coronary band. Buy boots that are heavy enough to offer true protection and are made of a durable material. It is worth the extra expense to buy good ones. Boots come in a wide variety of materials, ranging from felt-lined leather to fleece-lined cordura nylon (fig. 113). Whatever the material, I suggest you use boots that are washable and also have Velcro fasteners. You will find that many boots are made of lightweight material that barely covers the area from the knee to the fetlock—these are useless. There are other boots available that go up well above the knee and hock. Although these afford excellent protection, they are very cumbersome and may give some horses trouble when stepping in and out of the trailer. Remember that the purpose of boots is to protect your horse's legs from injury during loading, travel, and unloading.

113. Good shipping boots should cover the lower leg, including the coronary band, to prevent injury while traveling. The boots shown here are made of heavy cordura nylon with fleece lining. Photo: Karen Paulo

Loading

If your horse is difficult to load, or tends to toss his head while inside the trailer, it is a good idea to invest in a leather head bumper. This protects the horse's vulnerable poll area from injury. Some people use them all the time as a precaution.

Much has been written about how to load your horse into a trailer. Fact is, every horse is different—so whatever works for you is correct. I would only add this bit of advice: When you load your horse, be sure to secure the tail chain in place *before* you tie his head. I was once loading one of my horses and tied his halter before the tail chain was in place. While I was doing this he stepped back, and a hind foot went clear out of the trailer. At this point, he panicked, the snap broke, and he somersaulted out. I was lucky he wasn't injured—I've seen horses break their necks in freaky incidents like this.

Water and Food

During a long haul your horse will need water, especially in hot weather. It's a good idea to offer him water every two hours. An alternative is to attach a small rubber bucket near his hay supply, with just a few inches of water in it. If your horse has not drunk it during the trip and is becoming slightly dehydrated (see pp. 65–66), give him electrolytes mixed with bran mash at dinner time. (The mash will also be good for him, since it keeps his bowels active and moving, preventing colic, constipation, or, worse yet, impaction.)

Most horses are more relaxed when they have something to munch on. Rather than just dropping hay on the floor, I prefer to put it in a net and tie it securely to one corner of the trailer or the other, where it won't take up all of the horse's head room.

The hay net prevents a lot of hay from going to waste on the trailer floor.

Driving Prudently

Drive with consideration for your equine passenger. Every time you slam on the brakes, accelerate quickly, or swerve around a corner, your horse is tossed about and is liable to get hurt. And—very important—he will waste a lot of precious energy just trying to keep his balance. Some horses will develop nasty loading and hauling habits if they always have uncomfortable, unhappy experiences traveling in the trailer. They can easily come to hate trailers. So keep your speed within the limit on highways, and *under* the limit on back roads, particularly around curves.

Breaks and Overnights

On trips of over eight hours, give your horse at least one break. Unload and walk him around, letting him stretch his legs and get some fresh air. A good time to unload him is when you stop to eat lunch. Truck stops often have big parking areas with water available, and they usually don't object to horses. On long trips I often spend the night in these truck-stop parking lots. Some states have designated special horse areas along major highways where you're permitted to spend the night. Fairgrounds will usually welcome you and your horse. And there are even some motels and campgrounds with stables or corrals. When camping for the night, it's a good idea, if possible, to take an easy two-mile ride on your horse, mostly walking. If there is no place to ride, you can hand-walk the horse in a smaller area, which is preferable to lunging. If the horse has a corral to rest in, he can amble around all he likes.

Hay and Grain

Take along as much feed from home as possible. It is important for the horse's digestive system to have foodstuffs that are familiar. As you journey down the road using up your hay, I recommend buying a new bale as soon as you have room for it; then mix it with what you have brought along. Try to buy only good-quality hay similar to what you are already feeding. Finding the same grain as you use at home is usually not difficult, since most large milling companies distribute to feed stores nationally.

Final Tips

Your horse will weather a multiday trailer trip and arrive in optimal condition only if you care well for him along the way. Once you've reached your destination, ride him lightly to limber his muscles and stimulate circulation—this will prevent him from tying up during the ride. When the competition is over allow him a day or two of rest, if you can, before leaving for home. He will be far more comfortable in the trailer and less likely to become stiff.

Good planning, special care, and above all *consideration* are the keys to success while on the road.

19 *The Vet Check*
What Procedures to Expect

There are many different vet-check procedures in distance riding. They vary within both Endurance and Competitive competitions. Before you begin any ride, if possible, find out what types of vet checks and what recovery criteria will be used on that day, since this may well affect your ride strategy. In Endurance rides the vet criteria may depend on weather conditions, so they may be determined only the day before or even on the very day of the competition.

Types of Holds

Many Endurance rides used to have only mandatory "timed" (or "fixed") holds, requiring all horses to stop for a specific amount of time. The times varied from 15 to 60 minutes, and the horse was required to recover to predetermined pulse and respiration parameters set for that particular ride. This made the vet check easy for the timers and vet crews, but it was hell on the horses. Com-

114. Horse getting a thorough once-over from the vet crew at a ride in Virginia City, Nevada. While one vet is evaluating gut sounds, another is examining interference marks on the inside hind fetlocks. Photo: Charles Barieau

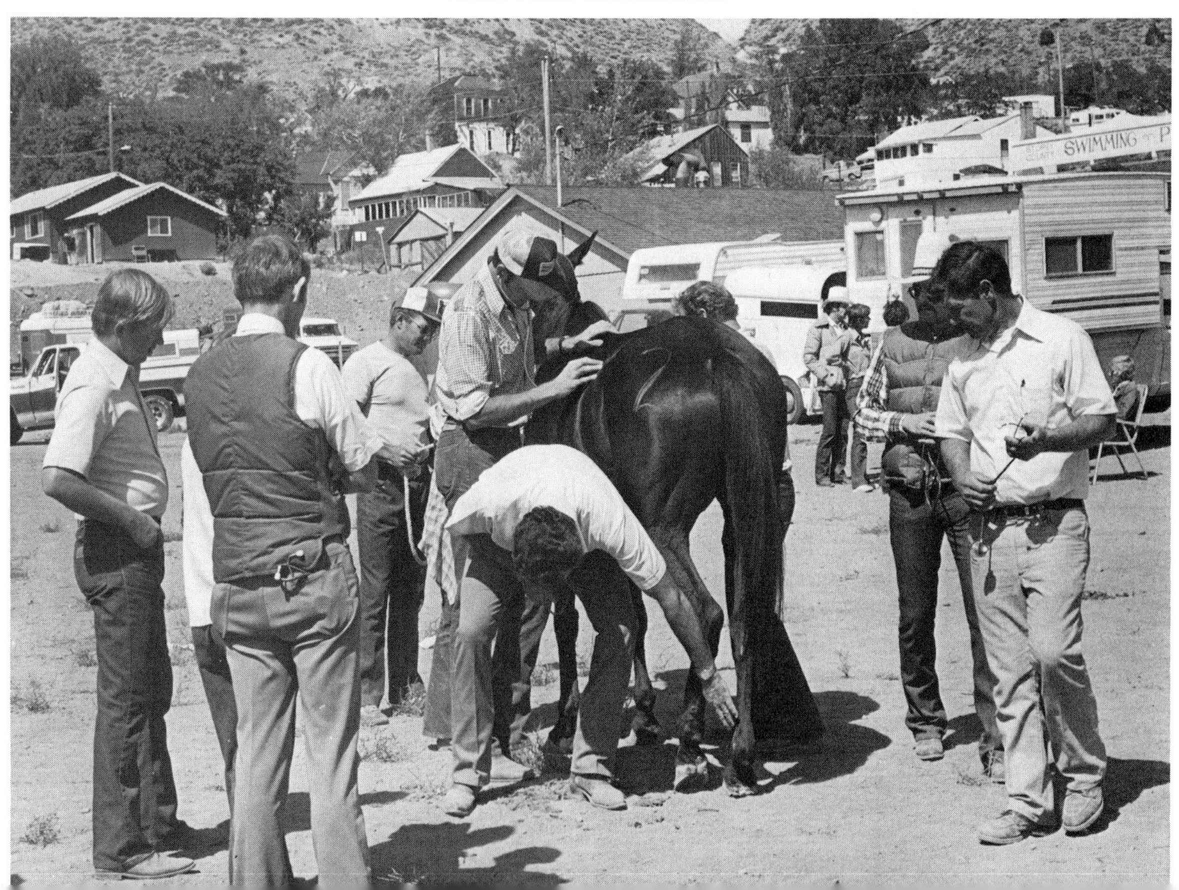

115. As a means of normalizing the horse's pulse and respiration rates to meet recovery criteria, you may lead him into a vet check at an Endurance ride. Photo: Terry Halladey

petitors would too often ride hard and fast into the checkpoint, knowing that they had a set amount of time for their horses to rest and recover. Hot horses were forced to stand around, leading to serious problems—tying up, stiffness, colic, and occasionally even death.

Many of these timed holds in Endurance competition were replaced by the "gate" (or "stop-and-go") check. Here, there are no timed (fixed) holds—instead, the horses come in and as soon as they meet recovery criteria they can resume the ride. This method is much easier on the horse's system because it encourages the rider to dismount and lead the horse into the check; as a result, the horse does not arrive in oxygen debt and with a racing pulse. The well-conditioned horse will pass through the check without any delay, allowing him to get closer to the front—where he belongs. Less-conditioned and inexperienced horses who recover more slowly take longer to get through the check and are therefore held behind the front-runners. This helps prevent these horses from being overridden after any given vet check, because they will not be straining to keep up with the top-conditioned athletes now farther along the trail. Some Endurance rides use only gate vet checks throughout the entire course, while others alternate them with preset timed holds that are not longer than 30 minutes.

A third type of vet check in Endurance riding is known as "meet criteria and hold," or "gate into timed hold." Many vets believe this is the ideal type of check; it has become widely accepted and is recommended by the AERC. It is similar to the gate check in that the horse comes in slowly and must meet the criteria set up for that checkpoint. The difference is that once he has been vetted and passed, he must still wait a mandatory timed period, which may be 10 to 60 minutes. This type of check avoids the problems created by the older type of mandatory check, since it encourages riders to arrive with their horses in good shape and ready to pass the vetting. In addition, the mandatory time period after the horse has been vetted gives him an opportunity to rest and eat for a while.

In Competitive riding, at the midway point there is usually a mandatory ten-minute hold, with pulse, respiration, and soundness checks at the end. Vets are also located at different places along the trail not known to the rider. These vets may at any time request a "trot by," a brief stop, or pulse-and-respiration spot check, if they feel the weather and trail conditions warrant. Occasionally, gate checks are used in Competitive rides.

Recovery Criteria

All vet checks have preset recovery criteria. These differ from place to place, depending on climate and terrain. Humid areas may have a pulse recovery criterion of 68 (the horse must regain a pulse of 68 or lower before he can continue) and pay little attention to respiratory rates, allowing the horse to "blow off heat" (pant for heat dissipation). In other areas, the horse's temperature will be taken in addition to pulse and respiration. A horse who has a temperature of 103° or higher is definitely overheated; the vet may hold him until his condition improves, or he may be pulled from the ride.

Some vets evaluate body heat by using the respiration rate instead of a thermometer. For example, a horse whose respiration rate is 60 after resting for 20 minutes will often have a high temperature—say 104°. A horse with a respiration rate of 20 after the same rest period will probably have a normal temperature of 101° to 102°.

Some areas use a 68-to-72 pulse requirement with a 40-count respiration rate. At rides in other areas, there is a pulse requirement of 60 to 64, with the respiration rate being equal to or lower than the pulse rate. The AERC recommends a recovery pulse rate of 64, with the respiration recovery rate subject to the vet's discretion.

Vet-check procedures vary with each Endurance or Competitive ride. Many Endurance events give you your own vet card at entry time and in-

116. Minette Rice-Edwards on Bright Hope rides slowly across a stream to get to a vet check at the 1974 San Antonio 50-mile race. Photo: Charles Barieau

struct you to carry it with you. Most Competitive rides record vet-check information on master sheets for each horse. Most rides have a timer who records your times in and out and the P&R crew will be there to take and record his pulse and respiration. It's a good idea to take the horse's pulse *yourself* before presenting him to the P&R crew in order to be sure his rate doesn't exceed the limits; some rides will give you a time penalty if your horse has not recovered sufficiently. You then proceed to the vet, who will check your horse's other vital signs—gut sounds, dehydration, and CRT. He will also make an overall assessment of your horse's condition and well-being. He will then ask you to trot your horse out so that he can check for soundness, coordination, and impulsion. He may ask you how much your horse is drinking and whether you have given him electrolytes. And he may wish to determine your horse's "recovery index."

Recovery Index

To find out a horse's recovery index (formerly known as the "Ridgway Trot"—named for its founder, Kerry Ridgway DVM) the vet first checks the horse's pulse, then has you trot out approximately 125 feet and back. At the end of the trot, the vet checks gut sounds, CRT, dehydration, and anal sphincter response. During this short time, the horse should be recovering from his trot. Exactly one minute after the trot-out started, the vet then rechecks the pulse: if it is at or below the initial reading, taken when you first arrived, the recovery index is good, indicating little fatigue; if just above the initial reading, the recovery is only satisfactory and warrants watching; finally, if the pulse is much higher than the initial reading, the recovery is poor, and the horse will be held until he improves. The recovery index is used particularly when evaluating marginally fatigued horses. It is not usually practiced at the first vet check. More often, it is used after the first 25 miles, when horses are less excitable and nervous, and recovery can be measured with greater accuracy.

Despite the seeming inconvenience of all these procedures, you must remember that the vet is not there to get in your way. He is there to help your horse complete the ride safely, and help you with any other problems—real or imagined—you may want to discuss with him at this time.

Time in the Check

Unless your horse's condition is problematic, your time with the vet should be quite short—perhaps two to five minutes. If his condition is marginal, the vet may hold you at the checkpoint until the situation improves and your horse is safely capable of continuing.

It is important not to waste any time when you are in the vet-check area. Be organized and take care of your horse quickly and efficiently. If the weather is warm, you can speed his cooling by sponging tepid or cool water on his head, neck, and lower legs while he is drinking. You can further cool your horse by sponging the large veins on the underside of his belly and inside his hind legs. Remember: do not douse the whole horse in very cold water. This will only constrict the blood vessels, allowing less blood to pass through them, which in turn can raise his pulse rate, defeating your overall purpose. You should also be aware that pouring cold water over your horse's back or over the large muscles of his rump can cause him to stiffen or tie up. Finally, whenever possible, give your horse a few mouthfuls of soggy bran mash with electrolytes and some grass or hay. If you are in a timed hold with access to your gear, use this opportunity to replace your grungy, wet saddle pads and girth cover. If you are using interference boots, this would be the time to clean them out to prevent chafing during the miles ahead.

In Endurance competition, every minute that is wasted in the vet check because of inefficiency on your part puts the other riders that much farther ahead of you. While you are standing still, they are gaining on the trail. For instance, if you are at a gate check which is followed by a timed-hold check reasonably soon (say under 15 miles), don't spend any extra time at the gate check, unless, of course, your horse needs extra rest.

All of this thinking and planning will not be important if your only goal is to complete the ride, but it is critical if you are looking to improve your performance and aiming to be a top contender for winning or for best-condition awards.

Number of Vet Checks

The number of checks will vary with each ride, depending on terrain, distance, and weather. For both Competitive and Endurance events the average distance between vet checks is 12 to 15 miles. On a Competitive ride, some of these checks will consist of no more than a trot-by or a quick informal stop.

117. Apprehensive rider watches Annie Burke taking her horse's pulse during the 1987 Vermont 100-mile competitive ride. Photo: Mike Noble

118. Drs. Bud Strauss and Dave Swaney vetting a horse before spectators. Photo: Mike Noble

An example of a 50-mile Endurance-ride scenario is as follows: A gate check at 12 miles, followed by a meet-criteria-and-hold check at 25 miles. Then at 37 miles there may be another gate. At the finish line your horse will have to pass a postride check after 30 to 60 minutes in the camp. This inspection may be lenient, stringent, or in between; AERC-sanctioned rides require the maximum pulse to be 72 and the horse to be sound at the walk. If he is in poor condition requiring veterinary treatment, or is obviously lame, you will not be awarded a completion.

This last check in an Endurance ride is simply one more means of protecting a horse from an overzealous rider. You will never be rewarded for abusing your horse. And in a Competitive ride, it's the final check that determines the horse's condition—and thus the winner.

Some may wonder why there are pulse and respiration criteria, why there are timed holds, and why the vet has the right to tell us, "Your horse is very tired, but I'm going to let you complete only if you lead him all the way to the finish." The reason for all these controls is that riders are very competitive. Sometimes, in their bid to place best, or even just complete the ride, they ignore their better judgment and allow selfish impulse to take over. The result is too often an overridden, sick, or possibly dying horse. The vet is there to be sure we make sensible decisions—otherwise the horse is pulled. The various check criteria allow the vet a quick, easy way to evaluate the horse. The timed hold gives the vet the chance to observe the horse and his behavior *and* gives the horse time to eat and rest, reducing the stressful effects of the ride.

It is a rare person who starts out with the intention of overriding or harming his horse. But errors in judgment occur all too frequently. The vet checks are there only to protect the horse and see that he finishes the ride safe, sound, and healthy.

20 The Pit Crew
How to Organize Your Helpers

The pit crew is an invaluable aid for any Endurance rider. A good pit crew will save the rider a lot of precious energy; and the horse will probably get better care than he'd receive from a rushed and tired rider. If you are lucky enough to find a crew, you're in for a real treat.

Here are some tips for you and your crew, based on my personal experience. Of course everyone's needs are different, so remember to use these guidelines only as they best serve your purpose. If the competition is a multiday ride, warn your crew that it will be a long and tedious week. The rig will have to be driven each day from campsite to campsite, stopping in between at vet checks and selected access points (sites on the trail where it is possible for crew and rider to meet). Camp will have to be totally disassembled and reassembled daily, and the truck will need to be checked frequently for fuel, oil, and water. The crew furnishes you and your horse with a daily supply of fresh water.

For things to run smoothly, you must tell your crew exactly what you need; work out as many details as you can in advance. They can't possibly anticipate your every need, so good communication is vital. Give the crew your estimated arrival times at the vet checks and/or access points—and be sure that you are talking about the same places!

119. Crewing at the 1987 Race of Champions, Nina Warren and Jock Johnston hold Pam Johnston's horse while Jon Warren does the pulse-taking. Photo: Howard Hartman

120. Pit-crew member Ellen Merwin cools Morgan gelding, Salty's Blaze, at the Sun River 50 ride. *Photo: Dorothy Petrequin*

It's your responsibility to tell or show your crew how to get to each checkpoint. However, some rides with a great many checkpoints will provide the crews with directions and even with a map.

If the plan is for the crew to meet you at certain vet checks and/or access points, you should pack your gear for each stop ahead of time. Several one-gallon (or larger) lidded buckets work ideally. You will need one bucket for each stop. Pack whatever you need in these containers and label them, for example, "Vet Check 2," "Highway Access," or "Vet Check 4." Use a felt-tip pen on masking tape for labeling. Large plastic trash bags are very useful for hauling hay and other bulky items. Have everything that you could possibly need on the trail packed and ready to travel *before* the ride begins.

You as Crew

If you are serving as someone else's crew member, be sure the truck has plenty of fuel, oil, and water before you leave the camp. And be sure you know your destination. If you can't drive all the way into a checkpoint, organize your materials so they are easy to carry by hand. As soon as you arrive at a stop, fill all the water buckets. Set them in the sun, if possible, to remove the chill; if you have a camper, you can also remove the chill by heating some of the water on the stove, then mixing it with the cold water. Lukewarm water doesn't shock a horse's digestive system the way very cold water does. If you cannot warm the water in some way, be sure to give the horse only small quantities at a time. If the weather is warm enough to allow sponging, have your wash water ready and the sponges in it.

121. Rider rests, letting the pit crew do it all. Shown here is Nina Warren at the 1984 ROC.
Photo: Jackie Mitchell

Brushes should be on hand to remove some of the horse's grit and dried sweat if there is time. Have a hay net full and hanging in place. A snack is welcomed by any tired and starving soul who has been eating dust all day, so have something ready for the rider. You should also replenish the snack and juice supply that the rider carries along the trail.

When the horse arrives at the checkpoint, give him whatever care the rider requests. This will vary with the time of day, temperature changes, and the distance into the ride; the rider will know best what his or her horse needs. For example, in the cool of the morning the horse may need blanketing, while later on he will need to be cooled by sponging with tepid water. The rider may ask you to feed the horse a little grain and give him electrolytes (see ch. 7). You may also be asked to present the horse to the vets while the rider rests and regroups for the next leg of the ride. I prefer to do the presenting myself, since it gives me a chance to evaluate the horse's condition with a vet. If the horse and rider are on a timed hold (see pp. 102–103), you may have a chance to change saddle pads and girth covers if they are sweaty, salty, and dirty.

After the Ride

There are some really special things a crew member can do at the end of a ride. Fill the "sun-shower"—a black plastic bag with a shower attachment, loaded with water and left in the sun to warm—and have it ready to use. You can purchase this portable shower at camping or hiking outlets. The rider will feel greatly refreshed if he or she is able to wash off the dust and dirt accumulated on the trail.

Offer to take the horse down to a creek, if possible, to soak his legs. And have the corral clean and ready. I've even heard of some crews setting out the candelabra and making mint juleps! That's real luxury, but of course no one has to go that far.

Good crew members are not easy to find, nor are they easy to keep. They all too often get tired of crewing and would rather be out there riding themselves. Treat your crew with the greatest kindness and appreciation—while they are around!

122. A very tired-looking horse being sponged at the Vermont 100-mile ride. Once the horse had a rest, he was able to finish successfully. *Photo: Mike Noble*

21 *Your First Competition*

Preparation and Campsite; Start to Finish

You have been conditioning your horse for months now, and both of you feel ready for your first distance ride. He looks like a lean machine, with nice, firm muscling and a tidy belly; he has an alert manner, a shiny coat, and no filling, heat, or tenderness in his legs. After a stiff workout, his pulse drops to 60 bpm in 10 minutes or less. His respiration rate remains lower than his pulse rate (except perhaps on very hot and humid days), and he bounces back full of energy after each workout, eager to do more. If you have accomplished all of the above, you are indeed ready to go for that first, unforgettable ride.

Equipment—Organizing and Packing

Make sure your horse's transport is in good running condition. Check all the tires, including spares, and make sure they are functional and safe. See that your jack and lug wrench are in their proper place (and that you know how to use them!) and that the gas tank is full and the engine has plenty of oil. (For more information on trailering and trucking your horse, see chapter 18).

About a week before the planned ride, begin to organize your equipment. You will need all of your tack and gear: saddle; pads; girth and girth cover; bridle; breastplate; crupper, or martingale, if used; halter and lead rope; blankets; cooler; anti-sweat sheet; rain sheet or tarp; sponges; interference boots (if allowed); and a couple of your horse's old shoes in case he loses one. Don't forget the grooming kit.

You should also put together a first-aid box with the following: liniments; sweat preparations; Domoso (dimethyl sulfoxide—a topical preparation for reducing inflammation); rubbing alcohol; topical ointments for wounds and chafes; emergency bandaging material such as gauze, cotton, and vetwrap; butazolidin paste (a pain-killing medication to be administered only with a vet's okay); leg-cooling items such as ice boots, cold wraps, or cryotherapy unit; and also postride leg wrapping of quilts and bandages (see p. 62).

Make several copies of your horse's registration papers, Coggins test (proof of negative blood test for equine infectious anemia), and any other health papers; put one set of each of these in your medicine box, one with your clothing, and one in the glove compartment of your rig. If one set gets lost you won't be without duplicates. Check with your vet to see what health papers may be needed if you are traveling interstate or out of the country.

Don't forget to pack horse feed, hay, buckets, a hay net, and portable corral materials (see p. 11). If your trailer space is limited, you can fasten an extra hay bale or two on the rig's fenders with elastic bungee cords. Once you've organized your horse's tack and gear, don't forget your own clothing and rainwear!

Plan the route of your trip *before* you leave home, and take the map with you. You may think that all ride camps are located in beautiful countryside in a semipopulated area, with stables, general stores, and a café nearby. Wrong! Very few are like that. Most are out in the middle of nowhere. You may have to drive for hours along back roads, often wondering if you are lost. More than likely,

123. Horse hitched to a picket line at the campsite. He has freedom to walk around and even lie down to rest. Photo: Karen Paulo

the stores, restaurants, and gas stations will be miles away from the camp—so get whatever you need *before* you head for the site. It's a good idea to check with the ride management before leaving home to find out just how far away the site is from all the necessary services.

Contacting the ride management ahead of time has other possible advantages. They can tell you about entry deadlines, entry fees, camp location, and trail terrain and condition. Some rides require that you preenter as much as two months or as little as two weeks before the ride. Some allow you to enter on the day of the ride. Check also to see if you will get an entry-fee refund if you can't make the ride; management policies vary widely on this point.

The Campsite

Since most ride camps are out in the country, there are often no stables or corrals provided. Your horse will either spend his time in, or tied to, your trailer; or else tied to a picket line, i.e., a line of rope fastened high between two trees (see fig. 123). Some riders construct a small metal or plastic portable corral consisting of interconnecting pipe units. Others use battery-operated electric-fence chargers, attached to various types of wire-and-post fencing. If you use electric wire, tie string or surveyor's flagging on it every few feet. This increases the wire's visibility and helps prevent horses or people from walking into it.

The water supply may come from a nearby well, stream, or pond; or it may be trucked in. Some horses refuse to drink strange water; you may have to spend a little extra time at home getting them accustomed to different waters. Some people place

124. Preride briefing—don't skip this meeting or you might not know where and when you start the ride. Photo: Mike Noble

125. Predawn at a Competitive ride in New England. Photo: Mike Noble

126. Ride manager Cole Still and Endurance rider Bill Ansenberger start frying some eggs for the riders at the Prineville ride camp. Photo: Karen Paulo

a drop of peppermint in the water to disguise unfamiliar smells, or put Vicks VapoRub in the horse's nose so he can't smell anything else. I've never had this problem—my thirsty horses always drink!

When you arrive at the campsite, find a convenient place to park. If you don't have a pit crew, set yourself up as near as possible to the water supply. It is also useful to be close to the vetting area. Now unload your horse and set up camp. Once you have done this, take a set of your horse's papers and your entry money to the registration office. If you have already preentered, just check in. Take some extra cash for any additional charges or fees. The ride secretary will give you a number, the veterinary card that you carry with you (in an Endurance ride), and any pertinent instructions. You should find out when and where the vetting will begin, and where the start of the trail is. Don't be shy about asking questions, even if you think they might be considered trivial.

Final Activities Before the Ride

All distance events start with a preride vet check, usually done the afternoon before the ride. The vet will examine your horse for soundness and overall good health. If a horse is lame or ill, the vet will not allow him to start. He may ask you to have your horse reshod if he feels the current shoes are in poor condition or if some aspect of the shoeing might jeopardize the horse's chances for a safe completion. As the preride check goes on, the vet may ask you a number of questions about your horse. That is normal procedure. If you are expected to carry your vet card on the ride, be sure to present it for signing at every vet check throughout the ride, and be very careful not to lose it. The card lets each vet know how your horse is doing in every respect from check to check.

If you find you have some extra time before the first vetting procedure, you may wish to saddle up and limber your horse after his long ride in the trailer. If you can, ride the last mile or two of the trail. The horse will usually remember this, and it will boost his spirits at the end of the ride the next day. There will usually be a preride briefing either the evening before or, for shorter Endurance and some Competitive rides, on the actual morning of the ride (fig. 124). The ride management should tell you about the trail, how it is marked, where the water sources are, vet criteria, types of checks, and other pertinent information. Don't skip this meeting or you might miss some essential information—like the starting time of the ride!

Many rides begin very early in the morning (fig. 125). At an Endurance ride, it'll probably still be dark when you wake up. Therefore, it is best to get everything possible ready the night before. Don't forget that many trails can be long, hot, and very dry; for this reason it is really important to carry along water or some healthy beverage for yourself. Prepare this in advance, too, in case you get rushed the next day.

Time really flies in the morning, so keep a constant eye on your watch. Try to organize your camp so that everything you need will be ready when you return. Have the horse's drinking water ready, and put out the wash water, sponges, and blankets. In clear weather, don't forget to leave the water where the sun can warm it. Have food ready for both you and your horse.

Try not to saddle up until about 15 or 20 minutes before starting time. Saddling up too early may well get your horse excited. Also, remember that he'll be wearing his saddle a very long time on the ride. Before you mount up, double-check that you have everything you need to take with you, including that vital beverage for yourself. Don't wear too many clothes. I often shed a layer right before the start, since I'm always surprised at how warm I get as soon as the ride gets under way.

127. And they're off! A group of horses at the start of the Prineville 50 ride. Photo: Gene Peterson

The Start

As starting time gets closer, walk or jog around to limber up yourself and your horse. In Endurance competition the start may be either a *controlled* start or a *shotgun* start. The controlled start usually has a lead-out rider on a horse or motorbike who guides the riders for the first mile or so at a controlled pace. The shotgun start simply turns everyone loose in a mad dash. Either way, you must decide where you wish to be in relation to the other riders. Ideally, the more experienced horses should be in front, because they'll set a faster pace; the less experienced horses should be held back, since it is inadvisable to let a young or green horse get sucked along by the speedsters. Many good riders think it's best to start a few minutes late, after the front-runners' dust has settled. In this way, your horse isn't surrounded by 50 other excited animals. He'll be easier to control and will use up less energy (fig. 127).

In Competitive events horses start individually at 30-second or 1-minute intervals, so it is very important that you know your own scheduled starting time in advance.

Different Courses for Different Horses

Distance rides vary according to the regions in which they are held. You can encounter every sort of terrain imaginable. The route is often marked with surveyor's tape or flagging, usually colorful, that is tied to trees, brush, fences, or whatever signposts are available. Most rides tie the tape or ribbon on the right-hand side of the trail, so that riders have consistent directions in following the correct course. Usually, three ribbons are tied together to signal an unexpected turn or dangerous area. At intersections, lime or gypsum arrows are laid down on the ground indicating the turn you should take. Sometimes directional signs are used. A road that you are *not* supposed to take will often be marked with a solid lime (or gypsum) line across it. Some ride organizers do an excellent job of marking the trail; others do not. Never rely on just following other hoofprints; this may well get you lost. If you think you are off the trail, it is best to double back, find the last ribbon, and look around. You will probably locate the next intended ribbon quite easily.

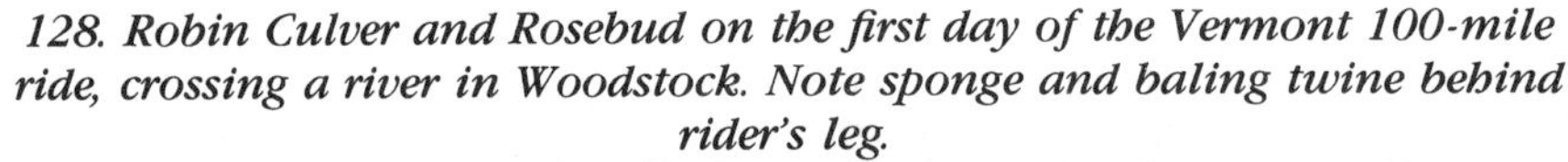

128. Robin Culver and Rosebud on the first day of the Vermont 100-mile ride, crossing a river in Woodstock. Note sponge and baling twine behind rider's leg.

129. Ham radio operators keep communications open between base camp, vet checks, and various points along the trail. *Photo: Judy Sutherland*

130. Trail spotter with walkie-talkie calls in a rider's number, time, and location on trail, enabling ride management to know exactly where the rider is at any given time. *Photo: Judy Sutherland*

The difficulties involved in marking a distance trail can be nightmarish. On the Lost Wagon Train ride, competitors were given a small pamphlet to carry with them. This outlined a description of landmarks on the trail, as well as the mileage between them. In addition, some ribbon was used on the trail—on corners and where no path was evident. This system worked very well.

Some distance events have radio-spotters along the trail (figs. 129 and 130). They record and report your competition number and the time of day you passed that point. This gives ride management an idea of where you are. A well-organized ride may have a big information board at main camp. As riders' numbers are radioed in, their progress is recorded on the board. This tells everyone in camp approximately where you are and that you are okay and saves your pit crew anxiety.

131. ***Above:*** *Group of Competitive riders led by Kathy Downs, Heather Hoyns, and Blakely Murrell coming through a covered bridge together in New England.* *Photo: Mike Noble*
132. ***Right:*** *Horses at a water trough in the middle of a ride.* *Photo: Mike Noble*
133. ***Below:*** *One often encounters spectacular scenery on rides. Shown here is Squaw Valley, with Lake Tahoe in the distance.* *Photo: Charles Barieau*

Vet checks, as you now know, are spaced out along the trail. Follow the prescribed procedure for every checkpoint. After each, be sure to pace your horse according to whatever data you learned about his physical condition.

You will probably ride alongside several different people throughout the day (fig. 131). It's always great to find someone who is going at your particular pace. Conversation helps pass the time, especially when you are feeling tired or lonely. Be sure, though, that you always ride your *own* pace.

Keep in mind, too, that many horses are quite sensitive to their riders' attitudes. Your horse will reflect your excitement, depression, or fatigue, and act accordingly. You'll notice, for example, that when you are tired your horse will be tired too. But if you whoop it up and get enthused, he'll most likely respond. Similarly, riding along with another horse that is tired may well tend to pull your horse down.

*134. **Above:** Rider receiving her finishing time at the Vermont 100-Mile ride.* *Photo: Mike Noble*
*135. **Right:** Officiating can sometimes be a boring job as the day gets long and the horses spread out. Here, timers Charlie Pettner and Paul Combs catch forty winks waiting for the riders at the end of the Oregon 100.* *Photo: Karen Paulo*

The End of the Ride

Seeing the camp in the distance, and knowing that the finish line is just ahead, you will undoubtedly experience a rush of pride and a surge of energy. You'll feel especially good if you've paced your horse well, and he is completing the ride in good shape. On 50-mile rides, there are usually people around the finish line to "hooray" you across. But on 100-mile rides, don't expect a welcoming committee to wait up half the night to greet you!

Once you have properly cared for your horse, it is wonderful to sit down with a cool drink and a snack and share your experience with other riders. Some distance events present their awards with dinner, some with breakfast the following morning, and some have an informal awards presentation at another time. All offer an opportunity to meet other people involved with the sport.

Whether you spend an extra night at the campsite depends on your personal schedule. But if you do have to leave right after the ride, try to allow your horse some well-deserved time to relax and feel good about his performance before you depart.

22 *How to Ride Your Ride*

Pacing, Strategy, and Groundwork

Although conditioning your horse is the most vital part of your preparation for a ride, there are other factors that can influence your success in competition. The most important ones are pacing, strategy, and, in Endurance rides, groundwork. You and your horse should learn to work together as a team, combining every possible ability and talent. It can take a long time for these components to meld, so here are some tips to speed up the process.

At the Race of Champions in 1985, Mary Koefod made a statement that every rider should heed carefully. Right after winning the competition she said, "I came to this ride with three goals: One, to finish the race. Two, to keep my horse healthy and sound. Three, to pass as many horses as I could, keeping goals one and two in mind. The third goal is important to me because I am competitive and I enjoy working with my horse to get the best performance we can. But that is the *third* goal. The first and second goals are always the priorities."

All competitors should share her wisdom. Never put goal three ahead of goals one and two, particularly when you start competing or you have a new or young horse. Don't think about goal three until you and your horse have gained experience. Be satisfied with "To Complete is to Win"!

How to Pace

Pacing is the most important factor on any ride; without it, you will probably fail to finish. The longer the distance, the more important it becomes.

In order to pace your horse correctly, you must be able to gauge how fast you are going at all times—how many miles per hour your horse is covering at a walk, jog, extended trot, and canter. Just like a jockey on the track, you must develop a "feel" for speed so you can rate your horse and not run out of steam too soon. The easiest way to learn your horse's speed is to time yourself over a measured distance of one mile. For example, if your horse trots the mile in ten minutes, you will be going at 6 miles per hour. By timing yourself over a measured route of 5 to 10 miles of varied

136. Take your time on the first few rides. Learn the ropes and enjoy the scenery. Photo: Karen Paulo

terrain using different gaits, you can figure out the average speed you have traveled. After enough time and practice, you will be able to estimate how long it takes to ride over most trails, and this will enable you to pace your horse accurately. By just looking at your watch you can calculate how far you have gone. For example, if you feel you are averaging 8 miles per hour and you have been on the trail for one and a half hours, then you have gone approximately 12 miles. This kind of information will let you know whether to speed up or slow down, depending upon your horse's overall conditioning.

137. Crocket Dumas does some groundwork with his Arab gelding, Sanjur Al Kim, conserving the horse's energy by giving him a breather.
Photo: Terry Halladey

Strategy

After you have completed a few competitions, pacing becomes essential if you aim to be a winner. However, when you start this sport, your strategy should be focused on completion, not winning. Don't concern yourself with how many riders are ahead of you; concentrate instead on completing in good shape—and learn as you go along.

The trot will be your staple gait, since it uses less energy, burns less calories, and is less concussive than the canter. The canter may be used for quarter-mile distances occasionally, to limber up muscles and break the monotony. The walk is a resting pace, and you should use it to give your horse a breather. (In Endurance competition you can dismount and lead him, which also loosens up *your* riding muscles.) When you are walking, use this time to take a good look at the horse—his respiration, motion, attitude—and check for injuries and loose or missing shoes. Evaluate his general condition so that you can accurately determine your continuing pace (fig. 137).

Start the ride slowly, allowing your horse to warm up over the first five miles before asking for more speed. Then realistically set a steady, working pace that you think you'll be able to continue all day. Try to keep your horse's energy output constant. An erratic pace of intermittent walking and cantering is far harder on him than a steady trot (fig. 138). I prefer to start slowly, and then assess

138. Sonya Kinney's Appaloosa stallion, MDK's Shogun, displays the ground-covering trot so vital to a distance horse.

my horse's condition at the first vet check. If his recovery is excellent, and he looks and feels good, I'll speed up. If he is only average in the check, I'll stay with the same pace. If I'm not pleased with his appearance, I'll slow down. You must evaluate your horse's condition frequently to avoid overriding him as the ride progresses. Of course your horse will tire to some degree as the miles accumulate, but he should be alert and interested throughout. At the end of a ride it's sad to see a horse with his head between his knees, ignoring food and his surroundings.

When your horse has miles of experience and conditioning under him and you really *know* him—his capabilities, his limitations, and his needs—then you can think about more than completion. You can focus on winning (see ch. 23).

In Endurance competition, it is a good strategy to come on late in the ride. If your horse is not up to par that day, then do not push—let him go as slow as he needs to. But if you've planned the ride well, your horse will still have energy when the others are tired from the faster pace. If your horse is strong on hills, that gives you a strategic place to pass. And when you pass someone, you should do so quickly—otherwise his tired horse may decide to run with you. This is known as "rabbiting," and it is both undesirable and unpleasant. So look invincible as you blow by, and apologize later for being unsociable. As my husband, Al, says, "Heaven is having enough horse left to pass the others near the end of a ride. Hell is having a tired horse and getting passed."

A horse with quick recovery rates will allow you to gain several positions in the vet check (see ch. 19). I recall the 1979 Mt. Burney ride in Northern California with my horse Sunny Spots R: I came into the 25-mile point in 24th place, left in 15th place. Then I passed a few riders and came into the next check in 11th place, leaving it in 6th place. I ended up 6th at the finish.

Some riders prefer to make their move early in the ride, opening up a lead of one or more miles, then continuing along the trail at a more relaxed pace. If they maintain this lead, they can avoid an all-out sprint to the finish line. Racing your horse to the finish can be great fun, but it's also an easy way to injure what may be an already strained horse.

Saving the Horse's Energy

Gradual climbs can be very deceptive because the grade is so hard to *see*. When you are not sure how steep a hill is, look behind you at the surrounding countryside to determine the grade. Endurance competitors can get off and walk, which quickly tells them how steep a hill is. (Remember, you are not allowed to dismount and move forward in Competitive rides.) If your horse is in very good condition, you may do an easy trot on a gradual climb. If not, you should alternate walking and trotting, one or two minutes for each, until you reach the top. If you have a totally wet horse, one who is breathing hard and rapidly, or one who keeps extending his head and neck in an effort to gain more air—these are all signs that you are climbing up even a gradual hill too fast. If you have to keep pressing your horse to make him trot, then you should probably be walking. In 1977 at the first Sun River 100 near Bend, Oregon, ten horses started and only five completed—because the first 25-mile stretch appeared flat when in fact it was all one gradual uphill climb.

Downhill riding uses very little of the horse's energy once he has learned how to carry himself and you efficiently (fig. 139). Some riders let gravity help "roll" the horse down the hill at a rapid trot or gallop. Not only am I scared to go down a steep hill fast, but I also feel that this practice can damage the horse's front end, since his front bears more weight and receives greater concussion this way. In Endurance riding, it is a good idea for the rider to dismount and jog down the hill with the horse to reduce these damaging effects. Without a rider hindering his motion, the horse will trot more freely and reach the bottom of the hill rested and ready to go on.

139. Rider saves his horse possible front-end injury by dismounting and jogging down a long hill.
Photo: Charles Barieau

Whether going uphill or downhill, your horse's center of gravity always shifts slightly. You can make him more efficient by helping him with your seat. When going uphill, raise yourself out of the saddle, using the stirrups, and bring your weight slightly forward. Never use the reins to hold yourself in this position—either grip the pommel area of the saddle or hold onto a bit of mane. On downhills you should shift your weight back slightly, allowing your horse to move freely in front and to use his rear end more efficiently. When you are trotting through a lot of rapid, short uphills *and* downhills, it may be easiest to stand in your stirrups and ride in a "floating" position. As your horse gains in strength and experience, it is even possible to canter in this position for short up- and downhill stretches.

Make the best use of your horse's energy by taking it easy on the long climbs and making up time on the flat. Also, go easy on the parts of the terrain that require extra energy to negotiate—obstacles such as logs, holes, ditches, as well as

140. Brian Johnson DVM shows us how to run with a horse on the flat—saving the horse's energy for later. Photo: Karen Paulo

deep sand and mud. Don't forget, too, about wind. Imagine how tired you would get, jogging with a 30-mile-an-hour wind in your face!

Another big energy drain is often the start of the ride. This is particularly true in Endurance competition. A lot of people like to start with a mad dash. Some start quickly because they don't want to get caught in the pack, or they think they can win by taking an early lead. And some simply take off because their horses are out of control due to the excitement of the start itself—horses and dust flying! This is silly. As discussed earlier, if you are fighting to keep your horse in control you are wasting both his and your energy. The problem is easily avoided by starting a few minutes late, after the trail and the dust have cleared.

Groundwork

In Endurance riding, groundwork will go far in saving your horse's energy. It is particularly important if your horse is not completely fit and is getting tired. Here, groundwork may mean the difference between finishing or not finishing a ride. In addition to walking beside your horse, you can help by jogging beside him, too—though obviously you have to be pretty fit to do this (fig. 140).

When you come to very steep hills, get off and lead him or "tail" him up. Tailing is having your horse walk ahead of you while you grasp his tail (see fig. 141). Don't let him pull all of your weight—remember, you got off to help your horse! Use his tail just as a partial aid for yourself in climbing. At the top, mount up and catch your breath as you start to ride. Tailing requires a horse who is not touchy about his tail. It also requires a long line on your bridle so that you can still remain in control. It is also a good idea to make sure you know what the terrain is like ahead. I learned my lesson at the 1980 Old Selam ride held in Boise, Idaho, when I was tailing Sunny Spots R up a very long grade. I didn't realize we were approaching a corner that dipped slightly downward before the uphill continued. Sunny, who could see the downhill ahead, picked up a trot, reached the dip at a canter, and then ran farther up the hill, dragging me behind him. My feet hit the ground about once every six feet. I yelled "Whoa" between wheezes and gasps. He finally stopped about a quarter mile up the hill—it seemed like an eternity—and I managed to haul my wobbly and exhausted body into the saddle, as he took off at a trot to catch the next rider. When the rider remarked, "I didn't know you could run so fast!" I realized, to my embarrassment, that he had witnessed the entire episode!

141. Tailing up a steep and rocky incline. Note the long line attached to the bridle, allowing the rider to keep control of the horse. Photo: Charles Barieau

Part Eight

Beyond the Basic Ride

23 *The Winning Edge*
Advanced Conditioning Practices

Once your horse is experienced in competition—perhaps after a couple of seasons—you may wish to raise your goal from completion to winning. Alternatively, you may just want to compete in longer, multiday, more difficult rides. Not every horse is destined to be a winner or a 100-mile champion. In any case, he won't even have a chance unless you prepare him carefully, thoughtfully, and thoroughly.

A distance horse should be seven years old or more before he is really pressed for a top-performance effort. Horses that have not had at least two years of prior competition will tend to break down when asked for a maximum competitive effort, or even when put on a rigorous conditioning program. A less experienced horse can complete 100-mile rides, so long as he is ridden sensibly and not pushed for speed. *Remember, it is speed that hurts a horse, not miles.*

- Begin his annual spring conditioning program as you've done before, with the mile after mile of trotting (see ch. 9). This is important, because without a sound base or foundation your training program will inevitably fail. There are no shortcuts.

The seasoned horse's condition will return to him quickly following a winter lay-up; and, depending on whether he has been stalled or pastured, this process may take one to three months. It will also vary according to the amount of time your horse was laid off. When he can handle 20 miles of varied terrain in two to three hours with absolutely *no* stress; when he jigs and bounces home because he still feels fresh; when his legs do not show any evidence of heat, swelling or lameness—then you can advance to the next stage.

Interval Work

At this point, I'll describe my own version of interval work. I have an eight-mile loop with four major hills. First, I trot the horse to warm him up and then let him canter up a hill. At the start of this training, I canter up only one or two of the hills, being sure to keep the canter speed slow. Then I walk the horse for a minute or two afterward. As he progresses, I eliminate the walking and let him partially recover at a trot for about a mile

142. Mary Koefod and Dana's North Lite making great time on a flat spot after 96 miles at the 1985 ROC. They went on to win. Photo: Susan Brannon

until we come to the next hill. As my horse gets fitter, I advance from a canter to a strong gallop up a couple of these hills. Later, I gallop all the hills. This is true and deliberate anaerobic work, calculated to put the horse in oxygen debt. I do this eight-mile loop about twice a week. (Incidentally, be aware that loop trails with several hills are not as monotonous as repeated runs up one particular hill.) If you condition your horse sensibly, this type of exercise will stimulate his cardiovascular system and build up tremendous strength and stamina, which he will need for the more challenging competitions.

Check your horse's pulse rate between hills to determine how well he is handling his workout. If you are walking him between the hill runs, his pulse should recover to at least 68 bpm. If you are trotting the in-betweens, his pulse may recover to 80–100 bpm. These readings are normal.

By using a consistent premeasured loop at least once a week, you have an excellent opportunity to monitor your horse's pulse and respiration. You should time yourself over the loop to measure his progress and to evaluate recovery rates. As the spring coolness turns to summer heat, you can also get a feel for how the higher temperatures will affect your horse.

While I refer to the above as "interval work," it really is not *true* interval work—which is much more precise, involving measured distances in conjunction with target heart rates during both work and recovery. The latter method may sharpen a horse more than my cruder version does, but it requires the use of an on-board heart monitor. If you are fortunate enough to own one, please refer to chapter 10. If not, you will find that my version of interval work will be adequate for most purposes.

Gallops

The next step in conditioning is to begin going for long, easy gallops once or twice a week—never more. The speed of the gallop should not place your horse in oxygen debt as it did in interval work.

These workouts raise the horse's aerobic threshold, which in turn makes him more efficient. Start this phase with slow gallops of one minute. On successive training rides increase the duration *gradually*, adding no more than a minute at a time, until you have reached the goal of five-minute gallops. If your horse is very strong, and you are really pushing toward a competition, you can increase his gallop time to seven minutes. Watch *very carefully* for any signs of stress and fatigue, avoiding them at all costs. Too much galloping is worse than too little. And be sure to gallop only when there is good footing on the flat or on slight uphills. If at any time your horse feels the need to slow down, let him do so. You increase his stamina by building him up, not by tearing him down. There is a fine line between the workout that triggers the conditioning response you are looking for and the workout that causes fatigue. You are the best judge of when the horse has had too much—ideally pulling up well before he reaches that point.

Remember that there is risk associated with speed work. You are adding stress and concussion, and not every horse can withstand such a tough conditioning regimen.

Using Early Competitions for Conditioning

When the competition season begins, use your first rides as conditioning rides. Unless your horse is really tough and ready, leave the winning to someone else. I have noticed that many of the

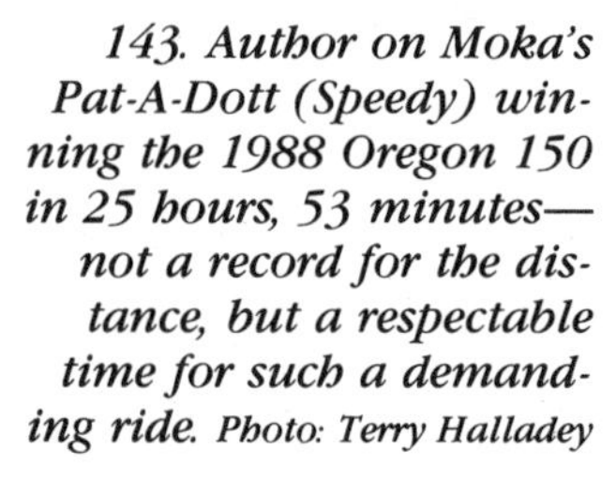

143. Author on Moka's Pat-A-Dott (Speedy) winning the 1988 Oregon 150 in 25 hours, 53 minutes—not a record for the distance, but a respectable time for such a demanding ride. Photo: Terry Halladey

horses that place first, second, or third in the early rides of the season are not to be found on the competition trail later that year. By using these first events only as conditioning rides, your horse will get fitter and tougher as he goes along.

If he has handled his long gallops well in training, and if, in a competition, you have breezed through the first two vet checks with absolutely no problems, then you can work in a little galloping—but only if the terrain is easy. This provides both the Competitive and Endurance horses with an interesting change of pace. Don't overdo it, since you must always keep some energy in reserve in order to complete the ride in good shape. After a few rides, your horse should be ready for a winning effort. A winning Endurance effort requires that a horse be able to travel consistently at a fast and steady trot, interspersed with miles of cantering—or whatever combination of paces allows him safely to travel his fastest. A winning Competitive effort means that your horse must complete the ride within the prescribed time and show the least change in condition of any horse on the ride.

If your goal is just to *complete* a 100-mile competition where the terrain is reasonably easy, you can follow a less rigorous conditioning program by simply leaving out the interval workouts that include risky speed work.

Further Conditioning at Home

If you are not using competitions as part of your horse's conditioning program, you will need to step up his work at home. Ride 20 to 25 miles, using all gaits—twice a week when preparing for an Endurance ride, and once a week for a Competitive ride. Each week, add a day of interval workouts and an easy day or two of walking and trotting for five to ten miles. While speed work is an important factor in sharpening your horse, you must not ignore the basic LSD work. All areas of your horse's body must be in top physical condition in order to achieve an optimum performance. In addition, give your horse as much free exercise as you can by turning him out at every opportunity.

Last Week Before Competition

Conditioning should be tapered off during the last week before a ride. One widely believed theory is that a horse doesn't actually derive the full benefit of a conditioning workout until five to seven days afterwards. So plan your preride workouts accordingly. I like to lay my own horse off completely three or four days before a ride. This gives him a competitive edge by allowing his entire body to restore itself following the rigorous training. During this time, I turn him out with his pals so that he can run about as much as he likes. This also reduces the chances of his tying up in the competition. If you cannot provide this sort of turnout, some good alternatives are ponying him, taking him for easy walks, or lunging him. Be sure to use a lunge line at least 30 feet long in order to minimize any torque that might strain his legs.

Competing Frequently

Later on in the season you may find yourself competing nearly every weekend. If you do, your conditioning program should be altered. If you allow your horse free exercise, you will need to ride him only once during the week, preferably on a Tuesday or Wednesday, for five to seven miles. Ride out just long enough for him to work up a sweat and get his circulation going; then head for home. Unnecessary workouts between competitions will inevitably lead to lameness or burnout. It is interesting to note that when the most experienced riders compete on a weekly basis, they do not push the horse for a top-performance effort on each ride.

144 & 145. ***Above:*** *A 100-yard dash at the end of a 100-mile challenge—left, Mary Koefod on Dana's North Lite; center, Darolyn Butler on Thunder Road; and right, Sherode Powers on Amon Tu—all racing for the 1987 North American Championship.* ***Below:*** *Moments later, victory at the finish line for Mary Koefod!* Photos: Susan Brannon

Resting Your Horse After Competitions

In chapter 9 I discussed the needs of the first-year horse and the amount of rest required for any horse after a 50-mile ride. After a 100-mile ride, I give my horse at least seven days of rest, depending upon his condition. He may need more time. If your horse must be kept in a stall, and you have no turnout area, you can exercise him by hand-walking, ponying, or riding him at a walk. Mild exercise is important for all bodily functions and for the horse's general well-being.

A rider must be willing to change his or her plans if a horse is recovering poorly from a ride. Taking a tired or marginally sore horse to yet another ride simply because it is on your calendar is liable to lead to serious trouble. If you *must* compete weekly and can't bear to miss a ride for any reason, it may be best to have two horses and alternate rides with them. Or else keep a backup horse to occasionally take up the slack when the ride season gets too hectic for your number-one horse.

Multiday Rides

If you are eventually planning to compete in multiday rides (50 miles per day in Endurance competition, and 40 miles per day in Competitive competition) you must get your horse fit enough to go the whole distance and get him accustomed to working several days in a row. If he does not get used to this kind of daily training effort, he will be stiff, sore, and annoyed after the first day of multiday competition. You should not ride *hard* every day, since you might end up without a horse to compete with. Your training schedule should be similar to the conditioning program—only without any speed work—that I outlined at the beginning of this chapter. Alternate each day of this conditioning work with a day of easy pleasure riding.

When my husband and I competed in the six-day Lost Wagon Train ride in 1986, our horses had the benefit of two 50-mile and three 100-mile rides under their belts. They were ready!

The AERC National Standings

If your goal is to place on the AERC national standings, be prepared to log a great many miles. It is very hard work! In 1985, the combined distance ridden by all the Top 25 horses was 37,930 miles—an average of 1,517 miles per horse. In 1986, Bandit, ridden by Smokey Killen, amassed 2,500 miles in a single year. This part Arab/part Tennessee Walker was eighteen years old in that year. He is the only horse to place on the AERC Top 25 seven times! In 1987, Rushcreek Lad, an Arab gelding then eight years old, ridden by Trilby Pedersen, completed a phenomenal 4,260 miles, making him the 1987 AERC National Champion. In 1988, Les Carr's eleven-year-old Morgan/Arab gelding, Astro Aries, went even farther. He did 5,005 miles, making him the AERC National Mileage Champion.

A rider can earn bonus points toward these standings by winning or placing in the Top 10 in several competitions, or by completing the mileage in many competitions. This system offers the rider a choice of either going fast and winning, or going more slowly but completing many more miles overall. These methods give different types of horses a chance to gain points. (There are, of course, some excellent horse-and-rider teams who have racked up many hundreds of miles in a year and won competitions as well.)

Your horse should be at least seven years old and have two years of prior competition experience before you try for a national position in Endurance riding. Riders who have learned to wait and be patient have completed 1,000 to 2,000 miles in a season *and* returned to compete consistently again the following year with the same horse.

24 *Go for It!*
Tips for Riding the 100-Miler

A 100-mile ride is the true test of any horse's mettle. Many veteran Endurance riders believe that practically any well-conditioned horse can complete a 50-mile ride, but not necessarily a 100-mile ride. The 100-miler truly separates the best from the rest.

Unfortunately, many horses never get to prove just how good they are. Too often, their riders feel that they cannot ride a horse for 100 miles and are scared off by the very idea. They feel that they can't handle the physical and mental stress. It is true that 100 miles presents a real challenge, but it can be successfully met through good planning and perseverance. The following points should help you.

Know Your Horse

It is essential to know your horse thoroughly. Don't overestimate his fitness and push him beyond his ability. There is room for error on a 50-mile ride, but not in 100 miles. *Listen* to your horse and ride him accordingly.

Terrain

There is no such thing as an easy 100-miler, but some are easier than others. Choose a ride that is not extremely difficult for your first effort. Summer rides offer more daylight hours than fall rides, but the weather is almost always hotter. A 100-mile ride that uses repeated loop trails will be easier when it gets dark. Loop trails make the miles seem shorter to me, though some people feel the horse gets discouraged by having to start the same trail over and over again.

It is sensible to find out about the terrain before you ride 100 miles. This allows you to pace the horse to your advantage. Some rides will open their trail a week or two before the competition. If possible, ride as much of it as you can. If you live near the ride site, an excellent way of getting a feel of the trail is to help mark it. At any opportunity, ask about the course from people who have ridden it before. Some riders bring along a motorcycle or all-terrain vehicle to view the trail. If you can only ride a small part of it on your horse beforehand, I suggest you ride the last 20 or so miles. Since it's possible that it will be dark when you reach this final stretch of the trail, it really does help to know what the terrain looked like in daylight. You may discover also that your horse will remember more of it than you do and will be encouraged by knowing he is close to camp.

Rider's Mental Attitude

As discussed earlier, the rider's mental attitude is very important, because a horse tends to pick up the rider's moods and feelings. If you are tired and depressed, your horse will feel the same. If you play positive mind games and conjure up a good attitude, the horse will respond accordingly. One popular trick is not to think in terms of the entire distance of the ride. Instead of moaning, "Twenty-five miles down, and 75 to go," look at it positively and think, "Only 14 miles to the next vet check."

146. Smokey Killen and Bandit climb the famed Cougar Rock at the 1981 Tevis Cup in California. This 100-miler is one of the oldest and toughest rides in the world. Photo: Charles Barieau

The most mentally trying time of an Endurance ride occurs usually somewhere between 50 and 75 miles. At this point, your body is tiring. Although you are past the midpoint, you still have many miles looming before you; and it is often the hottest part of the day, which makes it even tougher. This is also true in a Competitive three-day 100-mile ride, where both rider and horse often feel down after lunch on the second day. I was once told that an Endurance rider loses one IQ point for each mile he or she rides! Indeed, maybe that's the reason why, as we tire, most of us still persevere. Some riders have been known to give up at this point, surrendering to the challenge. Others simply grumble about it being the dumbest thing they have ever done, wishing that they had stuck with the 50-mile rides. They may have visions of themselves sitting comfortably in camp, eating a sandwich, and drinking something cool. Now is the time to fight off such thoughts. Ask yourself, What is the challenge of a mere 50 miles? Talk to your riding companions, your horse, or yourself—anything. I've been known to recite verses from the Dr. Seuss book *Fox in Socks*. They blend nicely with the rhythm of the trot. Do whatever works! I always begin to feel better at 75 miles and then feel really great at the last vet check because I know I'm almost home. The total experience is never a complete joy ride—if it were easy, there would be no sense of accomplishment and no satisfaction.

Pacing

It is absolutely necessary to pace your horse. A mistake could be very costly—you might not complete the ride. Remember, there are no prizes for riding the first 37 miles in the fastest time in the history of the ride; you have to make it through the entire 100 miles! Your goal should be to do as well as possible without wearing your horse out.

As in any ride, you should begin slowly at an easy trot so that your horse can warm up properly. Then, after several miles, set a pace that you both can live with during the entire ride. For most Endurance first-timers, the pace will be a trot averaging 6 to 8 miles per hour. In a competitive 100 miles, the speed is usually 5 to 7 miles per hour. A great deal depends on the terrain, footing, heat, humidity, and your horse's level of fitness and experience. For example, my husband, Al, and I placed first and second on a fairly flat, snowy, cold 100-mile winter ride in seven hours, 32 minutes; while earlier that year, in the heat of summer, we won on a somewhat hillier 100-mile ride, with softer footing, in over 14 hours. (I should add that the horses we rode in the summer did not have as much experience as the horses we rode on the winter ride.)

Vary your speed so that you and your horse do not become bored and stiff. An easy canter for a few hundred yards will stimulate circulation and relieve those muscles you use all the time when trotting. In an Endurance ride, do some groundwork on steep hills, up and down, to help your horse conserve energy while you help your own muscles to limber up. Depending on your horse's condition, you may want to get off and lead him up every grade. In fact, it's a good idea to dismount wherever you can move along on foot as fast as he can. And when you do get off, remember to check your horse over, evaluating his condition. If your horse is sweating heavily, your pace is too strenuous. He should be sweating lightly, perhaps even drying off on the flat and downhills (unless the weather is humid).

You must keep moving along. If you allow yourself the luxury of getting off and sitting in the grass while your horse munches, you will probably get so comfortable that you won't want to get back on again. In Endurance competition, getting off occasionally to walk for a short while is a good idea; but if you walk for too long, the saddle will be most uncomfortable when you get back on—and you probably won't exactly feel enthusiastic about getting back on the trail! Walking for too long, either on or off your horse, can be depressing for both horse and rider. You lose your momentum and feel you are not getting anywhere. Of course if your horse is spent, you must walk until he recovers.

Heat, Humidity, and Cooling

Ride veterinarians have observed that high humidity combined with heat can be deadly to the Endurance horse. Evaporation, the most efficient method of cooling a horse, is controlled by the level of humidity. For example, a horse will cool a lot faster in 110° temperature combined with 5 percent humidity, than in 60° temperature and 90 percent humidity. Matthew Mackay-Smith DVM says, "If the temperature is over 80 degrees and the sum of the temperature reading and humidity reading is over 150, you've got a red flag situation, so back off your pace."

In the hot summer months, 100-mile Endurance rides may start anywhere between midnight and dawn. It depends on the region in which you are riding, as well as the trail and footing. In the northwestern United States, it is common for the 100-milers to begin in the faint light of dawn, taking advantage of the coolness of early morning. Once your horse has warmed up, keep his pace up and make good time. You can slow down later when it gets hot. Then, in the late afternoon when the weather starts cooling, pick up the pace again. In hot weather, it's a good idea to jog your horse when you are in the sun. This allows him to create his own breeze to cool himself. When you find

147. Sixty-five miles into the 1984 Race of Champions, three riders give their horses a chance to cool off in a welcome, scenic lake. The center rider, Mary Koefod, is pouring water over her horse's head and neck using her helmet as a scoop. Photo: Purina

some shade, that is a good time to walk him. In other words, trot in the hot sun, and walk in the shade—your horse will appreciate it.

Offer your horse water at every opportunity. Some people will ride right past water, not even slowing down. I believe it's never too early for water. It's true that some horses don't like to drink early in a ride, but it doesn't hurt to offer. Sponge or scoop water over your horse's head, neck, and lower legs when the weather is warm. I personally like to wear an old, very thin, long-sleeved shirt over my T-shirt or halter top. I soak it at every water hole and wear it to keep cool. It takes about five miles for it to dry in 90° heat (though there are many humid parts of the United States where the shirt would not dry completely). The same can be done with a hat or with a bandanna around your neck. If you carry a sponge with a long string tied to it, you can dangle it into any lake, stream, or puddle that you ride through and then use it to wet your horse's head and neck. While you're at it, slosh some on yourself, too!

Heat can really affect rider or horse. It is important for both to take enough time at the water sources to cool down properly. Many riders care well enough for their horses, but ignore their own personal needs. Carry two bottles of water and drink even when you are not thirsty in order to avoid becoming dehydrated. Be sure to cool your own body, too, or you, the rider, will never complete 100 miles. I came very close to collapsing at the 1987 Oregon 100 because I failed to cool myself. At one of the vet checks my horse was fine, but my own pulse was over 160 bpm. At that point the vet crew poured water over me and insisted I wait there until I was in better shape. Of course the fool in me wanted to go and catch up to the next rider!

148. In a stunning expression of the bond between an Endurance rider and horse, Wendell Robie gives his mount a drink of water from his own canteen at the finish of the 1960 Tevis Cup. Robie established this race in 1955. He was later honored as the first inductee into the AERC Hall of Fame, 1975. Photo: Charles Barieau

Riding in the Dark

Riding alone at night can be very scary for some people, and darkness accompanied by serenading coyotes can be very disconcerting. But if you sing along with the coyotes, it's not so bad (and they won't bother you anyway). They're only telling their friends that some idiot on horseback is riding through their territory. A flashlight will make you feel better and will help you find your way. Use a small, lightweight flash that is easy to hold and to stow in your pocket. I like to hold mine up and shine it over my horse's head, right between his ears, lighting up the path ahead. This method seems to disturb the horse the least. It's also easy to trot along, following the bouncing beam. Some riders have devised a setup similar to a miner's light. The bulb and reflector are on a strap that goes around the rider's head; wires from the light travel down to a battery pack that is attached to his or her belt.

Remember that batteries don't last forever, so use your flashlight sparingly, checking mainly for directional ribbons that indicate the turns ahead. Depending on the ride, you may want to carry an extra set of batteries with you. Some trails use chemical glow-sticks to aid the rider. They are very bright and can be seen a half-mile away.

The flashlight is actually for your benefit only—your horse can see perfectly well without it. In 1986, during the Fort Rock 100 in Oregon, my horse was trotting along through the darkness when some creature ran across the trail ahead of us. I could hear the brush crackling as the animal continued on its way. My horse shied and I nearly died of fright. While I reasoned that it might only be a porcupine, and was probably quite scared of us, nevertheless it was very easy to imagine that it was a dangerous bear. I immediately got out my flashlight and used it all the way into the next vet check. The flashlight became my security blanket!

Two or three cyalume glow-sticks tied to your horse's breast collar (or around the base of the neck) with string will also light up your path. These glow-sticks are available in many sporting-goods and variety stores.

Riding in the light of a full moon can be an exhilarating experience. Everything looks beautiful and clear. A flashlight is completely unnecessary, because the ribbons and lime markers on the trail reflect brightly in the moonlight.

Pit Crew

A pit crew can definitely make things more pleasant for you. It's so nice to see smiling faces greeting you at a vet check. They will care for your horse, giving you time to rest, eat, and relax. Many riders do not have the luxury of their own crew, so they try to find someone who will take their necessary gear ahead on the course. Often another rider will have a friendly and willing crew that is more than happy to help and feed you, too. "Share and share alike" is the spirit of this sport.

149. This combination bridle-halter is equipped "Glo Nylon" on the brow and nose so that the horse can be seen in the dark. Photo: Karen Paulo

The 100-mile ride provides a physical and mental challenge to the rider. He must be able to maintain alertness, help his horse by doing groundwork (when possible), and continue to ride in balance. The mental part becomes a game—and a winning strategy is a waiting game. If all is going well, a rider needs only to wait and make his move at the right time. A simple error in pacing could well cost him a win, Top 10 placing, or even completion.

When you ride your first 100 miles, you will be amazed at your horse's stamina. If you are patient and pace wisely, he will appear to gain strength with each mile. You will find that the 100-mile ride is truly a team effort. You will be very proud of your horse—and even more proud of your great accomplishment together. In my opinion, no experience is as gratifying.

25 *The Pioneer Rides*
Multiday Rides over Historic Routes

Endurance riding brings out the pioneer spirit in many riders as they travel through the countryside on horseback. The multiday rides take it one step further, putting that same pioneer spirit to the test, as horses and riders continue on a trek day after day, literally eating, sleeping, and living together.

These rides last four, five, or six days, covering 50 or 55 miles each day. The route is point to point, with each day's camp set up in a different place and no portion of the trail repeated.

Multiday rides are sanctioned by the AERC, with one special requirement beyond the basic rules: the route must retrace a historic path. Each day's ride is an individually sanctioned competition, as well as being part of the multiday competition. This means that a rider has the choice of competing every day or for just selected days. He or she can also use the same horse for the entire ride or a different horse each day. Most multiday rides give awards for riders who compete on the same horse over the entire distance.

The pioneer rides take place all over the United States. They include the Pony Express Winter, Spring, and Fall rides in Nevada and Utah; Applegate to Lassen in Nevada; Lost Wagon Train in Oregon, Shore to Shore in Michigan; Capitol to Capitol in California; Death Valley Encounter in California; and the Great Texas Horse Race. These rides began in the early 1980s, so are a relatively new addition to Endurance riding.

The Lost Wagon Train Ride

All pioneer rides have a colorful past. The Lost Wagon Train trail has a most fascinating history. Over this route in 1845, 1,000 to 1,500 Oregon emigrants in several hundred wagons chose to follow a man named Stephen Meek, who promised them a shortcut between the Fort Boise Territory in Idaho and the Willamette Valley in Oregon. Meek thought this route—now known as "Meek's Cutoff" or the "Blue Bucket Trail"—would be less hazardous than the Oregon Trail, which passes through the Columbia River Basin, and that it would save 150 miles.

What the pioneers could not foresee was that the route went directly into some of Oregon's harshest high desert country. They got lost and confused. The rocky route broke up a great many wagons, and the oxen gave out and lay down, their feet bleeding from the stones. Water was scarce and provisions ran out. The hardships were immense. The whole story is told in the book *Terrible Trail: The Meek Cutoff, 1845*. If you ever plan to participate in this ride, I suggest you read this book for inspiration and some insight into the history and the countryside itself.

In July 1986, my husband and I rode the Lost Wagon Train ride. This was our first multiday ride. Our goal was to complete all six days, 310 miles, each on the same horse. Many other people shared this goal. Out of about 30 horse-and-rider teams

150. At the 1987 Lost Wagon Train six-day ride, Frank Bennett on his mule, Rufus, and Trilby Pederson on her Arabian, Rushcreek Lad, cross Buck Creek. Photo: George Bebee

that started, 13 completed the ride, and the horses suffered no ill effects from the effort. In fact, all went on to compete in other rides later in the year, and several won competitions and placed nationally. A few teams even competed in other multiday rides during the year—which proves to me that if you give your horse really good care, he can go a very long way.

When I rode the Lost Wagon Train ride, I learned a great deal about my own horse, as well as horses in general. Their recuperative powers are amazing! These well-conditioned animals grew stronger each day, and indeed our own horses peaked when we galloped in for first and second place on the fifth day. As we traveled along the rock-strewn paths, we had to marvel at the extraordinary strength the pioneers must have possessed to get those fully loaded wagon trains through such unforgiving countryside.

Important Tips for Multiday Rides

This extended form of Endurance riding became a new sport for us. The ride as a whole is extremely demanding. What made it possible to finish on eager and sound horses could only have been the proper and special care we put into the entire effort. Here are a few points I have discussed elsewhere in this book, but are well worth repeating here if you are planning to participate in a multiday ride:

Corral: Provide a large enough portable corral so that your horse can rest and relax easily. A horse that is tied up can't move around to prevent stiffness from setting in. The corral also makes it possible for him to lie down; this will help speed his recovery at the end of each day. The corral must be easy to assemble and disassemble, since you'll be changing campsites each day. Our corral is made of rope. But there are other types—see page 111. Remember that the lighter and less complicated your corral is, the easier it will be to pack up and move.

Tack: Before you enter a multiday ride, make absolutely sure your horse's tack fits him perfectly and that it doesn't rub or pinch him anywhere. On a ride of this length, you will find that rubs can appear on your horse where they never have before. Comfortable clothes for yourself are a must if you are going to mount up and ride 50 miles a day for several days. Use all your old and faithful equipment—this is not the time to experiment with something new.

Feed: Feed your horse often. Give him grass hay after each day's ride, since he'll be less likely to gorge himself or choke on it than with alfalfa hay. You can feed the alfalfa later, when he is less hungry. Give him several (up to six) small feedings of bran mash and include electrolytes as needed. Add his daily vitamin supplement. The small feedings prevent digestive upsets and colic. Get as much feed into him as you can before the next day's ride. Give him enough hay and water to last all night—a full hay net and several buckets of water. Feeding during the ride is equally important. Give him grass, hay, and mash with electrolytes whenever possible; his body needs refueling along the way. Grass is preferable to hay because it contains water. Hay absorbs water from your horse's body in the process of being digested, so feed grass wherever and whenever you can. The exception to this feeding plan is if your horse is overstressed or sick, since his condition could be made worse with feed.

Your Food: It's important for *you* to eat well, too. Good energy is essential if you are going to ride hard all day. It's easy to prepare wholesome meals ahead of time at home, freeze them, and then reheat them in the camp. Take plenty of snack food and carry an ample supply of water or juice with you on the trail.

Pampering: Prepare for the next day's ride by taking extra-special care of your horse at the end of each day. Nothing is too good for him; pamper him with lots of loving attention and treats. Stand him in a creek if possible. Massage and groom him. Wrap his legs in bandages. Blanket him when it cools off at night, so that he won't waste energy keeping himself warm. While it is possible to go for several days on one set of shoes, you should still check them daily to be sure they will last another hard day. If you use pads, check for rocks under them: add more silicone packing if necessary.

Vital Water: It is often difficult to get your horse

151. Here, Trilby Pederson gives Rushcreek Lad some grass and a short rest. Photo: George Bebee

152. At the Applegate-to-Lassen multiday ride, the competitors start out on the fifth and final day. Under a cold and dramatic sky, the riders begin at an easy trot to allow their horses to warm up. Photo: Deane Anderson

right to a water source on these rides, so it really pays to carry a 2½-gallon collapsible bucket on your saddle. If your horse leaves some water in the bucket after drinking, pour it on his neck and on your own head. Remember: never pass up water. It may be miles before the next opportunity comes along.

Ride Plan: Set a pace that is steady and that your horse can live with comfortably. Go fast enough to allow him plenty of time to rest at the end of the day, but not so fast that you tire him completely. If you blow your horse out one day, you'll have to slow down and pay for your sins the next. Start each day slowly to let his stiff muscles get warm and become limber. Your muscles will be stiff, too, so you probably won't feel like starting out fast anyway. (After the third day, many riders' morning stiffness will subside.) Remember to ride your own pace; don't forget your original plan by letting yourself be influenced by fresh horses who have just joined the ride that day—they will tempt you to go faster than you should.

Pit Crew: A pit crew is a great asset on a ride like this. More than anything, it gives the rider additional time to rest. The crew can drive your rig to all the vet checks, then into each new day's camp. You can manage without a crew, but it takes a great deal of organization. For example, we didn't have a crew at the Lost Wagon Train ride, so each morning a member of ride management drove our rig to the new camp for us. Every morning before we rode off at dawn, we had to have it packed and ready to go. And each day when we finished, we had to set it up again. There are a few rides where water is extremely scarce and you really should have a crew to provide water along the trail.

Mind Games: Mentally, don't think of the entire distance ahead of you. As discussed with the 100-mile rides, if you think about how you have the whole distance to go, it can be mind-boggling! It's so much easier, psychologically, to say, "We have only 50 miles today." Or better yet, "The vet check is only 22 miles ahead." Mind games help a great deal.

Weather Gear: During the first four days of the 1987 Lost Wagon Train ride, we experienced intense heat, hailstorms, and rain, along with some lovely weather. So remember to pack everything that you could possibly need for all weather conditions.

These multiday rides are what Endurance riding is all about. It is seeing the beautiful countryside, reliving a part of the history of our country, and traveling by horseback through the wilderness very nearly as our ancestors did. One also gets the feeling that all the riders are in this together—and indeed everyone helps each other. We may be competitors, but we are also friends. If you don't have this attitude when you begin a multiday ride, you certainly will at the end!

26 *Ride and Tie*

A Zany Sport

Ride and tie, an unusual variation of distance riding, combines the world of horses with one of the nation's leading sports—jogging. The result is a long distance scramble with eight legs!

Basically, ride and tie is a cross-country distance race, complete with vet checks like those on Endurance rides. The entries are three-member teams consisting of two people and one slightly confused horse! The team members combine their skills and physical stamina, with the two people taking turns running solo and riding the horse along the entire course. (It is a very good idea to have one or two friends along to act as your pit crew, too.)

One person begins the race on foot and the other on horseback. The rider goes as far as he thinks his partner can comfortably run (preferably a predetermined distance to a specific spot), then jumps off and ties the horse to something—say, a tree or a post—beside the trail, before taking off on foot farther along the course. When the first runner reaches the horse, he unties him, mounts, and takes off in pursuit of the second runner. He passes the second runner and, at an agreed-upon distance farther down the trail, finds another good place to tie the horse, then sets off running again. This equine leapfrog continues all the way to the finish line—anywhere from 10 to 100 miles.

Historically, ride and tie originated as an authentic form of transportation when two people were forced to share one horse over a great distance. It turned out that they could reach their destination faster by alternating riding with running than if they rode the horse "double." Needless to say, it was also easier on the horse. In 1970, Mr. Bud Johns, then a vice president of Levi Strauss & Company, in a promotional campaign for jeans, revived that mode of travel as a lively source of fun and sport. Thus the renowned Levi Ride & Tie competition was born, with the winning team receiving $15,000 in cash and other prizes. Often 150 or more teams compete in this race, and some of the best runners and Endurance horses in the nation are among them. Tight veterinary controls protect the horses from injury and abuse in case some riders get carried away with the lure of the money and prizes.

Visualize the spectacle of 150 horses and riders, plus 150 runners on the ground, all milling around the starting point. A gunshot sets them off and suddenly there are whoops and yells of excitement amidst mass confusion, as horses, riders, and runners all head for the hills. The Levi start resembles the California gold rush!

The American Ride and Tie Association was formed in 1987. Its goal is to unite ride-and-tiers throughout the United States. It publishes a newsletter that keeps its members up to date with information on the sport. In addition, the association has taken over the Levi Ride & Tie competition, now called the National Ride and Tie. It is usually held in California. Many other smaller ride and ties are held nationwide and are also recognized by the association.

153. At the 1987 Big Creek Ride and Tie, Maryann Truitt rides past her partner, Mary Ann Buxton, on her way to the next tying spot. *Photo: Hughes, Phelan's Equestrian Catalog*

Ride-and-tie competitions average 25 miles in length, though some organizations sponsor 10-mile novice races. The National Ride and Tie, which started out at 40 miles, is now 52 miles—the distance of two marathons. And, the Swanton Pacific Ride and Tie in Davenport, California, is 100 miles long. Ride and ties are held on all types of terrain, but are usually quite rugged with lots of hills, sand, and rocks. Of course, the trail needs to have trees or other objects available to tie the horses to. But every now and then there is a long, barren stretch with no place for tying, and the runner has to rely on fitness and sheer determination to get through it. The trail is usually well marked as in other distance events, and there will often be people along the way who provide water, juice, and cookies for the runners.

As mentioned, the vet checks are similar to those used in Endurance rides, although there are usually more of them since this sport is so demanding. While the horses are under strict control, the runners are on their own—no one is around to check *their* vital signs!

Qualifications Required of Horse and Riders

The sport of ride and tie requires the skills of both horseman and runner. Even if you or your partner were a world-class runner, the team would be severely handicapped if you didn't know how to ride. By the same token, if you were a world-class rider who could not run, you would also be disadvantaged. You don't need to be a marathoner, but you do need to be fit. It helps to be a fast runner, but being a consistent, even if slower, runner is equally important. You should keep moving at a steady pace and walk fast when the terrain gets too rugged for running.

Your horse must be *extremely* fit. Unlike the relatively even, comfortable pace he is asked for in a normal distance ride, he now has to be able to sprint a mile, or perhaps gallop for two or three miles, then be tied to a tree and stand virtually motionless for several minutes. This can be very stressful to a horse that is not very well conditioned, and should certainly not be attempted with a young, unseasoned horse.

The best ride-and-tie horses are older, with at least a few years of distance riding in their background. Their bodily systems must be developed to withstand the stress that ride and tie demands of them. The older, more experienced horse will also be calmer for mounting; he stands more quietly while tied, waiting for the runner to arrive. Many riders prefer smaller horses because they are easier to mount. But whatever the horse's height, he must be stronger and fitter than he would be for an Endurance ride, because with ride and tie he gets no groundwork help from the rider—there is always someone on his back when he is moving.

Strategy

Strategy plays a big part in these competitions. Every wasted minute adds up and can cost you a win or a place. One of the best ways to save time is to use a technique developed by Lew Hollander and my husband, Al: on one of the changeovers you hand the horse over rather than tie it. Al and I have this worked out to a science. I begin on the horse, with Al on foot. I ride a predetermined distance of about a mile, tie the horse, and then run on. Al comes along, unties, and vaults on, then gallops up to me. He rides up on my right, tossing me the end of the tie rope, and leaps off the right side of the horse, hitting the ground at a run. I then slow the horse enough to get my toe in the stirrup, mount up, and get going. I ride on ahead of Al, find my tree, tie the horse, start running—and the whole process is repeated.

154. Al Paulo's "flying mount" saves precious time at ride-and-tie races. *Photo: Nancy Cox*

Tying

A distance of approximately one mile between ties seems to work best. This relatively short distance helps to increase the communication between partners. They can more frequently swap information about how their horse is doing and how they themselves are doing. Another advantage of shorter ties is that the three-part team finishes the race at almost the same time. Long ties tend to place too much distance between team members—and they can lose each other! I'll never forget one ride and tie, where a runner picked up the horse, then rode four miles into a vet check. He was surprised to find out on arrival that his partner had not yet come through the check. But he decided to run on just the same, leaving the horse in the check for his overdue partner. He ran the last four miles to the finish line.

It soon became apparent that the partner had gotten lost. After several hours—and many people combing the surrounding hills—she was found, safe and sound. Moral of the story: if they had arranged a closer or shorter tie, this potentially dangerous situation could have been averted. (The one drawback of ties that are *too* short is that they deprive the horse of the valuable rest time he gets while waiting for the next runner to reach him.)

The only time a long tie should be used is when you have a pit crew and when it is the last tie before a vet check—say about two miles out. This gets the horse into the check far ahead of the runner and gives the pit crew time to care for the horse and have him vetted and ready to go when the runner comes in. The person who rode the horse into the vet check can also start running down the trail sooner, gaining more ground.

In general, it's a good idea to tie the horse

with a fairly short line. If you don't, he'll most likely play "Here we go round the mulberry bush," getting all tangled up in any surrounding brush, and you'll be there forever trying to get him unwound. Always tie your horse as near as possible to the trail so that he can be seen easily and your partner won't have to go out of his or her way to get him, wasting valuable time and energy.

Some Final Advice About Tying

- It's better to tie on a straight part of the trail rather than on a corner; this way you won't surprise your partner, and other competitors will be able to see the horse easily and not run into him.
- Don't tie him near a steep bank, ditch, or drop-off where he could slip or get hung up.

155. Al Paulo in high gear at the 1981 Levi Ride and Tie. *Photo:* The Western Horseman

• Always take a moment to look around for fencing wire, and never tie your horse to an old fence post, whether you can see wire or not. Old wire is often buried just beneath the ground, and if your horse paws it up he can easily become entangled and be seriously injured.

Pacing

In order to reduce the stress on your horse that results from sprinting, then suddenly standing still while you search for the ideal place to tie, you should slow his pace down. This will allow his body to adjust more gradually to resting than if you just gallop to a stop and leave him motionless. It will also reduce the chances of his experiencing a number of potential physical problems, discussed in chapter 12.

Another strategy for pacing the horse is for each of the partners, in turn, to run as fast and as long as they reasonably can, then rest on the horse as he *slowly* canters along. While this means that some riders will inevitably gallop past you, you will have the great advantage of being more rested than they are during the next running segment—often passing your competitors on foot. In the long run you will outdistance them completely, because their horses are so tired from all the galloping, while yours has been taken along more slowly.

Snafus of Ride and Tie

One of the most common mistakes made in this sport is when the runner passes right by his own tied horse! It sound crazy, but it actually happens. When a runner is cruising along, he can quite easily lose his sense of distance, forget to look around, or simply let his mind wander aimlessly—as so often happens while jogging. Runners have arrived at the finish line only to have their partner, who is already there, ask where the horse is. Since all three members of the team must cross the finish line in order to complete the race, the final runner must get back to wherever the horse was last left tied and then ride him back to the finish. He may have passed the horse several miles back. Needless to say, this sort of mistake at the end of a long day can be totally demoralizing.

Horses get left behind for other reasons, too. Sometimes ride and tie seems to be a world full of nothing but gray Arabians who all tend to blend together. If your horse has few or no distinguishing marks, try using a bright-colored saddle pad or breast collar in order to recognize him quickly. I've seen gray horses with their tails dyed red or green, with zebra stripes drawn on their haunches with a grease pen, or with pictures or a name painted on their hips.

Another nasty surprise that occurs in this sport is when the horse is not tied securely enough. There have been countless occasions where the runner is out in front buzzing down the trail, only to be suddenly passed by his own *riderless* horse! The horse must then be caught and tied again. This means that the unfortunate back runner has more distance to cover, since the horse is now tied farther down the trail.

156. At a lively practice session, Lew Hollander takes the ride-and-tie rope being handed to him by Al Paulo. Photo: Karen Paulo

Clothes

In order to ride and run, you need to wear appropriate clothing for both. Most ride-and-tiers wear T-shirts, shorts over biking tights, and some form of running or aerobic shoes. You need a very tough hide to ride in shorts alone—though some people do. Tights help protect your skin from the saddle. Some riders find that the answer is a fleece *saddle cover* that completely envelops the saddle, thereby eliminating chafing.

It is a good idea for you and your partners—both two-legged and four-legged—to practice your ride-and-tie tactics at home to determine which methods work best for you. If a particular strategy or technique goes sour, it is better that the mistakes happen there than in competition.

The sport of ride and tie may seem from this account to be a bit crazy and masochistic. But that only makes the satisfaction of finishing—and using the combined talents of each member of the team—all the more enjoyable. Once you have completed a ride and tie, you know you've performed a really great feat.

157. The author offers some water to her partner, Hanne Hollander, as she gets off Tuko at the finish of the Graveyard 20-Mile Ride and Tie. Photo: Nancy Cox

27 *Competitive Driving*

Horse-and-Carriage Competition

An interesting variation on Competitive riding is competitive driving. Most driving competitions are held in the eastern United States and are sanctioned by the Eastern Competitive Trail Ride Association (ECTRA).

Competitive drives are conducted under the same rules and scoring system as Competitive rides (see ch. 3). They are often held at the same times as regular trail rides—even using the same courses and covering the same distance of 25 to 40 miles. Drives have a maximum and minimum time limit: the 25-mile drives must be covered in 4 to 4½ hours; and 40-mile drives in 6½ to 7 hours over two days. This requires an average speed of 6 miles per hour.

As with Competitive rides, scoring is based almost entirely on the horse's condition: Time is a scoring factor only if you exceed the maximum or minimum limits. There are, however, some important differences for drivers to remember:

- The harness and carriage must both pass a safety check prior to the start of each competition. This ensures that no equipment is faulty or unsafe—for example, held together with baling wire, which could lead to an accident with serious consequences for horse, driver, and other competitors. If your equipment is defective in any way, you won't be allowed to start.
- The "carriage" harness used in competitive driving is different from the "fine" harness used in

158. Robin Culver and Deb Donahue driving Cricket at the end of the 1984 January Thaw Drive, South Woodstock, Vermont.

the show ring. A carriage harness with breeching, wider breast collar, wider girth, and wider padded saddle, is safer and more comfortable. A "draft" harness is too heavy and cumbersome.

• You may use any carriage you wish. However, it's important to have one that fits your horse. It should not be too heavy or large for him. You should also avoid wheels with inflatable tires, since these often go flat on hard competitive drives.

• You must remember that your horse's hindquarters work much harder when he is driven than when he is ridden, because he is *pulling* weight rather than carrying it. Consequently, you should condition your horse by driving him, not riding him. And if you plan to take a passenger along with you in competition, be sure to train with a second person in your carriage. (Incidentally, ECTRA has a rule that if you drive more than one horse in hand you must always take a passenger along with you to act as your groom.)

159. Steve Rojek and groom driving a pair in a 40-mile Competitive trail drive. Note the well-padded harness to prevent the horses from becoming sore. Photo: Joe Haynes

28 *Special and International Events*

Elite 100-Mile Competitions

As the sport of Endurance riding continues to grow, so does the caliber of competition. With this growth comes a different type of experience—rides that cater to the cream of the crop.

The Race of Champions

As Endurance riding became more popular in the early 1980s, David and Susan Brannon—veteran Endurance riders from California who publish the respected periodical *Trail Blazer*—decided that a major championship challenge was needed in order to truly separate the "best from the rest." Thus in 1984 a new annual ride was added to the sport—the Race of Champions (ROC), held in the mountain states of Wyoming, Colorado, and Utah.

A ride of this magnitude is very expensive to organize; normally it would mean prohibitive entry fees. But thanks to the main sponsorship of the Ralston-Purina feed company these entry fees are affordable. Other companies help, too, by sponsoring riders from different regions in the United States as well as other countries. The great publicity surrounding this event gets a lot of recognition for these companies and also helps the sport of Endurance riding gain respect from equestrians all around the world.

In addition to the race itself—which is controlled by a team of the best Endurance vets in the country—the riders, officials, sponsors, and friends get to attend a number of festive social functions. There is a barbecue and dance, champagne party,

160. Left to right: Nina Warren on Amir Nezraff, Annette Taschner on Annaleah Moonbeam, and Susie Niles on Kyobi Wizay walking through the edge of Lake Adelaide (altitude 8,600 feet) at the 1984 Race of Champions in the Big Horn Mountains, Wyoming. Moonbeam won this race (as well as the 1987 ROC, with Brian Weaver as his rider). Photo: Purina

161. Boyd Zontelli from California weighs in after finishing third on Rushcreek Hans at the 1984 ROC. He later received the Best Condition award. Photo: Purina

riders' dinner, and awards banquet. Although cash prizes are not given, the items awarded are very special—for example, vacation cruises, horse trailers, or saddles to the winners; and sterling-silver belt buckles or custom-made cooler blankets to all who successfully complete the competition. The Solo Award is given to riders who complete the distance without a pit crew.

When the ROC started in 1984, it stirred up controversy because it was the first ride to require stiff entry qualifications: the horses had to have previously finished in the Top 10 over 500 or more miles of competition, and completed at least two one-day 100-mile rides. It also required all entrants to carry a minimum weight of 155 pounds (rider plus tack). The event adopted all AERC rules, plus a few new ones that were soon to set a new standard for Endurance rides everywhere. For example, the postride check now required at all AERC-sanctioned rides originated at the ROC.

In 1990 the qualifications change. In order to enter the ROC the *horse* must finish five one-day 100-mile rides sanctioned by either the AERC or the Federation Equestrian International and place in the Top 10 in at least two of them. The *rider* must complete at least one one-day 100-mile ride. These qualifying rides can have been completed at any time during the horse's and rider's lifetimes.

The Tevis Cup

The Western States Trail Ride, more commonly known as the Tevis Cup, is the oldest and most famous Endurance ride in America, if not the world. Held in California, the Tevis Cup was the first one-day 100-mile Endurance ride anywhere and has remained the toughest and most grueling. Wendell T. Robie, president of the Western States Trail Foundation (an organization whose goals include the preservation of historic Gold Rush trails ranging from Nevada to California), founded the Tevis Cup in 1955 and issued the simple challenge, "Let's ride, really ride!"

Robie sponsored his 100-miler as an international riding competition with the purpose of bringing public interest to Endurance riding as a re-creation of Western history. The ride was inspired by the extraordinary feats of the pony express more than a century ago, when horse-and-rider teams were capable of delivering a mail pouch 1,960 miles away in ten days!

Traditionally, riders start out with the "Indian Rider's Moon"—the summer's longest full moon in late July or early August. They leave Squaw Valley at 5:00 A.M. and climb over the steep eastern barrier of the Sierra Nevada through Squaw Pass to the highest point at Emigrant Pass—elevation

162. Two riders crossing the No Hands Bridge near the end of the Tevis Cup. *Photo: Charles Barieau*

7,930 feet. The riders may have to avoid patches of snow. The trail continues on across Red Star Ridge to Robinson Flat before entering the toughest part of the ride, a 27½-mile stretch from Last Chance to Foresthill, with total descents of 6,150 feet and ascents of 4,250 feet. From there it is another 39 miles largely downhill to Auburn, where most riders arrive in the dark. The temperature en route may range from 40° at the top of the mountains to 110° in the canyons. The trail is as primitive as it was when it was the route of fleet-footed Washoe Indians, heavy-booted miners, and pony express riders. It is mostly in wilderness, and for a 70-mile stretch the riders may see only three or four cabins.

The Tevis Cup itself is awarded to the rider whose mount finishes first in good condition; and the Haggin Cup, another trophy, is awarded to the entry finishing among the first ten whose condition is superior to all others. Every rider who completes the course is awarded a sterling-silver belt buckle, and riders who complete the course without a pit crew to assist them receive a Frontier Award inscription on their buckle. Like the Old Dominion, described below, the Tevis has marathon runners on the course along with the horses and riders.

163. The late Will Tevis presenting the Haggin Cup for Best Condition to Minette Rice-Edwards, 1973. Photo: Charles Barieau

The Old Dominion —An Endurance Ride and Ultra-marathon Foot Race

The full moon closest to the summer equinox is when riders and runners congregate at Front Royal, Virginia, for the Old Dominion 100-mile competition. The riders must complete the course within 24 hours, and the runners must finish in less than 30 hours. This extremely tough trail in the Blue Ridge Mountains is known for its steep climbs and descents on boulders, ledges, and rocks. The Sherman Gap, a 2,000-foot climb, is dreaded by many, coming as it does some 80 miles into the ride. The Old Dominion ride is notorious, too, for its unrelenting hot, humid weather. Riders who manage to finish feel fortunate indeed. The Cavalry Award is given to riders who complete the course without pit-crew assistance.

International Events

In 1980, the Federation Equestrian International (FEI) became interested in the sport of Endurance riding and in 1986 sponsored the first official World Championship governed by FEI rules. Held in Rome, Italy, the race was won by America's Cassandra Schuler on Shiko's Omar, who finished in 10 hours, 50 minutes; her teammate Jeannie Waldron, riding Cher Habu, placed second and also won the prize for the horse in best condition. Third place was taken by Bernhard Dorsiepen, a West German rider. Eleven countries were represented, with the gold medal for team competition going to Great Britain, the silver to the United States, and the bronze to France.

The second World Championship was held in 1988 in Front Royal, Virginia, with riders racing across 100 miles of Blue Ridge Mountain country. There were entries from 15 countries, and 11 na-

164. Becky Hart and R.O. Grand Sultan gallop to victory and Best Condition at the first (1986) North American Championship 100-mile ride near Davenport, California. She later won the second World Championship ride, held at Front Royal, Virginia, in 1988.
Photo: Charles Barieau

tions fielded teams of four riders each. The team gold medal went to the United States, with Canada second, and France third. The individual winner was Becky Hart, riding R.O. Grand Sultan, and she finished in 12 hours, 51 minutes. This American rider also earned best-conditioned honors.

The 1990 World Endurance Championship is in Stockholm, Sweden, at the same time as all the other FEI equestrian world championships. It is a special occasion, since all the riding disciplines sanctioned by the FEI (which include dressage, show jumping, and three-day eventing) compete at the same time in the same place. This concurrence of scheduling happens only once every 12 years.

North America

The North American Championship, a 100-mile Endurance competition, was originally held in August 1986 at Davenport, California. It was the first ride run in North America under the international FEI rules. Teams came from the United States, eastern and western Canada, Australia, New Zealand, and West Germany; and individual riders came from Belgium and Switzerland.

The overall individual winner and national champion in 1986 was Becky Hart (USA) riding R.O. Grand Sultan in a very fast time of 9 hours, 36 minutes. Since 1987, when Mary Koefod (USA) won the event in 12 hours, 29 minutes at Front Royal, Virginia, the North American Championships have been held on a biennial basis. In 1989 the event was held in Flesherton, Ontario. Jeff Benjamin, riding for the U.S. East team, brought Cloud Valley across the finish in 15 hours, 55 minutes for the individual gold medal. The team gold medal was won by Canada East.

Europe

Many European countries have their own championship rides, but in 1979 ELDRIC (European Long Distance Rides Conference) was formed. Member countries included Austria, Belgium, France, Germany, Great Britain, Holland, Italy, Portugal, Sweden, Switzerland, and Norway, with the United States and Australia as associate members.

The ELDRIC Trophy (European Points Championship), first awarded in 1980, is a competition based on a point system and open to riders from all participating nations.

The European Championship, sanctioned officially by the FEI for the first time in 1985 at Rosenau, Austria, is an annual 100-mile event held in different countries. In 1989, it took place in Santarém, Portugal.

Great Britain

Britain has a number of long distance rides, some of which are sanctioned by ELDRIC, and one of which, the Goodwood 100, is run under FEI rules. There are also two organizing bodies—the Endurance Horse and Pony Society of Great Britain (EHPS) and the British Horse Society's Long Distance Riding Group (BHS LDRG). The two organizations, whose rules differ, are responsible for some of Britain's major rides, including the Good-

165. One of the happy outcomes of the first North American Championship ride was the camaraderie among people of different countries, customs, and languages.

wood, held in Sussex over two days; the Summer Solstice Ride, a 100-miler held in one day in Sherwood Forest in Nottinghamshire; and best known of all, the Golden Horseshoe Ride. This ride, held on Exmoor in Somerset, requires entrants to qualify in order to enter. It is not a race, but rather 100 miles over two days (50 miles per day), with the award going to the winning horse and rider on the basis of best time and the condition of the horse.

Australia

Australia has been involved in Endurance riding for many years. The sport is well established, with numerous competitions available for riders. Australia's principal ride, originally run in 1966, is the Tom Quilty 100-Mile Ride—better known as "The Quilty." It takes place over a very rugged, up-and-down bushland course in the Blue Mountains of New South Wales. This trail climbs over 8,000 feet and descends 10,000 feet. The Quilty is Australia's championship ride and has attracted riders from all over the world.

166. Cassandra Schuler on Shiko's Omar, left, won the first World Championship, held in Rome in 1986. Here she is seen with Patty Alexander atop Startez Too, riding the Swanton Pacific 100. Photo: Charles Barieau

167. Competitors at the Golden Horseshoe 100-mile ride held annually at Exmoor in England. Photo: Bob Langrish

Appendix I

Distance and Trail Organizations

United States (alphabetically by State)

Alabama Endurance and Trail Riders Association
Rt. 1, Box 100
Madison, AL 35758

American Endurance Ride Conference
701 High St., Suite 203
Auburn, CA 95603

Endurance Horse Registry of America
Box 63
Agoura, CA 91301

Heritage Trails Fund
5301 Pine Hollow Rd.
Concord, CA 94521

North American Trail Ride Conference
Box 20315
El Cajon, CA 92021

Quicksilver Endurance Riders Inc.
Box 71
New Almaden, CA 95042

Ride and Tie Association
Box 1193
Manhattan Beach, CA 90266

California State Horsemen
Endurance Division
897 3rd St.
Santa Rosa, CA 95402

Western States Trail Foundation
Box 1228
Auburn, CA 95603

Mountain Region Endurance Riders Inc.
4950 Shars Trail
Sedalia, CO 80135

Southeastern Distance Riders Association
Rt. 1, Box 397W
Altoona, FL 32702

Georgia Endurance Riders Association
Rt. 5, Box 170
Winder, GA 30680

Hawaii Endurance and Trail Association
Box 451, Kailua Kona
HI 96740

Southeast Idaho Trail & Distance Riders
6825 McGlochlin Rd.
Boise, ID 83709

National Trails Council
Box 44172
Indianapolis, IN 46204

Upper Midwest Endurance
& Competitive Riders Association
455 Moore Hts.
Dubuque, IA 52001

Trail Riders of Today
634 Wayne Ave.
Silver Spring, MD 20910

Great Lakes Distance Riding Association
1523 Cedar Lake
Stanton, MI 48888

Mississippi Endurance Riders Association
1316 E. 3rd St.
Forest, MI 39074

National Assn. of Competitive
Mounted Orienteering
Rt. 2, Box 46
Ogilvie, MN 56358

Icelandic Pony Trekkers
440 W. 62nd St.
Kansas City, MO 64113

Ozark Country Endurance Riders
RR 1, Box 92
Willard, OH 65781

Eastern Montana Distance Riders Association
Box 494
Baker, MT 59313

Hooves & Co. Distance Riders
Box 2091
Kalispell, MT 59903

Nebraska Endurance &
Competitive Trail Ride Association
Rt. 1, Box 23A
Denton, NB 68339

Nevada All State Trail Riders
Box 805
Virginia City, NV 89440

Eastern Competitive Trail Ride Association
RD 2
Voorheesville, NY 12186

Oklahoma Equestrian Trail Riders Association
Rt. 6, Box 82
Duncan, OK 73533

Pacific Northwest Endurance Rides Inc.
3736 SE Clay
Portland, OR 97214

Southeast Endurance Riders Association
Rt. 11, Box 9
Maryville, TN 37801

Texas Endurance Riders Association
Box 224
Canton, TX 75103

Vermont Competitive Trail Ride Assn.
RR Box 124
South Woodstock, VT 05071

American Recreation Coalition
1331 Pennsylvania Ave. NW, #726
Washington, DC 20004

American Trails Network
733 15th St. NW, Suite 427
Washington, DC 20005

Rails-to-Trails Conservancy
1400 16th St. NW, #300
Washington, DC 20036

Great Plains Long Distance Riders
Box 5122
Gillette, WY 82716

Canada

Canadian Long Distance Riding Association
RR 3
Stouffville, Ontario L4A 7X4

Ontario Competitive Trail Ride Association
1010-1600 Sandhurst Circle
Scarborough, Ontario M1V 2L4

West Yellowhead Endurance Riders
71 Bellevue Ave.
Spruce Grove, Alberta

Europe (general)

European Long Distance Rides Conference
Dr. C. Reidler, Sonnenterrasse
CH-60360 Ebikon, Switzerland

United Kingdom

Byways & Bridleways Trust
9, Queen Anne's Gate
London SW1H 9BY

British Horse Society's Long Distance Riding Group
Maggie Morton, British Equestrian Centre
Stoneleigh, Kenilworth, Warwickshire CV8 2LR

East Anglian Trail Riders Association
Jenny Kay, Toad Hall, Low Common
Deopham, Wymondham, Norfolk NR18 9DZ

The Endurance Horse
and Pony Society of Great Britain
15 Newport Drive
Alcester, Warwickshire

Highland Long Distance Riding Club
Candy Cameron, Drummon
Dores, Inverness, Scotland

Long Distance Riding Centre
Fosse Way, Bourton-on-the-Water
Gloucestershire

Welsh Long Distance Riding Centre
Jan Lloyd Rogers, Pine Lodge Stables
Rhydagaeau, Carmarthen, Wales

France

National Committee of France Endurance Riders
P. Passamond, Combelcau-Flaugnac 46170
Castelnau, Montratier, France

West Germany

German Endurance Ride Association
Hermann Schicker, Maasseustrasse 12
4235 Schermbeck, West Germany

Australia

Australian Endurance Ride Association
P. Harris, Box 235
Gawler, South Australia

Appendix II

Breed Associations and Registries Offering Distance Awards

United States

American Association of Owners and Breeders
of Peruvian Paso Horses
221 W. Alameda H 101
Burbank, CA 91502

American Bashkir Curly Registry
Box 453
Ely, NV 89301

American Donkey & Mule Society
2901 N. Elm St.
Denton, TX 78644

American Indian Horse Registry
Rt. 3, Box 64
Lockhart, TX 78644

American Morgan Horse Association Inc.
P.O. Box 960
Shelburne, VT 05482

Appaloosa Horse Club
Box 8403
Moscow, ID 83843

Ara-Appaloosa Foundation Breeders International
Rt. 8, Box 317
Fairmont, WV 26554

Colorado Ranger Horse Association Inc.
RD 1, Box 1290
Wampum, PA 16157

Endurance Horse Registry of America
Box 63
Agoura, CA 91301

Galiceno Horse Breeders Association Inc.
Box 219
Godley, TX 76044

Grade Horse Distance Program
RD 1
Cheswick, PA 15024

International Arabian Horse Association
Box 33696
Denver, CO 80233

Missouri Fox Trotting Horse Association
Box 637
Ava, MO 65608

North American Morab Horse Association
W3174 Fargo Springs Rd.
Hilbert, WI 54129

Pinto Horse Association of America, Inc.
1900 Samuels Ave.
Forth Worth, TX 76102-1141

Pony of the Americas Club Inc.
5240 Elmwood Ave.
Indianapolis, IN 46203

Racking Horse Breeders Association
(Trail, Field and Pleasure Division)
Rt. 2, Box 72A
Decatur, AL 35603

Southwest Spanish Mustang Association
Box 148
Finley, OK 74543

Spanish-Barb Breeders Association
188 Springridge Rd.
Terry, MS 39170

Spanish Mustang Registry Inc.
8328 Stevenson Ave.
Sacramento, CA 85828

Tennessee Walking Horse Breeders
& Exhibitors Association
Box 286
Lewisburg, TN 37091

United Kingdom

Arab Horse Society
Windsor House
The Square
Ramsbury
Wiltshire 5N8 2PE

The Endurance Horse & Pony Society of Great Britain
15 Newport Dr.
Alcester, Warwickshire

Appendix III

Distance-Riding Equipment Specialists: Stores and Catalogs

The Australian Connection
9274 Muir Way
Roseville, CA 95661

Equestrian Outfitters
Rt. 4, Box 313M
Fayetteville, AR 72702

Griffin's
881 Lincoln Way
Auburn, CA 95603

In the Long Run
RD 2, Box 347
Harmony, PA 16037

Phelan's Equestrian Catalog
184 Schoonmaker Point
Sausalito, CA 94965

Pony Express Endurance Tack
Box 740
Foresthill, CA 95631

Running Bear Farm
801 Valerie Dr.
Dayton, OH 45405

Skito's Enterprises
Box 311
Mt. Aukum, CA 95656

The Sport Horse
Rt. 1, Box 468
Powell Butte, OR 97753

V-V Saddle Shop
17500 SE McLoughlin
Milwaukie, OR 97222

Windridge Farms
14462 Old Auburn Rd.
Grass Valley, CA 95949

Appendix IV

Equipment Manufacturers

Bitterroot Outdoors Unlimited
581 Cash Nichols Rd.
Stevensville, MT 59870

Brown's Performance Saddles
Rt. 2, Box 132
Nevada, MO 64772

Cemar Enterprises
Box 157
Clovis, CA 03612

EQB-Equistat Heart Monitor
Box 185
Unionville, PA 19375

Equine Innovations
Box 2203
South Hamilton, MA 01982

Jan's Saddle Covers
Box 8
N. San Juan, CA 95960

John Ewing Co./Heart Monitor
Box 188
LaSalle, CO 80645

Kensington House Ltd.
Box 215
Chickamauga, GA 30707

Kreative Horse Products
1738 N. Moorpark Rd.
Thousand Oaks, CA 91360

Marciante Saddle & Leather Co.
214 Thompson Ave.
Glendale, CA 91201

Marvik Arabians, Inc.
Rt. 2, Box 255 DD
Mena, AR 71953

Plush Seat Bottoms
Box 1921
Sonoma, CA 95476

Sharon Saare Saddles
1267 Clover Dr.
Santa Rosa, CA 95401

Society of Master Saddlers
H. C. Knight (Cheif Executive)
The Cottage
4 Chapel Place
Bovey Tracey
Devon TQ139JA
England

Trail Tech
1021 S. Thompson
Springdale, AR 72764

Appendix V

Distance Riding Periodicals

United States

AERC Endurance News
701 High Street
Suite 203
Auburn, CA 95603

The Distance Rider
Rt. 1, Box 418
Kitts Hills, OH 45645

Hoof Print
NATRC
P.O. Box 1811
Loomis, CA 95650

Ride and Tie Journal
Ride and Tie Association
Box 1193
Manhattan Beach, CA 90266

Trail Blazer
5000 Carrizo Rd.
Atascadero, CA 93422

Trail Digest
Box 723
Virginia City, NV 89440

United Kingdom

Distance Rider
"Hillside"
Eastbourne Road
Blindley Heath
Lingfield, Surrey RH7 SJX

Distance Rider Magazine
May Garland Farm
Chiddingly Road
Nr Heathfield, East Sussex

Note: Most distance and trail organizations publish a newsletter. See appendix I.

Appendix VI

Available Booklets

AERC
701 High St. Suite 203
Auburn, CA 95603
Ride Managers Handbook
Veterinary Handbook
Rule Book

NATRC
Box 20315
El Cajon, CA 92021
Judges Manual
Riders Manual
Management Manual
Rule Book

ECTRA
Marilyn Miles
RD 2, Voorheesville, NY 12186
Management/Judging Handbook
Rider/Driver Handbook

UMECRA
Louise Riedel
455 Moore Hts.
Dubuque, IA 52001
Ride Managers & Veterinarian's Handbook
Rider's Handbook

PNER
Shelley Knezevich
3736 SW Clay
Portland, OR 97214
PNER Handbook

Appendix VII

Distance Riding Videos

Kerry Ridgway's Cardiac Recovery Index
AERC
701 High St. Suite 203
Auburn, CA 95603

Long Distance Riding
Farnam Company
(Available at tack shops)

Index

NOTE: Page numbers in italics refer to illustrations